NEUEN

Titles by Sheri Singerling:

ALFOM SHARED UNIVERSE
NOVELS
Nytho

Neuen

Blessed is the Rot

SHORT STORIES
The Badge

The Seed

Wireworks

Rogue

To Keep the Non-Euclidean at Bay

Paper Airplane Poet

All titles can be standalone reads and can be read in any order. Find the author-suggested reading order on her website at sherisingerling.com.

NEUEN

SHERI SINGERLING

Cover design by Geoffrey Bunting
Cover illustration by Vladimir Solnyshko

ISBN: 979-8-9914752-3-5 (paperback)
First Edition
HypIn Publishing

Visit the author's website at sherisingerling.com

Intro

Just so you know, I don't like getting myself involved in these kinds of things. I strive to be a—what's it called?—fly on the wall? It's that age-old refrain that god-like beings like to use, and I'm just following the precedence. So you must be wondering, "What's this all about?" Well, see, I promised little Levi that he could say his piece.

Truth be told, I'm rooting for the guy. I look at what he's done in his short, short life, and I'm just so blown away. I never would've thought one of my own creations could wreak so much glorious havoc. A chip off the ole block, he is. Primed for greatness. The central axis of an oh-so-interesting story. If nothing else, Levi is the heart of Neuen, and to you, Neuen is everything.

Just a few nuggets before his voice takes center stage. Number 1: He wasn't meant to be anything special. I didn't have a hand in anything he did. Remember what I said? A fly on the wall. Number 2: Levi took this little task on himself. I told him about you because I wanted to see what he'd do once he knew the truth. He decided he wanted to ask for your help. Now, I'm not going to tell you what to do about all of that. It's entirely your call, but we'll circle back to that later.

And number 3: He's a bit love-struck, which factors into his decisions. I, personally, don't get it, never having had that affliction myself, but I can imagine how it might make me do things a bit differently. All that to say, he's desperate to save his lovely little doll, Lyn. And she's very much a part of this. She'll be chiming in too. You'll hear from him, then her, then him and so on until it all comes back around to me.

Make sense? Sound good? Then, without further ado…

The Itinerate

Levi

I know nothing about you, but I suspect your life is wildly different from my own. With that in mind, maybe I should paint a picture of my world starting with Lyn's arrival because, in most ways, this is all for her. It wasn't at first. For one thing, I didn't know her. For another, my focus was solely on saving my people from our perpetual bondage.

Just before she came, I was working in my lab, a tent a few meters in diameter filled with books and notes and glassware. I say my lab because even though I was one of twenty-five botanists, I was the only one that used the space. It had a bad reputation owing to its previous occupant, but I wasn't superstitious, and even if I had been, I didn't spit at Rohn's name like the others. I looked up to him, even strived to emulate him.

"Don't forget to eat, Levi," Emyla said.

Her voice jolted me in that thrumming silence, and I almost dropped the tray of seeds I'd been looking at under the microscope. I glared over my shoulder at her. She sat on a stack of burlap bags, back straight, knees bent and pulled in towards her chest.

Emyla was small, almost wispy, especially so wrapped in her Reisender robes. Flowy and beige, high-necked, long-sleeved. Her pale blue eyes met mine, stray strands of her short, cropped, blond hair eclipsing the view. She leaned forward and pointed at the spread in front of her. Dried berries, nuts, pickled vegetables. My stomach grumbled, but I jammed my face back on the eyepieces.

"Once I'm done with this tray," I said.

I used a wooden stick with a sharpened point to push little black seeds, smaller than the finest human hair. Emyla sat in silence. Her eyes locked onto my back, no doubt, aching for me to acknowledge her. It was exhausting. I blocked her out and zeroed in on the luftor seeds, searching them one by one for any sign of disease. The majority were whole and smooth with no visible fractures or color irregularities, but those that didn't make the cut got put to the side. I'd save them for my own side projects.

After five or so minutes, I leaned away from the table and ran my hand through my hair. Emyla watched me, taking in every detail—the swaying of my russet waves, the symmetry of my square jaw, the alert gaze of my ochre eyes.

"Come over here and sit with me," Emyla said.

I moved to her and dropped down on the burlap bag pile. I inspected the food on offer and picked at it. She was silent for my first few bites, but I could tell that wouldn't last.

"I put our names in for the coupling assessment," she said.

I almost choked.

"You did what?"

Smile lines hovered at the edges of her eyes and the corners of her lips.

"The Itinerate will be here any sol now," she said. "And you said this year was as good as any."

I wanted to berate her for doing something so significant without consulting me, but I couldn't remember if I'd said the things she said I had. Exact words or not, I'd implied as much to her not so long ago, but I'd been distraught, trying to heal a heart wounded twice over in short succession. In such a state of mind, it was possible that I'd agreed to tie myself to her as life-long partners.

"I don't want to talk about this right now," I said.

Emyla reached out and stroked my cheek. She moved in for a kiss, but when her lips pressed against mine, they encountered lifelessness. She pulled away.

"Maybe we can meet here this somn and talk about it then? Spend some quality time with one another?"

I knew what that meant. I needed to stop leading her on, but it was probably already too late for that.

"We'll see," I said.

Emyla nodded then made her way out of the jurte, lifting the tent's inner flap and ducking out. I sat there and cursed under my breath. This wasn't what I wanted to devote my time or mental energy to. I forced myself to eat then headed back over to the microscope and tried and failed to regain my focus. The seeds jumped away from my pick, and the last thing I needed was to lose any of them. Every one was precious. The luftors grew the ONi crystallites, and the ONi were how we breathed on the too-thin air of Neuen.

I needed a break and a change of view. I donned my gloves, grabbed my rebreather, and fixed that mask on the lower half of my face. I grabbed a handful of ONi crystallites from the urn in the center of the jurte and tossed them into the satchel attached to my rebreather. ONi were a bio-engineered form of solid oxygen and nitrogen that changed to gas on heating. With a fresh supply of breathable air, it was safe to leave the jurte. I stooped through the two sets of flaps that held the air and heat in.

Then I was outside, surrounded by luftor fields, row on row on row of perfect specimens. That sight alone was a balm. That's not to say the luftors were beautiful. Other Reisende, those who didn't devote their life's work to the plants, would probably describe them as grotesque. Their smooth, black exteriors were more vine-like than tree-like. Warped and twisted, just gnarled spikes that reached about two meters when fully grown.

I leaned down and inspected the leaves on the nearest luftor. They were gray and occurred in couplets, each the size of a pinky nail. Normally, the larger the surface area of the leaf, the better the absorption from our faint red sun's rays, but everything about the luftors was designed to strike a delicate balance. Neuen's thin atmosphere would suck out any moisture in the leaves. Small ones reduced this tendency as did the leaf curling mechanism bred into the earliest of the luftors, ages ago.

But evolution is a clumsy thing. Even that ancient feature left room for improvement, and that's what I'd devoted my years as a junior botanist to—studying thousands of specimens, watching their reaction to temperature fluctuations, finding the ones that responded fastest and most consistently, and using selective breeding to make those traits become the dominant ones. And that had been child's play. My claim to fame was more ambitious.

I knelt down to the soil underfoot, careful to avoid the jumble of root fibers that blanketed the base of the luftors. I'd spent three years developing the new root structures so that the plants were an intertwined network, sharing nutrients and even information. After introducing my new breed, the productivity of our luftors had tripled.

I rose and walked down the row of plants until I reached

the edge of the luftor platform. I jumped down the meter drop from the metal base filled with the plants and their soil to the dirt of Neuen. I looked out on the Break, that ever-present twilight safely in the Goldilocks zone where the bitter colds of night and searing heats of day met and mingled. It was where we Reisende lived, nomadic, following the slow rotation of Neuen.

The nothingness of Neuen's endless, featureless plains stretched out in every direction. The sky was dim, like always, with just a faint glow heralding the rising sun that never did manage to crest. I scanned the horizon, and that's when I spotted Lyn. We'd been expecting the Itinerate, but her kind normally soared from the south with their gliders shining and buzzing. With Lyn, something was off. She was on foot and dragging an object behind her. I removed my rebreather and waved my arm.

"Hello," I shouted.

Her head jerked up, and she stopped. I fitted the half-mask back over my nose and mouth and trotted towards her. The gusts coming off the Break tore at my robes and tossed her long, thick braid of jet-black hair. When I got within a few arms' lengths, I realized the object she pulled was her glider, an elongated cylinder tapered on both ends with a color and sheen that matched her skin-tight, silver suit.

"Is something wrong?" I asked.

"Help me pull this to the Stamm," she said.

Lyn tossed her hand at her glider. The vehicle caught the yellow glow of daylight to the east and the black of the night to the west and reflected the two, split almost perfectly down the middle. I moved to one side of the glider then hesitated. As a Reisende, I was forbidden from touching tech.

"I give you express permission," she said.

That was all I needed. I grabbed the handle, and she

took the other. A splash of orange on her otherwise silver suit grabbed my attention. It was some kind of fabric braid serving as a bracelet. Itinerates rarely wore adornments, and the material and style told me it must have been gifted by a Reisender.

We both lifted and managed to move the glider forward without too much effort. It was just barely hovering.

"What happened to it?" I asked.

"Malfunction," she said.

I peeked back at the mass of metal. Its two sets of wings were currently folded back and in contact with the body. It was the closest I'd ever gotten to one.

"It's good that you made it," I said. "The Stamm will be relieved."

She nodded but seemed indifferent or else unconvinced.

"I'm Levi," I said. "Levi Zetmer."

"Lynev."

No surname, like every other Itinerate.

We walked in silence. If we hadn't been dragging the glider, we could have cut through the luftor fields and shaved several minutes off our trip. As it was, we couldn't risk damaging the precious plants. Our Stamm was the sole producer of ONi crystallites for the seven other neighboring Stämme and the nearly two thousand Reisende within them.

As we skirted the edge of the platform that held the luftors, Lyn eyed the plants. They were so familiar to me, spending all sol, every sol tending to and studying them. But to other Reisende in Stämme without luftors, those not on the nightside of the Break, they likely looked alien. To an Itinerate, whose whole tour only ever had them visit eight Stämme with luftor fields, the plants must have appeared equally strange. The ONi crystallites hanging on the twisted black branches were fresh and ready for harvesting, having reached the size of a human eyeball. They formed in complex geometries and glowed a soft pale blue. Lyn stared at them as we walked by.

"They're beautiful, aren't they?" I asked.

"You're a botanist?"

"That's right."

"Junior?" she asked.

"No, fully-fledged, since last year."

The rebreathers made it hard to gauge someone's age, but even if she had been able to see my face, she likely would have made the same mistake. I looked younger than my twenty-five years. I glanced at her and tried to guess her own age. I was at an advantage since Itinerates were always somewhere between twenty and thirty years old. A few stray strands of gray in her otherwise black hair told me she was erring towards the latter.

We neared the corner of the luftor platform and entered the Stamm proper. Without the plants obscuring our line of sight, we could finally see Vromdorf. Circular tent on tent on tent. Jurte after jurte after jurte. That's all it was, but to Lyn, it must have been a sweet sight after her travels.

"Let's leave this here," Lyn said, releasing her hold. "Take me to the oberhaupt."

I nodded and dropped my side of the glider. I moved into the Stamm with Lyn trailing. As we passed my fellow Reisende, they stopped what they were doing and watched. They knew who Lyn was, what she was, and had complex feelings towards her. If Lyn noticed the hardened glares or the respectful inclinations of the head, she didn't show it. She walked straight-backed and determined in a march that screamed of duty. She was telling us, "I'm here for you. I've braved the Break for you. When all is said and done, I'll have transited the whole planet from pole to pole, sacrificed three years of my life, lived amongst and for you Reisende."

But that's what every Itinerate told us either in so many

words or by their actions, and it changed no minds. You already either loved or hated them, saw them as saviors or jailors. The reality, of course, was somewhere in between.

We reached the center of the Stamm, and I stopped and turned. Lyn looked at me then to the tent beyond.

"The oberhaupt's jurte," I said.

I waved my hand towards the circular structure. It looked like the one-hundred-odd others, the only distinction—a yellow banner hung lengthwise over the opening. Lyn nodded, ducked in, and was swallowed by the folds of fabric.

***

I got to the Willkommen dinner a bit late that somn. The Essen Jurte was filled with all two-hundred and fifty Reisende of the Stamm, and it took six braziers piled high with ONi to provide enough air for everyone. The fabrics of the walls diluted some of the clamor. Bodies filled the benches set at long tables. I smelled the meal before I saw it—squashes and greens and corn and beans. It was a Willkommen dinner for the arrival of an Itinerate which meant a feast and a celebration.

In the center of the jurte, Lyn stood near the oberhaupt, erect and immobile, distinct from everyone else in her silver suit. It was the uniform of the Itinerates, revealing every perfection of their forms and in stark contrast to our Reisender robes. That was the point. We used our robes to hide external signs of our GLEtches, the manifestations of our flawed genomes. For the Itinerates, that wasn't necessary because they had no GLEtches.

Lyn's hair looked smoothed and less wind-worn. I also finally got a look at her face sans rebreather. Pursed mouth, pointed chin, sharp jaw. It was the kind of face that could look severe or serene depending on how she preferred to present herself, perfect for an Itinerate.

Then she locked eyes with me, hovering near the doorway,

hanging back. What did she see? A man with a mouth on the wide side and a nose with its bridge running flush with the brow. A square and hard jaw. But I had my advantages, and they weren't nothing. I was taller than most, nearing lanky but not to the point of awkwardness. I was also a rarity in having russet brown hair and eyes in a population otherwise dominated by recessive traits—blonde and redheads, green and blue eyes. If she hadn't noticed it before, while we were dragging her glider, she couldn't fail to see it now; I was different. I'd been told that I could pass as an Itinerate and that by an Itinerate.

Lyn looked away, and I scanned the room, catching sight of Emyla and two others of similar age at a table on the edges of the jurte. I headed towards them.

"There he is," Vena said.

She smiled at me and tossed her long, reddish-brown hair over her shoulder. One of her green eyes winked. I didn't love her anymore not after what she had done, but her little mannerisms still managed to exert an echo of a hold over me.

"I'd never imagine you'd be late for a Willkommen dinner," Cade said.

He was the reason for Vena's disinterest in me. My older brother and opposite in every way. Shorter and squatter with chestnut hair and blue eyes. Swarthy and brusque, a protector through and through, even down to the elaborate mustache that those types all wore. Never mind that they made the rebreathers less practical. What did they care? Fashion over function, swagger over substance.

"I got caught up with my work," I said. "A foreign concept for you, I know."

Cade grimaced. If he had a brain underneath all the bravado, he would have known that I only ever aimed to get a rise out of him, and he gave it to me every time.

"Let's see if you sing that tune the next time a labspawn

visits you in the luftor fields," Cade said. "Then you'll be begging for me and mine to save you."

"No, that's the point I'm making, Cade," I said, slipping onto the bench across from him. "Who do you think greeted our Itinerate? Who helped her drag her damaged glider to the Stamm and led her to the oberhaupt?"

"I didn't realize welcoming Itinerates was a protector's duty," Cade said.

"But the protectors are meant to be watching the Break, aren't they?" Emyla asked.

She'd been quiet like she always was, and I'd almost forgotten she was there, despite sitting beside me. Her butting in and taking on Cade was out of character. She looked at me and smiled, her pale eyes boring holes into me, desperate for my approval and hopeful I wasn't still angry with her.

"Did you really not see her?" Vena asked.

With even Vena questioning him, Cade's face turned red. He barred his teeth at me.

"We saw her. This one," he pointed at me, "got to her before any of us could. We figured we'd let him fawn over her like he does with every one of them that rolls into Vromdorf."

Emyla shifted on the bench, and Vena sighed. The two sisters had seen our bickering play out countless times over the years.

"Are you two getting into it already?" Vena asked. "The Itinerate hasn't even been introduced."

Cade ignored her and continued to glare at me. He sensed a weakness. I must have reacted in some way because he was ready to pounce.

"What did the two of you talk about during your nice little stroll, Levi?" he asked, leaning forward and clasping his hands. "Any juicy secrets about the Dipols? Think you can woo this one and convince her to whisk you away to Nord?"

Years ago, I had ached to go to Nord, the northern Dipol,

one of two permanent cities on all of Neuen. How could I not? It was the home of the Itinerates and their kind, our erstwhile kin, ages past before we marred our genomes and exiled ourselves in the process. But Cade was wrong. I didn't crave going to Nord, at least not in the way he imagined.

"I've no idea what you're going on about," I said.

My calm annoyed him and spurred him on. Vena and Emyla watched on helplessly. The switch had flicked, and Cade was out for blood.

"Oh, you do," he said. "The last one, what was his name? Artur? You were friendly with him but not like the others that came before. No, you were really, really friendly, you two. You say we protectors don't do our jobs, but sometimes we do them too well. One of mine, he saw something interesting on patrol one somn. Swore that he caught sight of you coming out of Artur's jurte late. Swore he saw Artur holding your hand as you slipped out, leaning in and tapping your foreheads. A rebreather kiss? No wonder he decided to stay on two whole extra weeks at our little Stamm."

Emyla slammed her fists on the table. We all leaned back in surprise, Cade most of all.

"Why are you like this Cade?" she shouted.

I glanced over my shoulder. Others were looking in our direction. The situation had all the makings of a scene, and I didn't want to give Cade a vehicle to spread his rumor.

"Emyla," I whispered, tugging at her robe.

She whipped her head at me, her hair swaying over her, for once, fiery eyes.

"You shouldn't let him tell such awful lies," she said.

"If they're lies, what does it matter?" I asked.

But they weren't lies. We had never talked about it, who had come before her, but somehow, I knew she knew everything. It was like she had sensed when I was most vulnerable and swooped in for the kill. If there had been no Artur and no

Vena before him, I wouldn't have looked twice at Emyla. Yet here we were, all but set to couple without my consent.

"Attention, attention."

Conversations cut off, and everyone turned their heads towards the center of the Essen Jurte. That's where our oberhaupt stood and, beside him, Lyn.

"I'm pleased to introduce the Itinerate visiting Vromdorf this year," Aarman said. "Many of you, no doubt, saw her arrival."

I didn't know exactly how Aarman did it, but he managed to make the most mundane routines feel more like sacred rituals. That's not to say Lyn's arrival was hum-drum, far from it. But even tedious events felt significant when Aarman made the announcement. To be fair, I didn't have anything to compare him against. He'd been the oberhaupt since my earliest years, but still, something about Aarman implied he was meant to be oberhaupt. Maybe it was his above-average height or the presence he exuded wherever he went. This despite not being anything near GLEtch-free what with the reddish-browns peeking out from his grays and his captivating but decidedly green eyes.

"Lynev is our Itinerate," Aarman said. "Please welcome her this somn or anytime during her stay with us. I know many of you were eagerly awaiting her arrival for the GenMapping of your children or approvals for coupling. Remember that Lynev has traveled a long way to be here and help us. If she requires anything of you, do what she asks without question, without hesitation. She is a Dipoli, after all. Show her the respect and reverence that she deserves. Now, let us eat."

Everyone stood and clapped.

"Let's grab some food while the best of it's still there," Cade said to Vena before rushing towards the platters.

"Would you like me to get something for you, Levi?" Emyla asked.

"No," I said, "I can get it myself."

She nodded and headed for the food. I hung back, wanting to put some distance between the two of us. I didn't like her acting like we were already coupled.

"Levi," Aarman said.

I hadn't noticed him come up to the table. Lyn stood beside him, her arms folded behind her back.

"Oberhaupt Greycher," I said, inclining my head.

"I wanted to thank you for helping Lynev earlier. She told me you carried her glider and showed her to my jurte."

"I'm always happy to help an Itinerate."

I glanced at Lyn.

"How is it? The glider?" I asked.

"It needs work," she said, "but that's nothing you need to worry about."

"I was hoping, Levi, that you and my daughters might keep Lynev company," Aarman said. "I think she would enjoy the evening better with younger Reisende, and I've got to make the rounds besides. Can I leave her with you?"

"Of course," I said.

"Good. Her jurte was erected before the dinner. It's the one with a red banner near Helmot and Vivan's."

Aarman smiled and dove back into the crowds.

"Are you hungry?" I asked Lyn.

"Very."

"Let's see what we can get."

I headed towards the central tables covered with platters, and Lyn followed. We stood in line. It was fascinating to see how people responded to the Itinerate. They all knew she was in the jurte somewhere, this Willkommen dinner being held for her, but even so, they looked startled when they spotted her nearby. Conversations dropped off and became subdued, smiles faded or switched to frowns, a ring of empty space floated around us. It was a no-go zone that had never been defined or declared. I was reminded of how lonely the existence of an Itinerate was. Lyn didn't seem to notice or else care.

"Will you start tomorrow with the GenMapping?" I asked. "Or take some time to recover?"

"Recover?"

"Dragging that glider for however long you did wasn't draining?"

"That's what sleep is for. Besides, the longer I stay, the longer my tour lasts."

So then, she was eager to make it back to Nord. Most Reisende wouldn't find that odd, but I knew things they didn't.

The line moved forward, and we were almost within arm's reach of the food. My stomach rumbled. The glazed rolls in particular were calling for me, rarity that they were. The cooks seldom bothered with baked goods since they took too much time and effort to prepare and didn't last overly long.

"What will you do when you make it home?" I asked.

She wouldn't answer that, couldn't, in fact, but I didn't know what else to say. There were countless questions I had for her and even more topics of conversation I was desperate to breach. But Lyn didn't know me, which meant she wasn't going to bare her soul. She wasn't Artur.

"What would you do after being away from home for three years?" she asked.

Answering a question with a question. Such an Itinerate response, but it was better than silence. I suspected she was warming up to me.

"Well," I said, "this is my home, and it's obviously very different than the Dipols. What I'd do isn't what you'd do."

"People are people. Reisende or Dipoli. We've all got the same basic drives. You might curl up on a mat in your jurte, and I might flop down on some elaborate contraption that serves the same role. We'd both say, 'I'd sleep in my own bed.'"

Reisende and Dipoli being the same? My mouth hung open. I couldn't tell if she was playing a game or not. Her face was impassive and her words matter-of-fact.

"We're up," she said, pointing in front of me.

I turned. Nothing stood between the steaming plates and us. We gathered what we wanted from the spread and made our way back to the table. Vena, Cade, and Emyla were already there eating and drinking away. They looked up and were dismayed to varying degrees on seeing Lyn.

"Lynev's joining us," I said.

I took my seat beside Emyla.

"Scoot down," I said to her.

Lyn sat to my other side and nodded at Vena and Cade across from us.

"I'm Vena Greycher," Vena said. "The oberhaupt's eldest, and this is Cade Zetmer. That's Emyla Greycher. We're glad to have you, Lynev. I'm actually a junior physician working with Kelica Zetmer, our lead physician. I'll be helping you with the GenMapping and coupling approvals."

"Zetmer and Greycher," Lyn said. "Is that a theme to this table or the Stamm at large?"

She took a bite of boiled cabbage and looked at us. No one knew whether she seriously expected an answer or not.

"You just happened on a table with two of each," Vena said. "Emyla and I are siblings, as are Levi and Cade."

"Kelica's our mom," Cade said with a mouth full of bread. "Levi's and mine. I'm sure you'll have a grand time with her."

"Kelica is very accommodating," Vena said, glaring at Cade. "She's always grateful for help from the Itinerates. And the four of us here are doubly pleased with your arrival. We're all set to couple if the approvals go through."

"Not all four of us together," Cade said, a burst of crumbs coming out at the end.

"Obviously," Vena said. "Cade and I and then Levi and Emyla."

I glared to my left at Emyla, but she stared down at her plate seemingly focused on each bite. She radiated tension. She'd been talking, telling people we were coupling even after our spat earlier that sol. She was crafty when she wanted to be. She must have assumed that if word got around about us, it would be too awkward for me to backtrack. Easier to just go along with things except she seemed to forget who I was.

"Emyla spoke too soon," I said.

Her head jerked up, eyes wide and panicked. It only spurred me on.

"I didn't agree to the coupling," I said.

Vena's gaze shifted left and right. Cade shrugged and shoveled a spoonful of corn into his mouth. Lyn watched me, her head tilted by degrees.

"If you wouldn't mind, could you strike our names from the list?" I asked Lyn with my warmest smile.

"Normally, I'd tell you to do it yourself," Lyn said. "But seeing how you did such an admirable job greeting me, I'll make an exception for you, Levi."

What was it that drew Itinerates to me more often than not? Could they feel my own fascination with them? Or was it more primal? A link between us, kindred code, and maybe that alone was enough to engender a bond? In any case, it was obvious to everyone that Lyn was flirting, and Cade sensed an opportunity to do some damage.

"It's so refreshing to have a friendly Itinerate who's willing to do some of the actual legwork for once," he said.

Lyn tore her eyes away from mine and looked fixedly at Cade.

"What does that mean?" she asked.

"Oh just, you Itinerates tend to punch a few buttons on your devices then sit back to wait for the results to come in. Not much effort. It all seems easy enough that we Reisende could do it. Makes one wonder why you Itinerates have to come to our Stamm at all."

Cade wiped his sleeve across his lips and pushed his empty plate away. I'd barely put a dent in my own yet.

"It sounds like you're trying to say something without saying it," Lyn said. "Why not just say it?"

"Don't pay him any mind, Lynev," Vena said.

There she went playing the diplomat as always. Did she do it because she liked to or because of who her father was? Then again, maybe just being around Cade made it a necessity.

"I want to know what he means," Lyn said.

She put her spoon down and leaned in. Cade brought his index and middle fingers to his eyes and wiggled them up and down.

"You're here to watch and report. I mean, I get it, I really do. I'm a protector. We're not so different in some ways."

"A protector, I see," Lyn said.

Normally, Cade would have pushed for more, more of a reaction from her, more discomfort from the rest of us, but he was interrupted by hoots and shouts. We glanced towards the center of the jurte and spotted an herbalist carrying a bag of powder and heading towards the urns with the sublimating ONis.

"Which is it?" Vena asked.

We looked at Emyla.

"A new batch," she said. "A bit of phoria and introspect. I haven't tried it myself, but the other junior herbalists seem to like it."

The herbalist tossed the entirety of the bag on the urn. Within seconds, the fumes started to work their magic. The edge was shorn down, the intensity subdued. Emyla was right. This new batch was good. Reisende moved tables and benches to the sides of the jurte. Drums came out, and the chanting started, deep and guttural and arresting.

I knew the voice to be Aarman's, not because it sounded anything like him, but because this was his duty as oberhaupt. He led the celebration and set the tone for the Stamm. It was primal somehow with the drums tethered to our own hearts, echoing the beat, or else forcing them to pump in time. Aarman's words were cracked and low, invoking an ancient past, of a time before time, the genesis of man on some distant homeworld that no Reisender knew the name of anymore.

We all rose from our seats, stamped our boots to the ground, repeated Aarman's refrain, swayed in a unified frenzy. It was hypnotic, and we all got pulled into the vortex of a collective. To stand by on the side as an observer was unthinkable. Something about the noise and emotions and general atmosphere demanded participation, but not for Lyn or any Itinerate. They weren't openly forbidden from taking part, but if they had, the aura would have gone foul. They seemed to sense this because they always stayed motionless and silent on the sidelines, gazing on, looking almost envious of us Reisende. And they were. Even though we were exiled from their glass city, they were the ones forced to wander along with us, utterly alone in their trek, even their memories having forsaken them.

I couldn't spend much time sympathizing with Lyn though. I was caught up in the moment, and then, as always, people clambered for my flute. In my rush to make it to the dinner, I'd forgotten to bring it with me. I was forced into the perpetual twilight in search of it, stumbling out of the Essen Jurte, so engrossed by the chant that I'd left my rebreather behind. One suck of air was all it took to remind me of its necessity. I whipped around to retrieve it and rammed into someone. I wheezed an apology, every word making my lungs ache. There was Lyn, wearing her rebreather and holding mine aloft.

"You left it on the bench," she said.

I fixed it in place, attached it to the satchel hanging on my belt, and sighed at the gush of oxygen-laden air that filled my lungs.

"Do you do that often?" she asked. "Forget the thing that lets you breathe?"

"Only when I'm fumed," I said. "Are you my escort in my flute hunt?"

"No," she said, wrapping her arms one over the other. "I want to go to my jurte. I would've asked someone where it was, but it's chaos in there. I figured you could show me while you were already out here."

"You won't get to hear me play," I said.

With another Itinerate, I would have avoided anything remotely flirtatious, but she had been the one to start it earlier. Besides, I was drawn to her. Part of it was the fumes and her being an Itinerate, but more than that, it was Lyn herself. Something I couldn't quite read. She was hiding, like me. The real version of herself nestled safely away.

"I'm a bit curious to see if you're any good," she said. "How about we stop by your jurte, pick up your flute, and you play a tune for me? Then you drop me off at my jurte. Fair?"

"Follow me."

We weaved through the jungle of tents. The Stamm was still and silent except for a faint throbbing from the drums and the occasional crunch of a protector's boots. We made it to the jurte where I lived with Cade and my mother.

"Come in," I said.

I held the outer flap open and waited for Lyn to move into the small entryway. Once she was inside, I let a few seconds pass then peeled back the inner flap. I removed my rebreather and checked the quality of the air with a few short breaths. It was thin, so I tossed a few of the ONi crystallites from my satchel into the urn in the center of the jurte. Lyn inspected our belongings while I tried to get the flame to catch below the large brass bowl. She was in Cade's corner of the seven-meter-wide circle that was our home. There were tapestries hung on almost every bit of wall, but those near his space tended to feature scenes of battle or sport. He had a little display of weapons near the foot of the mat that was his bed and a jumble of clothing spilling out of a woven chest. Even with the precious few belongings we Reisende had, Cade still managed to hoard.

Lyn wandered to Kelica's spot, between mine and Cade's. Hers featured artisan trinkets, fabrics with beads and a clump of necklaces that had seemingly fused together by their intermingling over the years. They were gifts, despite the fact that my mother never wore adornments. Either she was sentimental, which I doubted, or she wanted to show off what others had given her in case they visited.

"Cade's?" Lyn said, pointing to my brother's space then to Kelica's, "And your parents'?"

"Just my mother's."

I moved away from the urn now that the flame had caught and the ONi were sublimating. I rummaged through my chest and pulled out a thin, featureless box. I slid the top off and retrieved a wooden flute from within.

"And this is yours," she said.

She stood next to me, and I looked up at her and smiled.

"The yin to Cade's yang," I said. "Or yang to Cade's yin, whichever you like."

"Yin and yang?" she asked, sitting down beside me on my mat.

"Dipoli don't use those words?" I asked.

She shook her head.

"I don't know where they come from," I said. "I just know they mean opposite but complimentary."

"I'd never take you two for brothers," she said.

"You couldn't give a better compliment," I said.

I lifted my flute. Lyn watched me, the light beneath the urn casting strange shadows on her face. I breathed in deeply, the sensation smoother than when we had first arrived. Then, I touched the wood to my lips and forced the air out of my lungs through the slit of my mouth. My fingers found the small openings on the body of the cylinder I held, and they moved across them in a pattern I didn't even have to think about. The notes sounded and shifted. The volume followed the exertions of my lungs. Lyn's eyes were fixed on me.

I preferred somber tunes maybe because they weren't the norm for most music created by Reisende. We'd been in exile for generations, forced to wander Neuen, but our journey never brought us to new places. All sense of adventure and exploration were taken from us. We were stuck on set paths, those defined by the Lats, metal rails that girdled the planet like a series of ever-tightening belts from pole to equator to pole, all at fixed latitudes.

We dragged our belongings with us, trudging behind the fields that held luftors for our Stamm and food crops for the other Stämme. If it wasn't for those platforms, maybe we could have strayed from the Lats. But the Lats held the luftors, and the luftors were for the air we breathed. If we wandered too far from the Lats, we choked. They were our literal leash.

Maybe it was that desire to break free that drove most Reisende to play loud and lively music. Hear us, see us, feel us, they said. I liked a subtler approach. It seemed Lyn did too. She sat in silence, almost holding her breath until I pulled the flute away from my lips.

"I can see why they wanted you to play," she said. "You're good."

"They wouldn't want to hear anything like that," I said. "That was just for you, Lynev."

Something about my words made a switch flick in her. Her smile faded, and the brightness in her eyes died.

"Tomorrow, the Stamm starts to turn against me," she said.

I knew what she meant. I'd seen it year after year.

"Not every Reisender will," I said. "Plenty of parents have been waiting for their child's GenMap."

She shook her head and fidgeted with her fabric bracelet.

"They think they want to know, but they don't. Even one GLEtch is one too many."

"Those waiting to couple then. They'll be grateful at least."

"Except when I tell them the prelim assessment that the physicians did was wrong," Lyn said. "When I have to explain how they aren't, in fact, compatible. That any children they produce will be riddled with GLEtches, so they have to move on and find another mate even when sometimes there isn't anyone else."

She stared at the floor, looking worn and tired. It was clear that, like every Itinerate I'd known, Lyn's tour had taken its toll on her. She was bitter and jaded, but beneath that, there was something more. Rage? But it was gone before I could be sure I'd seen it at all.

"Maybe some people are secretly relieved not to couple," I said.

"Like you with that Emyla woman?" Lyn asked.

"Like me with anyone," I said. "I have no interest in coupling. Ever."

"I'm not sure you'll get that luxury. Based on what I see from the outside, I'd say you have an especially low GLEtch count."

My mind ran back to the year prior. I was with Artur again, staring at my GenMap he'd helped me run. The text at the bottom of his digital display throbbed in time with my rapid heart rate. It was impossible, didn't make sense—I was an anomaly, unnatural, the result of someone tampering with the forbidden? Everything we Reisende were supposed to be moving away from. I was our twisted and distant past come back to haunt us. I was the lock and key that would keep us further barred from the pearly gates of Nord. That wave of self-loathing passed through me again until I remembered what Artur had told me.

"Who cares what your GenMap says. The whole system is flawed. We all have mutations. The only difference between Dipoli and Reisende is how the mutations formed in the first place. You're perfect just the way you are, Levi."

Then the rush of thoughts faded, and it was just Lyn sitting in front of me again.

"I'm Vromdorf's prized cow," I said.

"That's a funny way to phrase it. You can have your pick of the Stamm, and here you are sulking."

She didn't know the half of it, but there wasn't any point in whining. I didn't need her sympathies. No, better to give her the version of myself that would pull her in. The intelligent, capable, charismatic Levi. Lyn rose. I grabbed my flute and stood.

"Not sulking," I said. "Just an insatiable desire for more, always more."

Her eyes flickered and a smile cracked.

"Your Stamm must have a parable about the dangers of greed."

"No doubt," I said. "But my affliction tends more towards limitless ambition, the worst curse for a Reisender. I'm a scientist with no tech, no access to all the stores of knowledge you Dipoli have."

"A tragic flaw," Lyn said, "which would make you a tragic hero. But you know what that means?"

"That I have to die?"

Lyn leaned in so that our faces were only a hand's width apart.

"Or suffer a fate worse than death," she said.

"Before things get any heavier, let me drop you off at your jurte. I need to try to be in a light mood for my performance."

I tapped my flute with my fingers, the wood clicking under my nails. Lyn nodded and donned her rebreather then we headed out.

Vromdorf

Lyn

I couldn't call my time in Vromdorf dull. My fifty-seventh Stamm, and it still managed to surprise me time and time again. Even that first full sol was filled with drama. I should have taken it as a sign of what was to come, but hindsight is twenty-twenty.

I was asleep in my jurte when a guttural howl tore through the fabric walls. I jumped up and scrambled into a crouch, wide and low. My rebreather was already in my hand, and I fixed it in place before I was even fully conscious. I grabbed my gun, leaning against my lockbox. Then I popped my head out of the outer flap and scanned the sky. Same as always. Perpetual twilight.

The only sign of the passage of time came in the form of the Reisende. The corridors between jurten were silent and still. It was early, and most of them were likely still recovering from the Willkommen dinner last somn. I held my breath and waited for that howl to repeat. After twenty long seconds, I doubted myself. Had it been in my dreams? But no, I never had any. Then a human scream sounded.

I tore through the Stamm in the direction of the cries. The occasional Reisender face peered out of a jurte. My frantic rush scared most back in, but for the curious ones that didn't retreat to safety, I threw a few curses to drive the danger home. Someone was already in trouble. I wasn't going to have a bloodbath on my hands.

Fortunately, I wasn't alone. As I got closer to the focus of the screams, protectors appeared, all heading in the same direction. The luftor fields. Baskets of ONi sat near the edge of the platform, overturned, spewing their precious cargo.

A few protectors huddled around something. I pushed my way through. They tended to a Reisender. He was old and gray, his face white from shock and blood loss. They were fumbling in their attempts to tie a knot above a gnash in his leg oozing dark red liquid. Even if a physician was on hand, he wouldn't have made it. The creature had hit an artery. It was a precision puncture. Round. Clean.

"Everyone on your guard," I said.

I took in my surroundings. I needed everything silent. I needed everything still.

"No one move or speak," I said.

"But Gerald needs help," one of the protectors said. "He's bleeding out."

I locked eyes with the protector. She bore a pigmentation anomaly on her jawline that plunged down her neck before being hidden by her robe's collar. A GLEtch.

"He's gone," I said. "The poison is already working its way through his system."

The old Reisender started to convulse. His mouth foamed, and his eyes rolled back.

"Don't move or make a sound," I said.

The ten-odd protectors around me went stock still. Wind

rustled the luftor leaves. ONi crystallites tap, tap, tapped against one another. Then, there was a gasp and an intake of breath. The protectors didn't hear it. It had to be over a hundred meters away. Only my ears were primed for those subtle cues. I dove into the nearest row of luftors and zipped past the plants. I stayed low and searched. Then, there it was. Labspawn.

This one was half panther and half scorpion. Muscular limbs, segmented tail, razors for claws and teeth and stinger. The eyes were the worst though. Black irises with white pupils, slit like a feline's but doubled in each eye. The worst manifestation of GenEn. Creatures that had no business sharing a body spliced into monsters for a fight long gone, now routinely turning against their creators' descendants.

But the creature wasn't alone. It had a Reisende in its sights. Levi, my botanist flutist. He was lying on the soil, back to the ground, legs pushing away from the creature advancing on him. The labspawn was toying with Levi. It was so certain that he was no threat, confident that the rest of us were too slow and far away to save this one little Reisender. It was stupid, and for that, it would die.

I swung my gun around and let the long-barrel sit between luftor branches. An ONi tapped against it, and the labspawn's ears twitched. We made eye contact. I squeezed the trigger. My shot pierced its left pincher, and blue-green blood erupted from the fractured exoskeleton. The labspawn howled and pulled back. The next bullet sank into its left paw. Its pseudo-feline face smashed into the dirt. Levi backpeddled. I closed in.

The labspawn chomped its jaw and mandibles at me. It was feigning defeat, wallowing in its false death-throes. I waited for the smallest tic in its hindquarters then sprang back just as the poison barb on the end of its tail slammed down. It sank into the soil where I'd been.

I sneered and lodged a bullet straight into the bulbed end of it. Blue-green blood spewed. It roared and howled. Another bullet traveled through its head then its cries faded into a gurgling. I whipped around to check on Levi. His eyes were fixed on what remained of the labspawn. I went to his side and looked him over.

"Are you hurt?" I asked.

There weren't any obvious wounds on him, but the Reisender robes made it hard to tell.

"I don't think so," Levi said.

"Did it hit you?"

Levi shook his head.

"Come on," I said, "I'll take you to the Medizin Jurte just to be safe."

I slung my gun over my back and helped him up. I let him use me as a crutch. He was shaking, but his legs didn't give out on him. By the time we made it to the edge of the luftor platform, he could walk on his own. The protectors craned their necks forward to see who or what was emerging from the fields.

"It's done," I said. "There's a carcass down that row of luftors. Take it out, but be careful. There's still poison in its tail."

"Don't damage the luftors," Levi said.

He stood looking down at the old Reisender who'd been poisoned, the white foam hovering in his mouth and dancing in the wind gusts.

"Why were you out so early?" Cade shouted.

He pushed past the other protectors and grabbed Levi's arm. Levi looked at him in a daze.

"Huh?" Cade asked. "No one is supposed to be in the fields until after the first bell. You know that. We don't patrol out here until then."

Cade shook his brother, and with each jolt, life flooded

back into Levi until he pushed Cade away. A few of the other protectors moved in and kept the brothers from attacking one another.

"You did this," Cade said, pointing at the body of the old botanist. "Gerald is dead because you couldn't follow a simple set of rules. Work, work, work. So obsessed, and for what?"

I moved to Levi's side and grabbed his forearm.

"That's enough," I said to Cade. "He needs to see a physician. You can berate him later, after he's had some time to recover."

Cade went to stay more but stopped himself. I tugged Levi towards the Stamm. Reisende were already heading in the direction of the luftor fields.

"It's not safe out here," I said. "Go back to your jurten."

They wavered. I released Levi's arm and stood with my legs wide and my hands on my hips.

"That's an order," I said. "Labspawn are out. Go back to your jurten. Now."

I'd used a few magic words, but labspawn was really the one that did the trick. Most Reisende were running to safety, and Levi and I had a free path to the Medizin Jurte. It wasn't hard to find considering it was nearly four times as large as a standard jurte.

When we got there, an older woman was already in, organizing the scrolls, prepping the space for the GenMapping. She looked up as we entered, her alert blue eyes sitting behind a set of rudimentary glass lenses. Her vision must have been particularly bad to call for those. A GLEtch.

She shifted her eyes from me to Levi then went gray in the face.

"What happened?" she asked.

I brought Levi to one of the dozen mats situated in the Medizin Jurte. The woman rushed over.

"He says he's not hurt," I said. "But you should make

sure he's not been hit. It was a labspawn. With poison. It got at least one Reisender."

She pulled Levi's robes off and inspected every inch of his skin for signs of injury. I stood back and watched. Levi's shock was fading and giving way to embarrassment. Without any clothing obscuring the view, his lack of GLEtches was apparent.

"Where were the protectors?" the physician asked.

"Some got there before me," I said, "but not by much. One of them said something about them not patrolling the luftor fields this early."

"Luftor fields?" the physician said.

She glared at Levi, who refused to meet her eye. It clicked. This wasn't just some physician. This was his mother, Kelica, the lead physician, as Vena had said the somn before.

"Why were you out there before the first bell?" she asked.

She grabbed Levi by the jaw and forced him to look at her. Levi frowned but otherwise took the punishment. It was fascinating. A man in his mid-twenties reverting to a little boy in his scolding.

"Gerald asked me," Levi said. "He was behind on the ONi harvesting, so I offered to help."

Kelica released his face, shook her head, and set about checking for injuries again.

"I take it you're the lead physician?" I said.

"Kelica Zetmer," she said.

"Well, Kelica, given the death, we might need to delay the GenMapping until next sol."

Kelica stopped her inspection, straightened, and stood.

"I don't think that's necessary."

Two-hundred and fifty Reisende in a Stamm. Even if Kelica didn't have fond feelings towards the one that had died, her coldness was a shock.

"A Reisender was killed," I said.

"And that is tragic, but it's no reason to punish those who are still alive, some of which have been waiting a year for your arrival."

She forced a smile. It was bold of her to be so direct with me, and maybe in someone else, I would have respected the forwardness. But I knew Kelica's type. The serious, stern lead physician that ran her operation like a machine. Maybe it had something to do with how the edges of her lips sloped downward or how she smiled without her eyes, but I didn't like her.

"You know your Stamm better than I do," I said.

"Let me finish up with him," she said. "My physicians should be here within the hour."

I took the opportunity to head to the Essen Jurte for food. The protectors were out in force patrolling the Stamm, and the Reisende were on edge. The few that were in the Essen Jurte ate in silence. It must have been some time since a labspawn attack in Vromdorf. I had to remind myself that even spotting the creatures from afar was a rarity for the Reisende. To have one enter the sanctity of their Stamm and kill one of their own? It shattered any illusions of security in the Break.

But it wasn't my problem to solve. The oberhaupt would calm his people, probably give a speech, use the opportunity to remind them of why they needed to stay true to their course. The Dipols awaited. Once they cleansed their genomes, removed all lingering traces of GenEn from the bygone past, then they could return to Nord.

I didn't waste any time returning to the Medizin Jurte. Kelica didn't either when it came to diving into our work.

"These are my physicians," she said.

She arced her arm across the line of subordinates. Nine Reisende stood in front of me. They held their heads up. Spines erect. Hands clasped in the small of their backs.

"I currently have four junior physicians and five fully-fledged ones, excluding myself," she said. "Juniors, please move one step forward."

Four younger Reisende followed her command. Vena Greycher, daughter of the oberhaupt, was among them. She smiled at me, probably imagining that our interactions from the Willkommen dinner somehow meant there was a familiarity between us. To be fair, she wasn't unlikable. She had a trusting face and good features for a Reisender, at least the features not shrouded by her robes. Any GLEtches she had weren't visible. She had to be a popular one among the males. Still, it was the fact that she'd clearly been doted on her whole life that was off-putting.

"If you need any assistance," Kelica said, "feel free to ask any of my physicians."

"Thank you," I said.

I glanced around the Medizin Jurte and spotted Levi still on that same mat, sitting with legs crossed and resting against his arms, watching the proceedings. I smiled and nodded. He did likewise. Then my eyes moved to the remainder of the jurte.

The space was taken up by woven baskets and light-weight tables. They were flimsy things but the best option when portability was prized. Scrolls covered all the surfaces. Those would be for the GenMappings and later the couplings. The Reisende were eager for me to start my work. That much was consistent across all Stämme.

Kelica moved in the direction of the tables. She grasped one of the still-rolled scrolls and held it out in both hands like an offering. I had to keep myself from openly sighing. I was tired. No, beyond tired. Exhausted. My tour had worn me down. My drive, eagerness, sense of duty, they'd all but evaporated long before I'd even set foot in Vromdorf.

It was like I was stuck in a perpetual loop. Each Stamm

a repeat of the one that came before. Every Reisender either hostile or groveling. Even if I had been inclined to make connections, there was never enough time to forge meaningful bonds before I had to move on. Besides, how could I hope to bridge the gap between Dipoli and Reisender? I was untouchable to them. To top it all off, I didn't even know myself.

Still, I played the part they expected me to. The physicians began to hum. I strode up to Kelica, took hold of the scroll, and unrolled in on the table. The cluster of physicians were attracted to the ritual like flies to shit, eager to see the mutations still running rampant in their genomes. On the stiff and brittle parchment, someone had scrawled the first offspring's name followed by the names of its progenitors. Besides other information related to the birth itself, the scroll was blank and waiting. I turned to face the physicians and nodded solemnly at each one.

"We begin with the GenMapping."

I turned back to the table and grasped the opened scroll. I lifted it above eye level. The hums shifted to whispers of a repeating strain in a tongue I didn't understand. Either an archaic dialect or gibberish. Meant to sound mysterious and foreign. The ritual had to have its weight.

"First," I said, "Tann Brome sired by Lilya and Thoms Brome."

Vena and another junior physician opened the inner then outer flaps of the Medizin Jurte and ushered in the first couple. While waiting for the Reisende to enter, I laid the scroll back on the table. Then I removed my supplies from the bag slung over my shoulders—cotton gloves, a large bottle of solvent, and a pipette. I put each on the table. I slid the gloves on with the gravity they all expected, the chant quickening.

I unlatched the GenMapper from my belt. On the handheld device, more akin to magic than tech to them, I checked the connection to the network and ensured that I was logging data for Vromdorf. Then I keyed in the names of the offspring and its progenitors before depositing the GenMapper on the table.

"Tann Brome," I said, arms lifted and wide.

I waited for the parents to come forward. Kelica stood to my side with a fresh needle point and vial in hand. The parents brought their red-haired infant to the lead physician. Kelica grasped the child's toes and pricked the heel. The chanting got louder. The child squirmed and started to whimper, but Kelica held the foot tightly. She pinched the flesh around the wound until the blood dripped into the vial.

The child's pouts turned to cries then screams. Kelica didn't flinch. She didn't even seem to register that she was causing the child discomfort. The parents looked unsettled and glanced at me. I kept a neutral expression and waited for Kelica to finish. Finally, when she had enough sample, she released the foot and let another physician step in to clean the wound. Kelica already seemed to have forgotten that the child existed at all. She focused on the vial and handed it to me in both hands. To her, this was the precious thing, not the howling creature it had been sourced from.

I took the specimen from Kelica, added solvent, and extracted the mixture using the pipette. I released a couple drops of the solution into the specimen slot on the GenMapper. The chanting reached a fever pitch in time with the falling of the drops. Then it stopped. The only noise came from the GenMapper giving off beeps and whirrings. It mesmerized the Reisende.

The physicians stood in an arc around the device and swayed in time with one another. I handed the contaminated vial and pipette tip to Kelica for cleaning. The parents were shooed away. The genome would be sequenced by the end of the sol, but it would be sols more until they received the results. The Reisende liked to make a grand show of it. Everyone got their child's GenMap at the same time—typically the end of my first week. Then it would be on to the couplings.

The rest of the sol consisted of me routinely checking the GenMapper as the physicians swayed and took up bouts of chants. It was mind-numbing. What made it worse was the fact that I wasn't even needed. Any one of the Reisende could have easily stood in for me, if they were taught what I had somehow instinctively known at the beginning of my tour.

But then, that would mean trusting them to oversee their own reproduction, and we simply couldn't have that. They weren't meant to use tech, even tech that was as much of a black box to me as it would have been to them. Fortunately, the tedium wasn't as bad as it could have been this time, thanks to Levi. Throughout the sol, I watched him from my post.

When the GenMapper grew quiet and still, everyone in the jurte did too. The swaying stopped. The chanting fell off. A final long beep told us the sequencing was complete. I checked the display for the telltale green box then hooked the device to my belt. It would take a good part of the somn for the data to upload to the network. It was best to do that in the comfort of my jurte.

I scrawled the date and time on the child's scroll. We'd have to wait until all the other children's GenMappings were complete to fill in the rest of the details, namely the GLEtch count. I turned back to the physicians and nodded at each. Kelica dismissed them. I collected the rest of my equipment; I couldn't leave it out for any Reisender to interact with. Although I'd need it in the Medizin Jurte for the next several sols, it had to come back with me every somn.

I glanced in Levi's direction. He sat on his mat, still, patient, obedient. I migrated over to him.

"So you got injured after all?" I asked.

"My mother seems to think some minor scrapes could have been from the labspawn. She said I had to stay here until the end of the sol, just to be safe."

"It's the end of the sol, isn't it?"

Kelica came up beside us.

"Until next sol then," Kelica said to me.

"Yes, next sol."

"Go home, Levi," she said.

Kelica turned and passed through the jurte flaps. Levi rose from his mat.

"She's angry with me for putting myself at risk," he said. "This was punishment more than anything."

I moved in towards Levi despite the fact that no one was around that could overhear us.

"Did Gerald really ask you to help him, or did you ask him to help you?"

Levi's eyes shifted, and I had my answer right there. Gerald was dead, so no blame could be laid on Levi's shoulders. Why should Levi take the fall when Gerald could, with no consequences? I found myself drawn to him even more.

"Good somn, Levi," I said.

***

It was well into the somn, and I couldn't find sleep. Typical. Was this true of the other me? The Lyn before my tour? Linked by our bodies, the insomnia etched into our genomes? I laid on my back and stared up at the folds of fabric that made up the ceiling. My hands strayed to my bracelet, unfastened the fabric, and worked and reworked the braid.

I sifted through my memories. From present to distant past. In order. The labspawn skirmish. Levi's flute playing. The long trek from the last Lat to this one after my glider failed. Stamm to Stamm to Stamm. So many hazed out and indistinct now. Nothing distinguishing them from one another. Until I went back far enough. The blur resolved when I thought of my first Lat. My first set of Stämme. My first GenMap. First coupling assessment. That first ride on my glider. My first view of the Break. But what before? Nothing.

The memories from before my tour were a void. Absent of anything, even a trace of a fragment. How could those missing memories be so completely lost? I mulled the possibilities. The bitterness welled up, but just when it felt as though it would crest and the anger would finally rise to the surface, it died back down. Every time. That happened every time.

A muffled chime rang out. I moved over to my lock box, unlatched it, and retrieved the source of the sounds. My comms, a hand-sized flattened rectangle with a digital display. After bringing the tech to life with a tap, I checked my received messages, expecting the latest to be from the Dipols. A smile escaped on seeing the string of alphanumerics associated with the sender. I hadn't heard from Moray in several sols, and the lack of contact was feeding into my lethargy. But when I opened his message and read the contents, my excitement gave way to unease.

<I hope you made it to the next Lat okay. Was hoping you'd send confirmation but then realized I didn't ask you to. Knowing you, that means you wouldn't. So this is me asking directly: Did you make it to the next Lat okay? Also wanted to warn you that weird things are happening on the Lats. Stämme going missing. I know, how does that even happen? Can't go into detail. Don't know how much of a handle the Dipols have on this situation. Be careful, Lyn.>

It wasn't what I'd hoped to hear. Then again, I didn't know what I wanted him to say. We weren't even supposed to be communicating with one another. Itinerates were kept spread out on the Lats for a reason. Our visits to any given Stamm were separated by at least a year. My contact with Moray had been unusual, and as far as the Dipols were concerned, it had been a onetime occurrence born of necessity.

It was several Lats back. I was between Stämme, about a sol from each. The normally pervasive chill of the Break was almost balmy, given that I was nearing the dayside. I was riding my glider, zoned out with my eyes fixed on the horizon. A haze of clouds glowed a blush pink, and I tried to guess where the sun would rise if I kept heading eastward to meet it.

Then there was a shout and the buzzing of a glider off to my right. I whipped my head in that direction and spotted a glint of metal topped with a human form in silver. Flapping just next to the glider, hovering mid-air, was a strange conglomerate of a creature. Scales and feathers and talons and teeth. I couldn't make it out clearly, but I didn't need to see it to know what it was. On Neuen, there were only humans and labspawn.

My instincts kicked in. I set my glider to coast. I reached to the side for my gun and pulled at it until the locking mechanism gave way. As I neared, I lifted the weapon and aimed down the sights. I used the scope to get a better view. I wasn't more than twenty meters away, but their movements were a blur. I could barely make sense of which limb belonged to which creature.

I shouted as loudly as I could through my rebreather, and the Itinerate glanced in my direction. The second of distraction was all the labspawn needed. One claw on the end of its forked tail whipped around and hit. The force of the impact almost knocked the Itinerate free of the glider. The labspawn rushed. Time slowed for me. I tightened my grip on the smooth metal of my long-barrel and aimed down the sights. I breathed out. I squeezed the trigger.

The shot hit. The labspawn gave off a piercing cry that

sounded like metal and static at the same time. It plunged to the ground, thudding against dirt sprinkled with a black blood. I sent two more projectiles into its mutated flesh. Once I was sure it wasn't moving, I slung my gun over my back and lowered my glider to the ground. I sprinted over to the labspawn and peered down at the mess of viscera. The thing was half avian and half reptilian with more wing than body. The combination of a beak with teeth disturbed me the most.

Confident that the labspawn was down for good and not just playing dead, I turned my attention to the Itinerate. The details visible through his skin-tight suit told me he was male. His glider had auto-landed. He was trying and failing to dismount, his feet caught in their holds.

"Hold onto me," I said.

I laid my gun down and grabbed him. Together, we managed to get him free of his glider. I helped him to the ground and inspected the damage. His eyelashes got caught in his black curls as they stuttered open and close. If I hadn't already seen the gash across his abdomen, his eyes would have told me of his pain. He grasped his rebreather and went to remove it. I'd heard that people sometimes did this when they were injured. It was like he wanted more air but saw the thing providing him with it as an obstruction. Some strange artifact from our distant past when humans lived on a more hospitable world?

I grabbed his hand and squeezed it. With my other one, I fished out some spare ONi from my satchel and dumped them into his. Then I focused on stopping the blood that was leaking from his wound. His suit was trying its best to repair the damage, but the rip was too wide and deep. I needed medical supplies. I glanced at his glider.

"Do you have medical supplies?" I asked.

He closed his eyes and nodded. His grip on my hand

tightened, but I pulled it free and dashed over to his glider. I rifled through his belongings. Opened boxes that weren't locked. Unclasped pouches. Eventually, I found what I needed and hurried back to his side. I'd never gotten injured and had never had to stabilize someone. Even so, my hands seemed to know what to do without any active intervention. I watched them work away. They pulled back his suit's fabric, sanitized the wound, stitched it up, applied ointments and gauze to it. I was mesmerized by the abilities I didn't even know I had. Was it her? The other Lyn? A doctor in the Dipols perhaps?

By the time I was done, the Itinerate was calmer.

"I'm Moray," he said.

He smiled behind his rebreather but kept his eyes shut. The oddness surrounding this Itinerate suddenly hit me. Somehow, there was another Itinerate on my Lat.

"Lynev," I said. "What were you doing here? This is my Lat. Are you lost?"

"Now, that would be telling."

He still smiled and still had his eyes closed.

That somn, we camped in that same spot. I managed to jerry rig our jurten together so that I could keep a watch on Moray. He had fitful sleep, but after several hours, none of the telltale signs of fever cropped up.

Moray was a different kind of Itinerate, and eventually he did do the telling. He dealt with certain situations on behalf of the Dipols. He was something like their fixer. There were jobs that required a human touch, literally. Drops were helpful in many ways, but sometimes the Reisende needed more than supplies. Platforms could get stuck on the Lats. The limited tech we gave them could fail. Not every Stamm could wait an entire year for their usual Itinerate to arrive to solve the issues.

But beyond being a general handyman of sorts, I suspected Moray did dirtier work. Rebellious Reisende could be dealt with by their oberhaupt. Corporal punishment for more minor offenses. Exile or death for more extreme ones. But then there were the Reisende or, worse, Itinerates who went Rogue. If they defied the odds and didn't die from exposure or labspawn in the Break, someone hunted them down on behalf of the Dipols. Moray was that someone.

Given the wide array of tasks he was assigned, Moray moved between Stämme and Lats in an irregular pattern. Not from Süd to Nord. I didn't know what that meant about his tour, specifically how long it was supposed to last. When I asked, he told me he'd been on tour for over four years already and had no idea when they'd call him home. It was one thing to have a long and arduous journey, like mine. But how much worse must it have been to have one without an end in sight?

We stayed in that spot in our jurten for five more sols, and by then, Moray was moving around again. Talking. Laughing. Flirting. I'd had to report the situation to the Dipols shortly after it'd happened so they would know why two of their Itinerates had been delayed. They weren't pleased with the development, but they agreed it was best I keep an eye on Moray until he was fit to move on his own again.

"You know," he said, "you could tell them I'm mending more slowly than I really am."

At that point, his wounds were almost closed.

"And why would I do that?" I asked.

"So you and I can get much-needed rest. I don't know about you, but I'm exhausted. Even before this."

Moray gestured at the bandaged bulk that was his torso.

"Also, this life is lonely," he said. "Maybe it's different for you, interacting regularly with the Reisende and all."

I shook my head and grimaced. It was strange actually talking without having to hide anything.

"It might even be more isolating for me in some ways."

"Then let's do a little something for ourselves."

We did a lot of things for ourselves and each other over the next five sols, but eventually we knew we had to move on. And we did. Me to my next Stamm and Moray to whatever covert task the Dipols had assigned him. But we'd gotten a taste for what life could be like when it wasn't so achingly solitary. We liked it too much to give it up wholesale. Instead, we opted to keep in touch. The life of an Itinerate was a lonely affair, so we'd decided to have an affair of our own. It was ephemeral and happenstance, but when we crossed paths, it was the only time I felt alive.

This message of his bothered me though. I didn't like the tone of it. Moray wasn't the type to embellish. If he was worried enough to give me a warning, it meant things must be bad. I read and reread his words but couldn't make sense of what "Stämme going missing" might mean. I responded in the hope that he would say more.

<I made it to the next Stamm, Vromdorf. Just some minor glider issues, but the Dipols are sending parts for repairs. I'll be in Vromdorf for at least two weeks. Do you think you'll be on this Lat anytime soon? I don't like your warning message. You're not usually so vague. What exactly should I be watching out for? Labspawn? Something else? Be safe yourself.>

I muted the comms. If I didn't, I'd be waiting all somn for the chime from his response. I set about connecting the GenMapper to the transceiver and initiating the data transfer of the sol's GenMap. My stomach growled, and I took it as my cue to head to the Essen Jurte. When I got there, it was mostly empty. I glanced at the few occupants but didn't recognize them as any Reisender I'd interacted with. I was relieved to have a solitary meal. After grabbing a plate that a red-faced cook piled with some kind of mushed mess, I took up a seat on the edge of the jurte. It was all a far cry from the somn before, but that's how it always was. A Willkommen dinner followed by monotony. From that point onward, the food would be dismal, the company minimal, and the work unending.

Except, Levi was a dash of excitement to break up the tedium. I saw him again the next sol. We'd just finished a GenMap of the second child when a horn sounded. Kelica instructed everyone to pack up the entirety of the Medizin Jurte. Time for a Reisen. The whole of the Stamm would gather their belongings, pull down their jurten, and cart everything in a series of chains. The crop platforms moved on their own at a snail's pace, along the Lats, powered by tech. A day on Neuen was a little over six-hundred and eighty sols, which meant the Reisen only had to move the Stamm about a kilometer a week to stay well within the Break.

I grabbed my equipment and made my way back to my jurte. When I got there, Levi was standing nearby, waiting. He nodded at me. The creases at the ends of his eyes told me he was smiling behind his rebreather. He ran his hand through his wavy hair, almost the same shade as the dirt that blanketed Neuen. The movement was impossibly sensual. That was his way. Every little thing he did—when he'd grasped the handle of my glider, when he'd toyed with a pea on his plate at the Willkommen dinner, and especially when he'd ran his fingers over his flute. Every movement, expression, gesture—borderline sexual.

"Your glider is still near the edge of the luftor platform," Levi said. "Did you need help moving it?"

I'd covered the vehicle after meeting with the oberhaupt, but I hadn't bothered to bring it any closer to my jurte.

"Sure," I said.

Levi started for the luftor fields. He had his hands in the pockets of his robes and was silent for the first long stretch.

"How's the GenMapping going?" he asked.

"As it usually does. Smooth. Predictable. Boring."

At the last word, his head snapped to steal a glance at me. I liked doing this with him. Letting my disenchantment with my work sneak out.

"The excitement only starts once the GenMaps are made public," I said.

"But then the Stamm turns against you, like you said, so not the kind of excitement you'd prefer, I take it?"

"I'm sick of GenMappings and GLEtches and couplings. Let's talk about something else."

"Okay," Levi said.

The silence came back and stretched.

"I don't know what to say," he said. "The things I'd like to ask you aren't things you can talk about."

"You're welcome to ask them anyway."

I side-eyed him. I was begging him to breach forbidden topics, not even sure what I'd do if he did.

"Are the Reisen the same in all the Stämme?" he asked.

He was being conservative to start with.

"Mostly, yes. Although some Stämme choose to move ahead of their platforms, where others opt to follow behind. By and large though, it's remarkably similar."

"Are the Reisende the same in all the Stämme?"

Now, he was being more daring.

"What do you think?" I asked.

"Yes and no, but I'm curious to know in what ways we're similar and in what different."

I tossed my braid behind my back. It bumped against my backside. Levi glanced at it before training his eyes on the ground in front of us.

"I only ever spend two weeks in a Stamm," I said. "It's not enough time to take in the differences. Some have different customs, use different phrases, prioritize different things. But everything everywhere is anchored by the Decrees from the Dipols."

"It's a little strange, isn't it?" he asked.

"You mean the Decrees?"

"I mean the whole system."

He waited for a response. I wasn't sure how to give one.

"How else should it be?" I asked.

"I'm not sure, but something about it feels off. We Reisende rely wholly on the Dipols. For the materials we can't produce, for certain crops, for the bulk of our water, not to mention the oversight in removing the GLEtches from our genomes. And yet..."

"And yet?"

He looked at me. I stared back.

"Why do you do it?" he asked. "Why go to all the trouble for us? Organizing the drops, sending your own people on tours that take up years of their lives, coddling us, all in an effort to save us from past mistakes."

I'd wondered this too on and off during my tour, but I didn't know enough about the Dipols or my own people to understand their motivations. So I gave him the only answer I had. The one burned into my mind. The one I was supposed to give if asked.

"It's our duty," I said. "If we didn't do these things, the Reisende wouldn't last very long out here."

Levi looked back at the ground and shook his head.

"My ancestors fought yours, killed them, created the labspawn and set them loose, and you expect me to believe that once the GEC was over and my kind had given our unconditional surrender, yours only opted to show them compassion?"

I stopped. Levi took a few steps before realizing I wasn't moving then did likewise

"The Reisende were Dipoli," I said. "They were family,

friends, lovers. Even if they'd made mistakes, it wasn't a reason to condemn them to death or permanent exile."

"A logical and reasonable answer," he said. "But people, Dipoli or Reisende, are anything but logical and reasonable."

An unease crawled up my spine. There was wisdom in Levi's words, but I couldn't admit it. He was a Reisende, and I was an Itinerate. He was asking too many probing questions. I had to lay down the law.

"It almost sounds like you doubt the word of an Itinerate," I said.

"I'd never be audacious enough to doubt an Itinerate," he said.

He didn't buy my act, but rather than be distraught, I was intrigued. Still, I couldn't let him see that. An Itinerate was only as good as the authority she exuded. I needed to back away. Reestablish my dominance. Then assess if I wanted to let him get subtle tastes of the real Lynev. We walked the rest of the way to my glider in silence. Once there, I removed the covering and stowed the fabric in a pouch on the side.

"It looks like this can still hover," I said. "You ought to assist the other Reisende. I'll manage on my own."

My words had the effect I was aiming for. Levi was disappointed.

"Understood, Itinerate."

He met my coldness with coldness, and it was surprisingly effective. I found myself regretting my rebuttal as I lugged my glider, gathered my belongings, and dismantled my jurte. I was in a sour mood by the time the cogs affixed to the platforms began to turn. I kept to the back of the Stamm until the process was over and opted to erect my little shelter near the outskirts.

While I tried to stabilize my jurte's posts, a cluster of protectors walked by. Cade was among them. I locked eyes with him, and he grimaced on realizing that he was obligated to help the struggling Itinerate. He broke away from his group and beelined towards me.

"You shouldn't put your jurte so far out," he said.

He grabbed a post from my hands and jammed it in the ground. I handed him the hammer I'd been using, and in one massive swing, he lodged the post several centimeters into the dirt. With two more, it was solidly in place. He moved through the other five posts in short order then tossed the hammer in the dirt near my boots. I didn't say a word. He huffed then jogged along the edge of the Stamm in the direction his cohort had gone.

Wanting to avoid the Reisende for yet another somn, I waited until it was late to grab dinner from the Essen Jurte. By the time I laid down on my mat, my mood was abysmal. I still hadn't heard back from Moray, and my attempts to distract myself from that unpleasant fact had only upset me in different ways. But all of that was inconsequential, and soon enough I'd find myself wishing that my only sources of disquiet were a comms silence from my sometimes lover and the growing crush I found myself having on a Reisender.

***

I had four uneventful sols before a catastrophe reared its head. The GenMapping for child number seven was churning along. I was sitting near the device and keeping an eye on it. I let the sounds and whisper chants of the physicians act as a kind of lullaby. Then voices sounded outside. I didn't think much of it until Vena left the jurte then rushed back in and hurried over to Kelica. I couldn't make out the contents of their whispers, but Kelica's widened eyes told me something was at play.

My first thought was another labspawn attack had happened, but no one came to me. No one asked for my help. If it was an internal Stamm affair, I shouldn't get involved. I was an Itinerate. I was meant to be stoic and impassive. I played my little part. Another quarter of an hour elapsed then the protector I remembered from the attack, the one with the GLEtch on her neck, came into the jurte. She caught sight of me and approached.

"Itinerate Lynev, Oberhaupt Greycher would like to speak with you. It's urgent."

She was ready to move, one foot angled back to the entry. I looked at the GenMapper. It still had a few hours more to go. Interrupting a GenMap was unheard of. No one asked anything of an Itinerate while we were working. Whatever was going on was obviously important enough to usurp tradition.

"Kelica, please keep a watch on the GenMapper while I speak with the oberhaupt."

I didn't give her a chance to respond before I donned my rebreather and trailed after the protector out of the Medizin Jurte. When we got outside, a crowd was loitering. I caught snip-bits of conversation. The words "traders" and "Zeindorf" kept popping up, but I couldn't piece together what exactly had happened. As we neared the oberhaupt's jurte, I spotted five wagons piled high with crates of goods.

"Please, go right in," the protector said. "He's waiting for you."

I entered, removed my rebreather, and adjusted my hair. Aarman glanced in my direction and gave me a solemn nod. He was talking to a worn and weathered Reisender.

"I don't have any answers for you, Jorniv," Aarman said. "But here's our Itinerate who will surely have some insights. Please, Lynev, come join us."

Aarman and the Jorniv man sat cross-legged on thick, circular cushions near the center of the larger-than-usual jurte. This was Aarman's work space as well as his home. Any signs of the home-side of things were obscured by a series of screens that split the jurte in half down the middle. This reception area was meant to seat guests and visitors. It was taken up by tables, benches, and cushions acting as seats. The lighting was dim, but the air was wonderfully thick and full. A heaping pile of ONi crystallites was nearly spilling out of the urn nearby.

I walked over and took a seat on the cushion nearest theirs. Jorniv stared at me like I was a rain shower in a desert.

"What's going on?" I asked.

"She doesn't know?" Jorniv asked.

"That's why I asked her here," Aarman said. "Lynev, there's been a development, as you no doubt ascertained from all the commotion in the Stamm. Jorniv here and nine of his fellow traders just returned from a meet with Zeindorf. They were meant to exchange goods. The meet was planned well in advance."

Aarman stopped to gauge my reaction. I had none to give. I didn't care about the rare moments when Reisende from adjacent Stämme met to trade supplies with one another. I was waiting for news. None of this was that.

"We never miss a meet with Zeindorf by more than a few hours," he said. "We rely on Zeindorf completely since we have no other neighboring Stamm. Zeindorf as well as the other six Stämme on our Lat rely on us for our ONi crystallites. You can imagine how they would make every effort to be timely to a meet."

"I understand the situation of meets between Stämme, Oberhaupt Greycher," I said. "I'll ask again. What's going on?"

Jorniv looked at Aarman then back to me.

"Please tell her what you told me, Jorniv," Aarman said.

"They weren't there," Jorniv said. "We went to the meet coordinates, and no one was there. The platform was, of course, like it should be, but no Stamm. We couldn't even see their jurten on the horizon looking east. We talked with ourselves, us traders, and decided to move along the Lat further in case Zeindorf was delayed. We went two whole extra sols east before turning back. We didn't see anything."

"You did the right thing," Aarman said.

Jorniv looked torn, as if the whole debacle was somehow his fault.

"Has this happened before?" I asked.

"I was going to ask you that same question," Aarman said. "No, not with us."

"I've not heard of something like this," I said and then stopped.

Moray's message came to mind. This is what he meant by Stämme going missing. Zeindorf was somewhere far back along the Lat. That wasn't good. If Zeindorf was stalled and they delayed their Reisen too long, the day would catch them. That, and they would get ever more separated from their platforms. Then, who would be around to tend to their crops?

"The Dipols need to know about this," I said. "If Zeindorf is delayed for some reason, they're the ones that will know what to do."

"My thoughts exactly," Aarman said.

"What about all our goods?" Jorniv asked. "Some of them will spoil. The ONi, for one, won't last."

"We focus on what we can do," Aarman said. "We'll use the things that will otherwise spoil while Lynev finds out how the Dipols want us to handle this situation. Now, you tell the other traders to sort the goods. Lynev and I need to talk."

Jorniv took the hint and made his escape. Once Aarman and I were alone, he sighed and rubbed his mustache with his fingers, stroking the thick part and twirling the ends.

"Food will be a problem very soon," he said. "We only

have minimal crops of our own since our botanists focus on the luftors."

"Could you send some of your people to collect crops from Zeindorf's platform?" I asked.

Aarman stared at me like I'd said something in a foreign tongue.

"That's very unorthodox," he said. "Besides, I don't know that sending my people all the way over to the next platform is advisable. I would need some more specifics on how best to do that."

Such stubborn rigidity. Of course the Reisende would balk at the smallest hint of something novel. But Aarman was right. This problem was something the Dipols would need to weigh in on.

"Alright," I said. "Have your people do a calculation to see how much food you have and how much rationing needs to happen. I'll go back to my jurte and contact the Dipols right away. Maybe they can do a food drop for Vromdorf. In any case, I need to know what they want us to do."

"Hopefully, you just informing them will be enough, and they can handle everything else."

I rose from my cushion. The vivid yellow fabric caught my attention for the first time. The stitching was elaborate beyond what I would have thought a Reisender capable of. I was mesmerized by it. Sucked in by the swirls, almost fractal in form. When I came out of my reverie, Aarman was staring at me.

"I'll let you know more when I do," I said.

I left his jurte and barely registered the throngs of Reisende turning to stare at me as I marched to the outskirts of the Stamm. As soon as I was inside my jurte, I unlatched my lock box and retrieved my comms. I still hadn't received a reply from Moray, and with everything that had happened with Zeindorf, I was increasingly worried. It was all linked, no doubt.

If Moray was hurt or worse, who would the Dipols send to help Zeindorf? How many Morays were there? How long would it take another, Lats distant, to make it here? I stopped the frantic rush of fears with a long, slow breath. I unbraided and rebraided my fabric bracelet several times. Then, I brought the comms to life and sent the Dipols my message.

<Traders from Zeindorf missed a meet with traders from Vromdorf. Vromdorf traders moved a full two sols further east. Still with no sign of Zeindorf traders or Stamm. Vromdorf will run out of foodstuffs without a meet with Zeindorf. Zeindorf and all Stämme further east rely on Vromdorf for ONi crystallites. Please advise on next steps.>

I knew they knew which Stämme relied on which, but I didn't want there to be any room for misinterpretation of the severity of the situation. I sat on the ground, cradling my comms and waiting for the reply.

I wasn't actually being selfless or worrying on behalf of the Reisende. No, this was a problem for me too. My tour took me east. Zeindorf was my next Stamm, and if they weren't there, where was I to go? I could skip a Stamm if need be, but in all my travels, I hadn't had to do that. Besides, if Zeindorf was missing, it meant something bad had happened to them. Rushing headlong into danger wasn't my idea of a sound plan. The Stämme were supposed to be my little oases in the hostility of the Break not active threats.

Each minute that ticked by brought surges of nausea. Nearly half an hour passed. The Dipols rarely took so long to respond to even the most mundane exchanges. Then the device emitted a chime, and I propped myself up on my mat.

<Begin. Dipols investigated situation re: Zeindorf via orbital optics. Preliminary assessment inconclusive re: cause of Stamm delay. Zeindorf located 240 km east of Vromdorf. Other Itinerate personnel not available for in-person assessment. Itinerate Lynev nearest personnel. Dipols order

Itinerate Lynev to investigate Zeindorf. Causalities observed. Prepare for multiple possibilities on arrival—labspawn attack, plague, or blight. Dipols order Reisende of skill-sets protector (1), physician (1), and botanist (1) to accompany Itinerate Lynev. Bring protective equipment and testing apparatuses. Estimate one-way travel time via land-based vehicle: 15 hours. Vehicle drop near Vromdorf circa 6 hours. Supply drop on outskirts of Zeindorf for Itinerate and companion Reisende. Foodstuff drop(s) implemented for Vromdorf once need has been assessed and submitted by oberhaupt. Dipols suggest immediate departure (read: next sol) for investigation. End.>

It wasn't at all what I'd expected, and it meant something had happened to Moray. But I didn't give myself time to react. I marched back through the Stamm, tore into Aarman's jurte, and delivered the bad news.

"They're sending me to Zeindorf to see what's happened, and they want three of your Reisende to go with me. I'll need a protector, a physician, and a botanist. I'll leave it to you to figure out who. It'll be about two sols one way. In the meantime, you'll get a food drop once you've let them know how much you need."

"When do you leave?" he asked.

"Next sol. Get me those Reisende, oberhaupt."

Zeindorf

Levi

In my twenty-five years, I'd never left Vromdorf. Never ventured past the edge of the luftor fields, let alone anywhere near another Stamm, and now it was happening. Lyn was going to Zeindorf, and I was going with her. I checked and rechecked the contents of my two bags. One crammed with clothes and dried foods, the other with my botanist's supplies. For the latter, Aarman's instructions had been vague.

"Bring anything that might help with identifying the cause of a blight," he'd said to me in his jurte last somn. "Protective gear and materials for sampling."

It was clear he didn't know what was going on, which was unsettling. All I'd been told was that Zeindorf had missed a meet, the Dipols had investigated remotely, and they had seen bodies, many of them. Lyn was going to check the scene in person to try to make sense of what had happened. The Dipols ordered a set of Reisende to tag along, and Aarman had asked for a botanist in the group. This was my way to make up for having cost Gerald his life; I would be the only botanist putting himself at risk.

The idea of the trip itself was equal parts exciting and terrifying. The main downside would be the company. Not Lyn; I was eager to spend the next few sols with her. The problem was the other two Reisende. Vena had stepped up to fill the role of physician, probably knowing it was what Aarman expected of her.

I was apprehensive about traveling with her. I'd kept my distance ever since she'd chosen Cade over me and smashed my heart in the process. That had been over a year ago, but the sting refused to fade. As if to drive the point home, Cade was the other Reisender tagging along. Of all the thirty protectors they could have chosen from, I was stuck with him. He wasn't coming because he wanted to protect the Itinerate. He was only interested in protecting one person in our little party.

Despite my disappointment, I was resolved to be civil. Besides, Cade didn't know the particulars. He must have thought my angst towards him was just from us being brothers too close in age with such different temperaments. He hadn't even known we'd been rivals for Vena. She and I had kept our little rendezvous a secret, and we'd kept it well. Cade was oblivious, but maybe that's what made the whole thing hurt worse for me.

But my stalling in my jurte wasn't from wanting to avoid Vena or Cade. It was because of who was loitering just outside. I'd heard her voice when Cade had made his way out several minutes before. I half hoped Emyla would leave and see us off like all the other Reisende, but it was asking for too much. Despite her outward show of meekness, she was stubborn. She wouldn't leave until she'd seen me, so I grabbed my two bags, put on my rebreather, and left the jurte. There she was, waiting, not even acting as if she'd been doing anything else.

"Are you really going? To Zeindorf?"

She moved to my side and stood too close, pinching her fingers and fidgeting.

"No, I'm carrying these bags for show," I said.

She was quiet for a few seconds.

"I don't appreciate the sarcasm when I'm trying to have a real conversation, a conversation that isn't easy."

"Yes, I'm going to Zeindorf. At your father's request."

She grabbed my arm, and I had to fight the urge to shake her off. She was at her worst in the moment when she was trying her hardest to appeal to me.

"I'll ask him not to send you," she said.

She held my sleeve with both hands, but I pulled it free.

"Stop doing that," I said. "You'll rip the fabric. Look, I want to go, Emyla. Aarman didn't even need to ask me. I would have volunteered so please stop with the drama."

"Please don't go. It's not safe. Something could happen to you. Something almost did not even six sols ago, and here you are trying to act like that was nothing."

I didn't like the reference, not least because it was still a sore spot for me. I'd made a mistake, and Gerald had died because of it.

"It was nothing. I was fine, am fine. Besides, I'll have better protection this time. Cade will be there and the Itinerate too. They need a botanist for this trip. I'm the youngest fully-fledged one, and the only one willing to go after what happened with Gerald."

The name stuck in my throat. She narrowed her eyes and tilted her chin down.

"I don't want you to go."

I laughed, the exhalations exaggerated by my rebreather.

"Well, that's not your call, now is it?" I said.

I moved in closer to tower over her. I was exhausted by her blindness or unwillingness to see our relationship for what it was. First, the forcing of the coupling, and now this demand of hers. She was growing bold, and I wasn't going to let her think she could get what she wanted from me. She was delusional, and I needed to correct that, sooner rather than later.

"Emyla, we're not coupled, and we won't be coupled, ever. At some point, you mistook our fling for something more meaningful. In case you're still confused, it's not."

"But you said we would couple," she said.

"When did I say that? Last year? Right after Artur left? When you could sense my weakness and tried to take advantage of it?"

She looked away, but I had to keep going. She needed to understand exactly how I felt so she would finally let go of this silly dream of hers.

"You think you know me and want me, but you don't know the half of it," I said. "You see a man with minimal GLEtches and the esteem of the Stamm, but that's not who I really am. Deep down, there's something different, and if I let any of you see it, you'd shun me. Rohn was lauded and loved until he wasn't, until he showed too much of who he really was. So long as he followed the rules, he was a genius, but when he dared to test the waters, he was a maverick and eventually a traitor."

Emyla lifted her eyes to mine at the mention of that name. Rohn was a black sheep, and even she felt the need to hammer that home. She was conditioned and conditioned well. Not surprising given who her own father was.

"Rohn left the Stamm," she said. "There's no excuse for that. And besides, you're nothing like him."

I continued to tower over her, barely tilting my head and instead just angling my eyes to meet hers.

"What do you know about him?" I asked. "What do any of us really know? Secondhand knowledge. And you might be surprised by how similar I am to Rohn. I mean, half my genome came from him, but you don't like to think about that, do you? Ignore the fact that my own father deserted the Stamm except I'm telling you, that's part of the real me. The pushing of boundaries, the flirting with the forbidden." I leaned in. "That's who I am. That's what gets me fired up, not you, not this monotonous existence. For now, I'll settle on going to Zeindorf and getting the thrill of danger from traveling the Break. But just know, this is me. I told you you wouldn't like it."

I pulled back and watched for her reaction to my blunt truth. She stood still and just looked at me. I waited a few seconds for something, anything, from her. When she continued to do nothing, I turned and headed towards the center of the Stamm. Before I moved around the side of a jurte, I glanced over my shoulder. She still stood in the same spot. Maybe I'd been too harsh, too honest, but the little lies she told herself about what we were and who I was needed to stop. I was doing her a favor in the long run.

When I made it to the oberhaupt's jurte, a thick hoard of Reisende were surrounding the structure. I had to push and shove in order to make it through. When I finally broke into the center, I found my companions and Aarman standing together in a circle.

"You're late," Cade said.

He had at least three different types of weapons slung across his chest and hanging off his belt. He was decked out in full protector gear, still wearing the Reisender robes, but ones that were slightly more fitted for ease of movement and contained pockets and loops with pouches attached. On his torso, he had a padded vest that was meant to serve as armor.

"You're not actually late," Vena said.

She shook her head at Cade. She wore the standard Reisender robes but had her hair pulled back into a low and loose ponytail. Like me, she had two sets of bags, and in one, the shapes and forms of medical equipment showed through the burlap.

"We're just making sure we're all on the same page," Aarman said. "You brought materials to test plant specimens, Levi?"

"All the standard supplies we use when evaluating health and robustness."

"Air-tight containers for sampling?" Lyn asked.

With the exception of her gun, metal rod, and bag, she alone looked unchanged, like our sols' long trip was business as usual to her. And in some ways, it was. A trip to another Stamm was something she undertook every couple of weeks, but a missing Stamm? That had to be out of the ordinary even for an Itinerate.

I opened my bag and pulled out some of the storage materials. She seemed satisfied with the lot and turned back to Aarman.

"The Dipols said fifteen hours to get there. I'd say at least two sols to travel and rest, one sol to investigate, and then another two sols until we make it back."

Aarman gestured us closer until we were all nearly shoulder-to-shoulder in a little human pentagon.

"Please be careful, each of you," he said. "You're doing a very selfless thing for Vromdorf, and I won't forget it. Now, take the next several minutes to say any last goodbyes, then you really should be off."

"Meet at my jurte," Lyn said. "I'll be waiting there along with our ride."

She moved, and the Reisende parted. Once she'd passed, they filled the void she'd created within seconds like a repulsive force existed between her and them. It was like my own polarity was somehow flipped with respect to the Itinerates. I wanted to follow after her, but I had at least one goodbye I needed to give. Cade was with her already.

"Watch after him," Kelica said to Cade while looking at me.

"He's meant to watch after all of us," I said. "Even though we all know there's only one reason he's going."

"It doesn't matter why he's going," she said. "The fact is he's going. That's all I care about. Watch after Levi," she repeated to Cade.

Cade inclined his head and held it down for a few seconds. He was such a different person around our mother. She put him in a kind of trance, suppressed his demons, made him almost bearable. Kelica looked at me, serious and grim. She didn't want me to go, but she'd never say so and never ask me to stay. She nodded. That was all I got from her. No words, just that tilt of the head and that look of suppressed pain before she turned away and melted into the crowd.

Cade and I set out for Lyn's jurte. When we got there, she was staring eastward, her silver suit catching the fixed dawn's light and emitting a muted glow.

"Never understood why you Itinerates wear that get-up," Cade said. "You're just asking for labspawn to attack. With all that fancy tech you've got in the Dipols, why the hell would they go with chrome?"

Lyn turned around and put a hand on her hip.

"Do you really not know the answer to that, protector?"

Cade bristled and grumbled but avoided commenting outright. Vena must have told him he had to be on his best behavior if he was going to tag along.

"Most labspawn see in the infrared," Lyn said. "So even though, to our eyes, your beige robes blend in with the dirt and, to some extent, the day sky, they stick out to labspawn. My suit insulates and masks the heat signature I give off. To labspawn, I'm almost invisible."

I'd always suspected as much, but Cade didn't bother with much in the way of critical thinking. He kept his mouth shut, and we waited for Vena in silence. Everyone was lost in their own thoughts, the realization of what we were about to undertake sinking in. Finally, Vena strode over to Lyn's jurte, and the four of us were together and alone. No one from the Stamm had followed us to see us off, just as Aarman had ordered. No point in making the departure more difficult.

"Let's try to fit your supplies in the side compartments," Lyn said.

She pointed to a strange vehicle a few paces away.

"Is this the thing we're supposed to go to Zeindorf in?" Cade asked.

He walked around and eyed the thing. It was about three meters long and half a meter wide. Silver and sleek, open to the air, with a metal hull and large wheels that looked like they could handle a variety of terranes. It was huge. No wonder the drones delivering it earlier that sol had been so much louder than the usual ones that made drops.

"I'll be driving," Lyn said. "The protector does his protecting. Now, put your things in, and let's go."

Vena and I carried our bags over and peered into the open hatches. A few were already nearly full. Jurte fabric and foodstuffs mostly. I did the best I could gently squeezing my lab equipment in. Once Vena and I were done, Lyn closed the hatches and waved her hand at the vehicle.

"I take the front, and the protector gets the back. You two can choose either one of the middle seats in the landrover."

I already knew which Vena would take, which was fine by me. Let her sit as close to Cade as possible. At least it meant I had some distance from him and was closer to Lyn. We hopped into our seats, Lyn looked back to check that everyone was on board, and then she started the engine. There was a whirring not dissimilar from the gliders. We lurched and crawled forward. The slow start gradually picked up pace, and within a minute or two, we were cruising as fast as an Itinerate's glider.

It was a strange sensation, zipping by faster than our legs could carry us. Lyn leaned forward and gripped the controls. I glanced back. Vena was squeezing the sides of the landrover with her eyes shut tight. Her lips were mouthing something, but I couldn't make it out over the whoosh of wind. The light bounced off of Cade's gun as he trained it on the horizon. How long could he keep up that kind of vigilance? Suddenly all the marching, jogging, chanting, and drilling that the protectors did sol on sol made more sense.

I gazed at the endless plains through the haze of fine dust that the landrover kicked up. We wouldn't be traveling very far into the dayside of the Break, only 240 of the nearly 2,000 kilometers, but even that distance would mean a noticeable change. The temperature would rise, and with that, the volatile-laden ices on Neuen's surface would melt and release their stores. A mist would hover over the ground, making breathing without a rebreather possible though still far from pleasant. The winds would die down, the twilight would brighten, everything would be so alien to what I'd always known. Warmth, air, calm, light.

A finger tapped my shoulder. I glanced back, and Vena was leaning towards me.

"Yeah?" I asked.

"I talked with Emyla before we left," she said.

"The goodbyes were only temporary," I said. "We'll be back soon enough, and she won't need to worry about you."

"We talked about you," Vena said.

I had to force myself not to sigh. There we were, setting out on a journey that few Reisende ever got to take, going into the Break, bound for another Stamm, and Vena wanted to gossip. It was so like her, and it just hammered home how foolish I'd been to get hung up on her.

"You were about to leave our Stamm and face all the dangers of the Break, and all Emyla wanted to talk about was me?"

"She was upset," Vena said. "You upset her, Levi."

I wasn't going to do this. Not then, not there.

"I know I did. That was the point. Listen, Vena, we're not getting into this. We're not far from the Stamm, but we are in the Break which means danger. We need to be alert. Not just them," I angled my head forward and back to Lyn and Cade, "but us too. We've got bigger issues to deal with."

Vena pulled back, no doubt surprised by my directness. I was usually more tactful with her, softer, kinder. But that had been before she'd made her choice, before she'd rejected me and lost her special treatment. Vena leaned back in her seat and let the issue drop.

The rest of the ride was uneventful. We advanced, and the world slowly altered. I planted my elbow on the side of the landrover, rested my jaw in my hand, and watched. There were specks on the horizon and in the sky, too distant to resolve but likely labspawn. Fortunately, we got through that first sol unharassed. Eight hours into the journey, Lyn brought the landrover to a stop and jumped out of her seat. She flexed her fingers then leaned her torso to one side and the other. The rest of us got out and stretched.

"Are we breaking for the somn?" Vena asked.

"Yes," Lyn said. "We need to set up the jurte."

Cade went to open a hatch, but I beat him to it. I wasn't about to have him rummage through my lab equipment. He was all thumbs, and the last thing we needed was for him to damage the supplies necessary for our work. I set my and Vena's things aside then tossed the stacks of jurte canvas on the ground. Cade grabbed them, while Lyn kept an eye on our surroundings. I helped him untie and unroll the fabric.

"How does she manage to do this on her own with no one watching her back?" I asked.

"I guess her fancy suit makes her less of a target," Cade said. "All this scanning the horizons is probably because of us three. Here, grab that corner."

We spent the next several minutes fumbling with the jurte, too large to be the one Lyn used for her travels. It looked like the four of us would be bunking together for the somn.

Lyn came over to inspect our handiwork.

"The protector and I will split the watch for the somn," she said.

"It's Cade," he said. "If we're going to be wandering through this wasteland for sols together, you calling me 'protector' is going to get real old, real fast, Itinerate."

Vena came to the rescue with foodstuffs in hand.

"Is the jurte ready?" she asked. "I have some things we could have for dinner."

Cade glared at Lyn for a few seconds then finished securing his side of the jurte. He moved over to Vena and tapped his head to hers, the rebreather kiss.

"Good on that side, Levi?" he asked.

I gave the structure a few pulls.

"I think so."

Vena ducked into the jurte. After grabbing some of the bedding from the cart, Cade followed. I lingered outside, stealing glances at Lyn who continued to scan the featureless, flat landscape that stretched in all directions. I walked up beside her and looked straight ahead towards the north, a blackened sky to my left shifting to a yellow-orange glow to my right. The sun was hidden behind the horizon, and being so far towards the nightside of the Break, I had never actually seen it with my own eyes.

Artur had told me about the sun. How it burned a deep scarlet, how you could gaze at it for just a few moments before it made your eyes tear up, how it left a ghost of itself stained on your vision long after you looked away. It was an inverse shade, a phantom brilliance. I wished that we could move further into the Break, past wherever Zeindorf had stalled, so I could see it for myself.

"You should go inside," Lyn said. "Get something to eat."

"What about you?" I asked.

"I'll be in after I set up proximity detectors."

I nodded and followed her instructions. When I moved the inner flap of the jurte aside, Cade and Vena pulled apart. She laughed and her face burned, while Cade smirked. I rolled my eyes and removed my rebreather.

"I thought you were getting the food started," I said.

I settled down on a cushion. The space was cramped, but the air was smooth.

"There's not much to do for that," Vena said.

She pushed an assortment of dried and unappetizing options towards me. I nudged a few bricks of pulverized grain before grabbing a handful of nuts and desiccated berries. They were tasteless, but I was hungry. Eating was mostly about quieting the rumbling in my gut.

"Where's Lynev?" Vena asked.

She followed my example and nibbled on some of the rations. Cade joined in as well.

"Setting up tech for protection," I said.

Vena nodded then stared at me. I knew what that meant.

"Can we continue our conversation from earlier?" she asked.

"What's that?" Cade said.

I grinned, took a savage bite from a grain brick, and shook my head.

"You're relentless," I said to Vena.

A small urn sat between us, releasing fumes from the

ONi crystallites. The light and vapors made her features shift. Her pawing with Cade had dislodged her hair so that her right ear was visible, showing itself to be abnormally small and malformed. She always hid it. I remembered stroking it and planting soft kisses on it and telling her she was beautiful despite her GLEtches.

"Can we talk about Emyla then?" she asked.

"There's nothing to talk about."

"Nothing, oh really? She told me you said you'd never couple with her. I think there's something to talk about with that."

"Did he now?" Cade asked.

He crammed a handful of nuts into his mouth.

"I don't want to couple," I said. "It's that simple."

The flaps to our jurte rustled, and Lyn ducked inside. She removed her rebreather and squeezed into the only open spot, between me and Vena. We four surrounded the urn and took up nearly the entirety of the jurte. I smiled at Lyn, grateful for the interruption, and gestured to the food spread.

"It's no Willkommen dinner," I said, "but it's food."

She looked down and started to pick through the options.

"I have proximity detectors set up around our camp," she said, mostly to Cade. "If anything passes through the laser linking them, an alarm will sound. It's directional too, so that'll give you an idea of where the threat is coming from."

"I don't know what 'laser' means," Cade said, "but sounds like I just listen, and if I hear a noise, I go towards it, yeah?"

"Yes," Lyn said. "But we still need to do a watch. Even with the jurte hiding some of the heat signature, certain labspawn will see it. The detectors just make it so we don't have to watch all 360 degrees at once."

"Sounds good," Cade said.

"I'll do the first watch and wake you once it's your turn."

He bobbed his head up and down more energetically

than he needed to. He was in a good mood. Maybe he felt as trapped by the Stamm as I did and was revealing in his newfound freedom. Maybe all the Reisende did and just did a better job at hiding their discontentment than me.

Lyn focused on eating, and the jurte fell silent. I hoped the conversation wouldn't go back to Emyla now that an outsider was in our midst, but when Vena had set her mind to something, she wouldn't let it go. That was the Aarman in her.

"Levi, I'm sorry," Vena said, "but I don't think you've thought things through with Emyla. She's perfect for you. You two are complementary, she's clearly devoted to you, and you're compatible. I just honestly don't understand the issue."

I lowered a grain brick away from my mouth and locked eyes with Vena.

"I don't want to couple," I said. "That should be all you need to hear. Now, let it go."

I couldn't help but steal a glance at Lyn. She was sitting upright and leaning forward, listening attentively.

"But you're clearly attracted to her," Vena said. "I mean you two already—"

Cade flopped one of his heavy hands on Vena's knee, and she stopped.

"Lay off Levi, Vena," Cade said. "If he wants to spurn a good woman, let him. It's his mistake, and he'll have to be the one who lives with it. Emyla's better off with someone else anyway. She deserves a man who wants to be with her, not one who'd run after every Itinerate that comes to Vromdorf, year after year."

Cade looked at me sidelong and beamed. He'd been almost professional on our trip up until then. I'd made the mistake of thinking the good streak would last.

"Cade," Vena said in a warning tone.

"What? It's true," he said. "It wasn't just the Artur one

either. He fawns over all of them. That Artur just happened to enjoy the attention enough to give it back and then some."

I didn't want to talk about Artur, but if I was silent, Cade would keep pushing. The only option was to admit it outright and shut him up for good.

"Why are you fixating on Artur all of a sudden?" I asked. "That was a year ago."

Cade pointed to Lyn.

"Her coming to the Stamm brought it all flooding back," he said. "Speaking of which, maybe Lynev here will give me some insights into all that strangeness."

He grinned at me then looked at Lyn.

"Why would an Itinerate stay beyond his two weeks in a Stamm?" he asked.

"You know I can't go into details about other Stämme," she said.

"Sure, sure, but I'm talking hypotheticals. Is there any reason an Itinerate would need to stay on in a Stamm say two weeks past their expected departure? No injuries, health concerns, weather-related problems, or tech issues. Any reason for them to linger?"

"Unless the GenMapping or coupling assessments were taking an unusually long time, I don't see why they would stay. It would only prolong their tour."

Cade nodded and put his hand to his chin, tapping the dimple there.

"So, Artur didn't want to leave. Not that he couldn't, just didn't. Wonder why that might be. Any thoughts, Levi, since you and him were such good friends and all?"

"We did talk about it," I said. "But I don't feel like sharing it with you. Anyway, Cade, this is getting tiresome, you constantly bringing up Artur. What are you trying to do by it? Embarrass me, make me feel ashamed? Well, you won't. How about this: I laid with Artur, several times in the month he was in Vromdorf. I liked him, and he liked me. Satisfied? Now you know the truth and can let it go."

The jurte fell silent. Vena looked uncomfortable, and Cade was stunned. He didn't know how to react. They both avoided looking at me, but Lyn stared at me more fixedly. There wasn't much more in the way of conversation that somn, just scattered and empty phrases. Lyn headed back outside to take up her watch, and I arranged some bedding to sleep on. Vena and Cade whispered to one another probably about me, but I didn't care. What did bother me was the two of them starting to fool around.

Maybe they thought I'd fallen asleep or assumed they were being subtle enough. I shifted my position, and they froze, but it wasn't long until they were back to it. I tried the same tactic again without much of a reaction from them. I could have called them out but was too distracted to sleep anyway. Instead, I grabbed my rebreather, shoved on my boots, and left the jurte. Vena giggled as I let the flap close behind me.

Lyn was sitting on the ground and leaning her back against the mostly empty landrover. She straightened up on seeing me. I sat down beside her.

"Is the jurte not to your liking?" she asked.

"You try sleeping in there. Those two can't keep their hands off one another. Did you really have to choose them?"

She resettled in her spot, her gun propped against her knee. It shot a glint in my eye. It was different from Cade's in almost every way except the overall shape. The sound it had given off when she'd shot the labspawn in the luftor fields was more of a zapping than a bang. It used some tech we Reisende had no concept of.

"I left the choosing of the Reisende up to your oberhaupt. You can blame him for the less-than-desirable company."

"Vena's usually not so bad, but she's protective of her

younger sister. I should have known she'd badger me about that whole thing. I'm just sorry you had to witness it. You must think us Reisende so petty to be focused on our little dramas given what's happened with Zeindorf."

I pulled my legs in and crossed them then looked out at the horizon. Still that perpetual twilight. A somn to us didn't mean any changes in the environment, just a time for rest. I wouldn't be getting any of that though until Cade and Vena got their desires satisfied. I'd give them a half hour before heading back in. Knowing Cade, that ought to be double the time they would need.

"I don't think it's petty, the dramas of you Reisende," Lyn said. "It's human is all it is. If I stayed in any Stamm long enough, I'd be sucked into all the little stories too. You seem to have many. A shy, pale Reisender woman who pines after you. An Itinerate man who you loved and loved you back."

"Does it surprise you that I was drawn to a man?"

She shrugged and pushed her braid over her shoulder, the black so stark against her silver suit.

"Not really. I've been in Stämme where it's accepted."

"Some Stämme allow it openly?" I asked.

"It's the oberhaupt's call. The Dipols just want the coupling to be what it ought to be. They don't care which Reisender lays with which so long as it doesn't result in unsanctioned births. I take it from their reaction," she angled her head towards the jurte, "it's not openly accepted in Vromdorf?"

"People let it happen, but you're supposed to be subtle about it. I think with me and Artur, it's more that he was a man and an Itinerate."

She repositioned her gun so that it leaned against the cart and freed her legs. She drew them into her body and rested her chin on her knees.

"Did it surprise you when you realized you preferred men?" she asked.

"I don't prefer one or the other," I said. "I'm drawn to the person, a man or woman."

Unlike Vena's questioning, Lyn's was almost therapeutic. I found myself wanting to answer, wanting to confide in someone who was a neutral party. Vena wanted me to couple with Emyla, so it was less explaining my feelings and more defending them.

I was reminded of Artur and knew this, at least, was part of the draw of Itinerates. They didn't have a stake in our Stamm. They would come and go so it didn't matter if you made a fool of yourself. You could be vulnerable with them, open up, pull your guard down. It made me want to test the waters with Lyn, just dip my toe in and gauge her reaction.

"Are you coupled?" I asked. "To someone in Nord."

I had my eyes trained on the ground in front of me but was watching her reaction as best I could indirectly.

"You know I can't answer that," she said.

"Right, not won't, can't. Literally."

I lifted my head. Her face stayed impassive, but subtle twitches in the muscles around her eyes told me everything I needed to know about the conflict roiling within her.

"Rules are rules," I said. "Don't worry, I understand, Lyn."

Her shoulders lowered, and the strain in her limbs loosened. Testing those waters told me what I expected they would. She wasn't just on high alert because a Reisender had asked a question she wasn't supposed to answer. I'd hinted to her that I knew more about her situation than a Reisender was supposed to, courtesy of Artur. And her reaction told me Artur's affliction wasn't a one-off one but was one shared by at least one other Itinerate.

Such a strange and sad existence to not know one's

self, for their past the be a blank slate, sent into our world without knowing a shred of knowledge about their own, their memories stolen and, with them, all sense of identity.

"Who said you can call me Lyn?" she asked.

"I figured if I was pouring out my heart, I at least got the privilege of some familiarity. Do you not like Lyn?"

"Only one other person calls me that," she said. "But sure, Levi, you can too when no one else is around."

***

We continued in a similar rhythm the next sol—riding in the landrover with our Itinerate driving and Cade watching in the rear. Vena and I were crammed in between, simultaneously bored and nervous, alternating between tedium and anxiety. All the worry was wasted though because the second sol saw even fewer signs of labspawn. The only excitement came in the form of a half-hour of gales that forced Lyn to stop the landrover. By the time the winds died down, it was essentially somn. Lyn set up her defenses, and we all ventured into the jurte to share a meal and get some air from fresh ONi. We'd reach Zeindorf the next sol.

"I want to approach Zeindorf slowly and methodically," Lyn said. "I want a full sol to make our way in and investigate."

We were eating food more closely resembling a proper meal—grains that we mixed with water and spices and heated on the urn.

"Cade and I will cover the two of you," Lyn said. "We'll approach together and try to make sense of what happened to the Reisende."

"They're all dead, right?" Cade asked. "We just need to figure out why?"

"More or less," Lyn said, "but keep in mind that whatever got to them could get to us. Hence the need to always wear our rebreathers and protective gear."

"But if they wore their rebreathers," Vena said, "and were

killed by something microscopic, ours won't do much to save us."

"Once they went in their jurten, they took them off," Lyn said. "We won't be doing that. Unless we're back here, in our jurte, we won't remove our rebreathers. Understood?"

The silence hung heavy in the vapor-laden air. The mood was shifting, anxiety rearing its ugly head, the gravity of our situation hitting us hard. Lyn sensed it and tried to mitigate the rising doom.

"Let's have a story," she said. "I like to hear your Reisender folklore. I'm collecting tales from each Stamm."

"Writing a book?" Cade asked.

"Thank you for volunteering, Cade," Lyn said.

We all turned to him and waited. He stuttered and grumbled but eventually cleared his throat and smirked back at her.

"Fine, sure, I've got a good one for you. There was a Reisender once, ages past. This was back when the exile was young. Only a few years after our kind had been driven from Nord and Süd."

Lyn raised her hand, and Cade blinked a few times.

"What?" he asked.

"Your kind didn't come from Süd," she said. "The Dipoli, and the Reisende back when you were one and the same with us, all lived in Nord."

"Then what's Süd for?" he asked, getting red in the face. "That's where you lot start your tour, isn't it?"

Lyn smiled and shook her head. She loved telling Cade how wrong he was, and I enjoyed the spectacle.

"Industry. Mining, manufacturing, that all happens in Süd. The south pole. The Itinerate tour starts there only because it needs to end in Nord, where the Dipoli actually live and work. We get flown out to Süd to start our tour. I thought all Reisende knew that."

I did, but Cade clearly didn't. He tried to brush off his

lack of knowledge and gloss over how flustered her comment had made him.

"Can I get back to the damn story you begged me to tell in the first place?"

"Go on," Lyn said.

Cade muttered under his breath, but a pat on his thigh from Vena's hand cooled his blood.

"Like I was saying," Cade said. "There was a Reisender. He'd lived in Nord. Not Süd. He would dream about the life he'd lost. He'd picture those glass towers reaching up into the yellow sky. He would imagine walking those stone streets, clean and tidy, rocks set into the very ground. Everything fixed and permanent. Safe and whole. Then he'd wake up from his daydreams and see the jurten and dirt of his Stamm. He hated his new life, just couldn't adapt. There were others like him, those who grumbled about their fate, those who murmured about hitting back at the Dipols."

"Careful," Vena whispered to Cade.

Cade narrowed his eyes at her.

"It's a folktale, Vena," he said. "Not my story. Besides, wait until you've heard the end before you go cautioning me."

Vena frowned and pulled her hand off his thigh. I'd never have talked so dismissively towards her, but then again maybe that's why she'd chosen Cade, wanting to be treated like a lesser rather than an equal.

"The Reisender was unhappy with his lot. The more time that passed, the more restless he got. He tried drumming up support for returning to the Dipols, but no one was willing to go so far. To end their forced exile would be an act of war, and the GEC was still fresh in their minds. The labspawn that the Reisende had created for the conflict were roaming free and slaughtering their former masters. And GLEtches were becoming more and more prevalent from the GenEn that had started the whole war in the first place. In short, everyone was fine with bitching and moaning, but no one had the balls to do anything about it. No one except our little hero.

"The Reisender decided to do what everyone else was too afraid to. He thought, 'They all just need a strong leader. If I take the leap, then they'll follow.' He was so sure of his superiority that he couldn't imagine the Reisende not flocking to him in support. He did the unthinkable. He went Rogue. The man traveled north along the Break, fighting off labspawn and braving the elements. He almost died countless times, but after months of walking, the glass towers of Nord rose in the distance. His city. He was almost home.

"He trudged with a lighter step, and eventually he came to the city's wall. It shimmered with an iridescence. He approached the gate and let the tech scan wash over him. In seconds, Nord knew everything there was to know about him. It saw into his very mind and registered his intentions. Then, to his shock, the gates opened. He walked into Nord, his city. The stone streets were packed full of Dipoli hurrying along in their busy lives, but no one seemed to notice him. He tried to stop a few, yet everyone acted as if they couldn't even see him.

"The man was at a loss. He didn't understand. He'd expected fear, hatred, disgust, but the Dipoli didn't even deign to acknowledge his existence. He wandered the city, trying and failing to get anyone to speak with him. He eventually got so frustrated that he reached out to grab for a woman's arm to stop her, but then his hand disappeared. He shouted in alarm, but no one seemed to hear his cries. In a panic, the man tried to grab another Dipoli with his remaining hand, but that one too faded from view. He ran around screaming and shouting, but again, no one gave him the slightest heed. The Reisender dropped down in the middle of the stone street. Dipoli walked by. A child brushed against his foot, and that too disappeared. The man curled into a ball with what remained of his body and rocked himself.

"To no one in particular he said, 'What's happening to me? Why can't they hear me, see me, feel me? Why can't I touch them? What is this foul trickery? Why let me back into the city only to make me invisible?'

"A voice from everywhere and nowhere responded, 'Because this is your exile. You cannot be allowed to interact with Dipoli who are pure of genome. Yours is tainted beyond repair. We offered you the kinder fate of physical exile, but you opted for this metaphysical one. You loved your glass city so much, that we let you return, but your exile must remain. If you wish it, we will restore the lost limbs and release you back into the wilds of Neuen. You can return to your Stamm and do your part in purifying your genome. Otherwise, you will remain in Nord and live out the remainder of your days as a ghost. The choice is yours, wayward one.'

"The man was a fool. He loved the memory of his former life too much to leave it. And so instead of living in the present, adapting to his new way of life, contributing to society, he stayed in Nord, invisible, untouchable, and unloved. After he died from neglect and malnourishment, his bones crumbled into dust. The winds of Neuen picked him up and sprinkled him across the plains that he'd denied. The dust of his bones fertilized the Reisender fields. Neuen itself had done what the man could not—gave him purpose."

Cade had been more eloquent than I'd ever heard him be, and by the time he was finished, we were all at a loss for words. I knew what he was saying by choosing the story of the Nostalgic Fool. It was a jab at me, at least what he thought I was trying to do. In Cade's mind, I wanted to be Dipoli and live amongst them. To be fair, I had a long time ago, when I hadn't understood what exactly was at play on Neuen. Before

I'd glimpsed beyond the veil and seen the system for what it was—a lie, a false promise twice over.

The Reisender would never return to Nord. We would never again be Dipoli. Our genome was marred only because they said it was. GLEtches were mutations, created by GenEn true, but mutations nonetheless. Dipoli had those too. Every living organism did. GenEn wasn't an evil to be shunned but a tool to be used. The problem wasn't GenEn but that we'd lost control of it precisely because we had treated the very knowledge of it as taboo.

"I haven't heard that one before," Lyn said. "What do you call it?"

"The Nostalgic Fool," I said.

"It has a powerful message," Cade said. "Nord is not the paradise some Reisende imagine it to be. We're out in the Break for a reason. It's where we belong."

He stared at me, but I refused to look away.

"If that was true, why is it so hostile to us?" I asked. "Labspawn, the lack of water, not even air for us to breathe. The message isn't that the Reisende belong in the Break. It's that we have to atone for the sins of our fathers."

"And we do," Vena said.

"Levi thinks he's special though," Cade said. "He thinks he ought to be able to go to the glass city."

"Maybe I have much to offer them," I said.

"That wouldn't matter," Lyn said. "Reisende won't ever be allowed in Nord until their collective genome is cleansed."

I let a few seconds pass then smiled.

"Never say never," I said.

I wasn't aiming for a debate though and just laid back on my mat and rolled over. Lyn left the jurte, and Vena and Cade settled in for rest. As I tried to find sleep, my mind kept veering back to Zeindorf. I pictured bodies strewn on the ground between jurten, faces contorted, limbs twisted at odd angles, eyes frozen open staring at the infinity overtaking them, terrified by the impending unknown.

I woke drenched in sweat a couple of times. Then sometime during Cade's watch, a piercing wail went off. It rose and fell in pitch and volume. It sounded several times then Lyn sprang from her mat and darted out of the jurte. Vena gasped.

"Don't move," I said.

We both stayed perfectly still and silent. The jurte blocked most of the sound, but I could just pick up scampering, the thumping of boots, and mumbled shouts. A shot went off. Then another. A few seconds passed then there was one final noise, that same zapping sound I'd heard from Lyn's gun. Vena and I stared at one another, listening. Not long after, Lyn came back into the jurte, alert but calm.

"Labspawn," she said.

"Is Cade okay?" Vena asked.

She rose into a crouched position like she was about to rush outside.

"He's fine," Lyn said. "Go back to sleep."

Vena hesitated, looked at me, and back to Lyn.

"Don't distract him," Lyn said. "Sleep."

Lyn laid down on her mat and closed her eyes.

The next sol, I fully expected Cade to boast about killing the labspawn. But he was silent and lost in thought while we ate our morning meal. Even Vena had trouble rallying him. Had that been his first real one-on-one encounter with one of the creatures?

Before we set off in the landrover, Lyn pointed out Zeindorf, a blur on the horizon. It resolved into discrete jurten as we neared. Still somewhat distant from the outer ring of jurten, Lyn stopped and searched for the drop the Dipols had scheduled. If she hadn't used her tech, we probably would have wandered around for a couple of hours trying to track it down.

Instead, she tapped a smooth surface on a matte black object. It told her the location of the coveted supplies which included more robust protective gear, the type that Itinerates might sport but that we Reisende were normally barred from using. Gloves made of some synthetic material that fit perfectly to our skin, goggles that covered our eyes, white clothing that was smooth and baggy and had a shine to it, and a different kind of rebreather that used bands of stretchy material instead of the usual buckles. Everything fit snugly and ensured that whatever was outside our bodies would stay that way.

Then we were ready to approach the Stamm. We did so like Lyn had said, advancing at a crawl, constantly scanning our surroundings, stopping, watching, waiting. But there was nothing. No movement, no sounds other than the gusts coming from the nightside of the Break.

When we finally made it to the first jurte, I was all tension, flooded with adrenaline. Lyn gave hand signals to Cade who hung back with us while she crept further into the maze of tents. I shifted the pack on my back and gripped one of the straps until my fingers ached. After several minutes, Lyn returned.

"I did a quick scout and didn't spot labspawn or other obvious threats," she said.

"Did you find any bodies?" Cade asked.

"Yes, a lot. The whole Stamm, I'd guess, assuming some are in their jurten. Let's head in and have Levi and Vena see what they can find."

Within a couple of minutes, we were in Zeindorf. I found the first body. It was laid out in the dirt, stomach facing the ground, but there were no stiffened fingers reaching out or stilled veins bulging in the neck. I came in for a closer look.

His head was turned on its side with the left eye peeking up. The lid was just barely parted, and within it, there was a trace of blue. A gust of wind brushed the white-blonde hair against his pale forehead. He looked almost peaceful.

Vena came to my side and crouched. Cade and Lyn watched the horizon.

"Should we turn him over?" Vena asked.

I nodded and moved back. She rolled him over with one gentle push, and we both inspected the other side of the Reisender. No wounds or trauma from what I could tell. Vena searched for something, anything, that could tell us what had happened to him.

"Maybe we should remove the robes," she said.

"Cut them off?" I said.

She fumbled in her bag before drawing out a hemp pouch. She pulled a scalpel from it and set about slicing his robes in two, from neck to navel. At first, we weren't sure what was GLEtch and what was something more recent. He bore a mottled rash on his chest that wrapped around to his back. It was purple and looked like it might come from a deeper layer of his skin.

"Is that from a GLEtch?" I asked.

Vena leaned in and touched her gloved hand to the skin. When she pressed, the purple gave way to a white before settling back to the previous shade.

"I think so," she said. "Some kind of pigmentation abnormality."

She pointed to small, circular depressions near the sternum that were black and clustered in groups of a dozen or so.

"Those are more recent," she said. "Some kind of necrosis, perhaps. Let's get a sample."

Vena fished a container from her bag then used the scalpel to cut a chunk of the skin out. She balanced the mass on the knife and dropped it into the hemp bag lined with non-porous material.

"Since your hands are clean, can you write the label?" she asked.

A paper tag was attached to the bag, and I used my own pen to scribble on it as she read out what she wanted it to say.

"Do you see anything else?" she asked.

I peered into the open wound we'd made and shook my head.

"I don't really know what I'm looking at. Humans aren't my specialty."

"Let's check another Reisender to see if we notice similarities," she said.

We moved further into the Stamm and found a group of three Reisende clumped together. They looked like they were comforting one another, reaching out for each other's hands. But like the first one, something about their postures and lax muscles told me they had felt calm at the end.

We started with a woman who was facing the sky. Vena again used the scalpel to cut her robes away. There was no mottled, purple rash this time, but those same black spots were on her chest too, only larger and more numerous and with something coming out of them, a fiber or filament. Vena took another sample, and I helped with the labeling.

We continued this routine and saw traces of the same black spots on each. On the fourth body, whatever had happened to the Reisende was more pronounced. The filaments sprouting from the spots were more numerous and larger.

"They almost look like vegetation," she said.

She poked one with her scalpel. I moved in and grabbed a stalk between my gloved thumb and forefinger. I plucked it free and inspected it.

"It is," I said and bagged it.

About an hour into our investigation, we moved into a jurte. That's when we found the most advanced stage of the affliction. The urn was long cold. Whatever ONi had been in it had sublimated away even without heating. The room had a haze in the air.

Vena approached the body then back-peddled. I moved up beside her and peered down at whatever sight had spooked her. We didn't even need to cut the robes away this time. The Reisender was saturated with stalks, bursting through the fabric of his robe. He was staring at the ceiling with the foggy eyes of the dead. Near his sternum, a seedling, several centimeters tall, sprouted. I immediately recognized it.

"Luftor," I said.

"The plant?" Vena asked.

I nodded and moved in for a closer look. I brushed the nascent leaves with my hand, looking at their fronts and backs, so familiar except for the fact that it was sprouting from the dead flesh of a Reisender.

"I don't know why it seems to be growing out of a body," I said.

"Bag it," Vena said.

I grabbed a sampling container of my own and cut the sapling free from the Reisender, along with a serving of the fleshy mass it was attached to. Filaments reached deeper into the body, but they didn't look quite root-like to me.

"Let's turn him over," I said.

Vena hesitated. She'd been nervous ever since we'd entered this jurte. I glanced up at her and tried to read her emotions behind her rebreather and the goggles. Her eyes darted left and right while she clenched her fists. Then it hit me. She was terrified, but why wasn't I? We clearly had a plague on our hands, one that had wiped out a Stamm, and yet all I could think about were the connections forming in my mind.

A new breed of luftor, but it was too soon, didn't make sense. I'd given Artur the spores to release into the Break about a year ago, too little time for the new breed to take root and spread on this scale. These couldn't be mine. Could they?

"Are you okay?" I asked.

Vena tried to erase the fear, but it lingered then started to grip her.

"What do you think it means?" I asked.

I was trying to distract her. The tactic worked as she focused back on me.

"What do you mean?" she asked.

I angled my head at the Reisender.

"A plague?" I asked.

She shrugged and moved to kneel down beside me.

"It doesn't matter what we think," she said. "It's better if we don't think about it at all. We're just here to get the samples. The Dipols will make sense of it."

"Sure, but we can hypothesize, can't we? The Dipols aren't all-knowing, and besides, what's the harm in us running through theories?"

Vena furrowed her brow.

"There's plenty of harm in sticking our noses where they don't belong. The Dipols will handle this."

"Maybe," I said. "Or maybe not. They didn't manage to do much of anything to save this Stamm so who's to say Vromdorf will be any different?"

Vena tilted her head and stared at me.

"You haven't changed at all," she said.

"What's that mean?"

She tried to wave the question away, but I pressed.

"No, Vena, tell me what you mean by that."

"Can we get back to the task at hand?" she asked.

"Sure, just as soon as you say what you meant."

Vena sighed and threw up her hands.

"Your silly defiance, Levi. Your constant questioning of the Dipols. It was cute when we were teens. You were dangerous and edgy then, but now it's just exhausting."

My eye twitched. The comment stung, more than I would have thought it would. I was tempted to bring up our past, but it wasn't the time or place for that. Besides, my attention was divided. The sapling was calling to me, begging me to make sense of its presence.

"Fine," I said. "I'll drop it. Now, help me flip this Reisender over."

Vena nodded and stationed herself on the opposite side of the body. I lifted as she guided the torso. We both gazed down at his back. The same filament-like material that permeated the body also penetrated it, making its way through the textile rug then into the dirt below.

Vena sprang up and paced back and forth.

"What is it?" she asked.

I shook my head, still staring at the filaments. I had an inkling what they were, but I wasn't going to breathe a word of it to her. I was hardly willing to entertain the possibility myself.

"I'll take a sample," I said.

She turned away while I moved the rug aside and dug into the ground. I made a wide circumference all around the site of interest. When I lifted the cluster of soil on my trowel's blade, a thick mass of the same filaments hung like an interconnected web. I dug adjacent to the hole, moving progressively away until the fibers thinned then disappeared. They were clearly linked to the bodies and whatever the black dots on the sternum signified.

I knelt there and stared into the hole flecked with what looked like white strings. Then a rustling sounded and shifted into something else. I glanced at Vena, who had stopped her pacing, her ear angled in my direction. She was listening for something too.

"Do you hear that?" I asked.

She nodded, and we strained to hear what was barely registering. I leaned forward, closer to the hole I'd dug, and heard whispers. I couldn't make out what they said. The sounds were less words and more noise, but some inherent quality kept forcing my mind to categorize them as whispers. They rushed forward in an uninterrupted stream, growing in volume and urgency. Then, they were gone. We waited for them to come back, but after a few minutes of silence, we dusted the dirt off our white clothes and made our way out of the jurte.

Vena and I did our due diligence and moved through the remainder of the Stamm, thoroughfare by thoroughfare, jurte by jurte, but we only found the same variation on the themes already noted. We had what we'd come for. We told Lyn as much.

"Are you sure you don't need anything else?" Lyn asked.

"We have everything we're likely to require," Vena said.

Lyn didn't question us further. She inclined her head, accepting our decision. Now, we just had to make it back to Vromdorf in one piece.

Plague

Lyn

Levi emerged from the jurte, and my lips peeled into a smile.

"Are those two at it again?" I asked.

He shook his head and ran his hand through his hair.

"No, I just can't sleep," he said. "I can't stop thinking about Zeindorf. What we found there, and what it might mean."

"What do you think it means?" I asked.

"I don't know yet."

We'd investigated Zeindorf the previous sol and spent the past one traveling back to Vromdorf. Our journey had had us share three somns together so far, and on two, he'd come out to join me on my watch. With a third, it was becoming a ritual. One I looked forward to.

Was this typical? I'd never spent so much concentrated time with the same set of Reisende before, and I was finding it hard to keep my guard up, especially considering the strange situation we found ourselves in. Up to that point in my tour, routine had made things easy. Just perform the preordained movements and speeches, but the trip to Zeindorf had usurped everything. Without the usual constraints, I was letting myself slip, at least around Levi.

There was a sadness to him that I was pulled in by. He put on a good show, but I could see through the act. Levi was haunted by something. A few stray remarks told me where the treasure I sought was buried. GLEtches.

Levi was in the elite class of Reisende with few GLEtches, a label that most would gloat about. But a hint of disdain floated behind Levi's words when he talked about his genome. It was at odds with everything a Reisender ought to feel. He was a step on their path to redemption, and yet he seemed to resent it. Why?

"What's your GLEtch count, Levi?"

I avoided looking at him. I instead watched the desolate horizon, broken only by rock and dirt. Browns lorded over by a sky of yellows and oranges.

"Minimal," he said. "Why?"

"You're a rarity," I said. "In all the Stämme I've been to, all the Reisende I've seen, I've only met a handful in your class. GLEtch count is such an important metric for your people, but most of you don't know what it really means. What do you know about it?"

"Just what I've been told," he said. "Whether that's the truth, who's to say?"

"How about you tell me what you know, and maybe I'll elaborate with what I know?"

"Okay," he said. "Should I start from the beginning?"

"If you like."

"Neuen was first colonized by the company," he said.

"BayDeut AG," I said.

Levi stopped and took a few moments, most likely to commit that fact to memory. He was almost vibrating with anticipation, hungry for the truth, not unlike most Reisende, but his stomach seemed to growl and rumble exceptionally loud for his kind. Maybe that's part of the reason I decided to feed him little bite-sized morsels.

"BayDeut AG," he continued, "was studying terraforming, using Neuen as a test case for a planet with extreme day and night cycles."

"Almost. They were more interested in how to use genetic engineering to aid with the terraforming process in such extreme environments. Less about the actual terraforming. The terraforming was done elsewhere or by other companies."

"Right, the GenEn," he said. "So it was more about the GenEn and less about the actual terraforming."

"Go on."

"At some point, a schism formed in the ranks of the company."

I locked eyes with Levi. His brown eyes danced. Had his Itinerate lover ever divulged this kind of information to him? Based on his reaction, I doubted it.

"Whether GenEn ought to pass a point of no-return," I said. "Move past the ultimate taboo. To germline edit or to not?"

Levi's brow wrinkled. He didn't recognize the jargon.

"That's where GLEtches comes from," I said. "GermLine Editing trace. You change the genome, edit it, at most stages in a person's life, and it doesn't get passed on to their offspring. That's what everyone is fine with. The sticking point is if you do the editing to the embryo or at the very earliest stage in the fetus's development. In that case, the alterations get passed on. That's when you change what it means to be human."

Levi nodded and hummed a bit. The system had been designed such that he was taught a skeleton of the science, but was he putting the pieces together? Seeing the awful context?

"The schism became an actual war," he said.

"The Genetic Engineering Conflict."

"There were the ones who wanted to breach the taboo, do this germline editing, and the ones who wanted it to stay taboo. The former were my ancestors and the latter yours. Mine lost the GEC, and yours won. The punishment for performing the taboo, for marring our genome, was to become the Reisende until our genome was pure again and purged of any GLEtches."

"Bravo."

"But it doesn't make sense," he said. "The system in place."

He paused and watched my reaction. This part of the conversation had put him on thin ice the last time we'd talked about it. He was being delicate in approaching it again.

"Why not just sterilize my ancestors?" he asked. "Why all the song and dance of the Reisen and Itinerates?"

At least he was phrasing his doubts in a way I could respond to this time.

"You know the answer to that," I said.

"Punishment?"

"The Dipoli were too forgiving to kill the Reisende, but there did need to be some kind of consequence for all the pain and suffering they'd caused."

Levi didn't follow up, and I took it as a sign that he was satisfied with my explanation.

"And now," I said, "I'll bet you know far more than any other Reisender. Just make sure to keep it to yourself, or you risk getting me in trouble."

"I have a habit of making Itinerates do bad things."

"You're referring to Artur?" I asked.

Levi looked down at the ground, his eyes defocusing.

"I don't want to talk about that."

I wanted to ask why he'd even hinted at it then but just kept my mouth shut. I knew, given enough time, he'd tell me.

Maybe I should've been more focused on the journey and less on Levi and his secrets. I was slipping, but the slide was subtle. The slope barely discernible. That one attack that had happened during Cade's watch, the one with the labspawn I took down, had lulled me into a false sense of security.

It was on the next sol, just several hours from Vromdorf. We were in the landrover in our usual positions, me driving, Cade in the rear, and the other two sandwiched in between. I was too focused on driving, and Cade wasn't watching directly overhead. Maybe there had been an unusually strong gust? My eyes squinted, one hand raised to ward off the flux of air, my other gripping the controls? Maybe that's why I hadn't heard the whoosh of the thing's wings?

It was right on top of us. On me. It didn't go for the three warm bodies adjacent. No, for some reason, the labspawn honed in on me and struck with talons grasping and serrated teeth chomping. When I think back, I can feel the terror. And then, there's only a big blank.

The others told me what they saw play out. Cade said it had been at high altitude and dove vertically down, using the wind as aid and cover. It had been a clever one. Too much so. If I'd been alone, it would've won. Luckily, Cade reacted as soon as the creature entered his line of sight. While it busied itself with me, he took aim and fired. I doubted he was as good of a shot as he let on. He'd wasted two rounds on the last labspawn that had attacked. I'm certain he got lucky with this one. Me too. That little projectile of his could have easily embedded itself nicely into my own soft flesh. Instead, it cracked through the hard exoskeleton covering the labspawn.

The first thing I remembered after the blankness receded was seeing the body. It was a complex mess, half on the landrover's hood and half in the dirt below. Part bird, part arthropod, with too many of everything. The mouths alone were horrifying. There were rows of teeth that ranged from sharpened triangles to needle-like spikes, and they were black set against bone-white gums. Tucked further back in its throat, rings of teeth traced circles down into the thing's esophagus. Two mouths set in two heads, and those on two eerily slender, meter-long necks.

Vena rushed over to me. She shouted for Levi to lift me free from my seat.

"I need to be able to get to her," she said.

Then Vena was rushing between her supplies in the hatch and me, back and forth. It was distracting. I wanted to tell her to stop, but it was too much effort to even form the words. She lifted a bundle of gauze and shook it at Cade.

"I need her lifted to wrap this around the torso," she said.

Levi moved in close so I couldn't see much else. My head kept shifting, my eyes trying to catch sight of what Vena was up to. Levi bobbed his head to keep eye contact. Eventually, he used his hands to cradle my jawline. I gave up my attempts at watching Vena. Cade lifted me near my shoulder blades, and a searing pain gripped my abdomen. That's when I knew. The thing had got me, and got me bad.

"I'm putting her under," Vena said.

She lifted an amber bottle, removed a fat, black stopper, and put a clean rag over the opening. Two inversions.

"Take off her rebreather," Vena said to Levi.

He slipped the fasteners from behind my ears and removed it. Vena knelt beside me and put the cloth bundle over my nose and mouth.

"Take a deep breath," she said.

***

I awoke on a mat in Vromdorf's Medizin Jurte. My whole body was numb, but when I made the mistake of trying to sit up, everything radiated pain. My gasp alerted the attending physician, who bolted to my side.

"She's awake," he shouted.

A whole cluster of them seemed to materialize around me. The air was too close, too hot, and smelled sour. I opened my mouth to say something, but my throat was desiccated.

"Give her space," Kelica said.

She pushed a few of them aside to make room for herself. The physicians retreated then immediately moved back in. Kelica sighed and turned back to them.

"Everyone out except Vena," she said.

"Keep an eye on her," Kelica said to her junior. "She'll want to move. Don't let her. I'll tell Aarman she's awake."

"Thirsty?" Vena asked.

I nodded, which sent another shock through me. I hissed and closed my eyes.

"Like Kelica said, don't move," Vena said. "If you can talk, do that. Otherwise, maybe blink your eyes to tell me yes?"

She moved out of my line of sight and came back with a ceramic cup. After using pillows to elevate my head, Vena poured the water into my mouth. It tasted almost sweet.

"How long?" I asked.

"Since we got back?"

"Since you knocked me out."

Vena smiled and lifted the cup.

"More?" she asked.

"In a bit," I said.

She put the vessel down by her foot and crouched next to me, her knees resting on a cushion.

"Two sols," she said. "You were lucky we were so close to Vromdorf. Levi managed to drive the landrover."

I hadn't given him express permission to touch the tech. It was a breach, but if he hadn't done it, I wouldn't be around to report anything to the Dipols. Besides, flouting the Decrees required punishment that could be excessive, no matter the cause. In this, it would be a branding of the hands that had touched the tech. There was no reason to put Levi through that. To gift his risk-taking on my behalf with searing pain. The Dipols didn't need to know just how we'd made it back to Vromdorf.

"How bad is it?" I asked.

Vena's smile lessened before a forced rally. That told me everything I needed to know.

"You need to rest," she said.

"Internal bleeding? Damage to any organs? It got me in the gut, right?"

"The abdomen, yes. The organs seem to be intact, but we can't rule out internal bleeding."

"We're glad to see you awake, Lynev," Aarman said.

He ducked into the jurte with Kelica trailing. Levi and Cade followed. Everyone looked at me doubly hard. I was worse off than even Vena had let on.

Aarman came over and knelt beside Vena. I shifted under my sheets. My hand grazed the soft skin of my thigh.

"Where's my suit?" I asked.

"We had to get to your wounds," Kelica said. "It was in the way."

Reisende touching tech yet again. This would be two lies of omission when I sent my report to the Dipols.

"But once you'd done your Reisender bandaging," I said, "why didn't you put it back on? It speeds up the healing."

Kelica smiled without her eyes, her pursed lips peeling back into parallel lines.

"Not with your wounds, it wouldn't."

"How would you know? Suddenly an expert on that tech?"

Kelica's blue eyes shifted behind her glass lenses. The movement was exaggerated by the magnification.

"An educated guess," she said.

"If you want, we could put it back on," Vena said.

"I would," I said. "And my bracelet. The orange one. Where's that?"

"With your suit," Kelica said. "We can put you back in it, but you have to agree to stay here in the Medizin Jurte until I say otherwise."

"Agreed."

Kelica jerked her head in what passed as a nod. Aarman cleared his throat and eyed her.

"I'll be nearby if you need me," she said, then left the jurte.

"Now that it's just the five of us," Aarman said, "I'd like to have a little chat about Zeindorf. I wish I could give you more time to recuperate, Lynev, but we don't have that luxury. The others told me what they saw and found in the Stamm, but I wanted to check with you before trying to send anything to the Dipols."

"Good, because I want you to hold off on that," I said. "The Dipols need to hear from me about what we found. Did you reach out to them yet?"

"I just informed them that you all had made it back to the Stamm, but you had been injured."

"That's enough for them to know right now. While I'm mat-ridden, I want Levi and Vena, and those two alone, to study the samples they retrieved. I want them to tell me, and only me, what they find. I'll synthesize the observations and send them along to the Dipols. I'll tell you," I said to Aarman, "what you need to know, but I'm afraid that won't be much. This is an investigation that relates to another Stamm."

"But it could affect my Stamm," Aarman said. "It is affecting it already with the rationing."

His face was stern, stone-like. He wasn't used to being left in the dark. Still, it was exactly what the Dipols would want, and I was their agent.

"I understand, oberhaupt," I said. "But we have procedures in place for a reason. You don't get to know everything. None of us do."

Aarman pulled at his mustache. Surprisingly delicate fingers twisted the coarse, red-brown hairs.

"I'd like to talk to them alone," I said to Aarman.

I used my eyes to indicate Vena, Cade, and Levi. Aarman took the hint and made his way to the exit.

"I'll check on you next sol," he said.

He disappeared into the folds, and I waited for several seconds while the others looked at me. I cleared my throat, and a spasm of pain shocked me. I kept forgetting what being seriously injured meant.

"I think it goes without saying," I said, "but everything you saw, everything that happened, stays with you. This goes for the journey to Zeindorf, our time in Zeindorf, and our return journey. You don't talk about this with anyone, any other Reisender, not Aarman, not even each other. Only me and only when it's necessary."

Cade moved in closer but didn't kneel. His knee was level with Vena's face. He gazed down at me with his arms crossed over his chest.

"Aarman's already told us this," he said. "We've kept it to ourselves."

"But you didn't, did you?" I said. "You told him what you found."

"He's the oberhaupt," Cade said.

"That doesn't matter. You don't speak to him or even each other about any of it. Do you all understand?"

They nodded at different speeds with different levels of eagerness or sulkiness.

"Good," I said. "In that case, Cade, give us privacy."

He opened his mouth. A few huffs and scoffs accompanied a scowl.

"Are you serious?" he asked. "You're not even going to thank me?"

I saw what he wanted. It wasn't praise for praise's sake. It wasn't a stroking of his ego. He craved confirmation of his prowess precisely because he was so uncertain of it. I remembered the labspawn that had attacked during his watch on our way to Zeindorf. The one that I had had to shoot down after his misses.

"You're right," I said. "I should thank you, although you could have just as easily hit me as the creature."

He got the insinuation and looked away.

"But thank you for at least trying," I said. "It worked out better than it could have."

"I guess that passes as appreciation for an Itinerate," he said.

He uncrossed his arms and took a few long strides to the exit. We all watched him as he ducked through the flaps. With Cade gone, the jurte was more relaxed. He emitted a kind of aura that promoted a strange combination of nervous energy and mania. It could be infectious and was the last thing I needed.

"You heard what I said to Aarman?" I asked Levi and Vena. "About studying the samples?"

They both nodded, eyes locked on me.

"Good. Make that your priority. If your superiors complain, tell them this is a directive from the Dipols. It supercedes everything else."

Vena leaned in.

"Lynev, I don't know that I'm the best person to study the samples," she said. "I'm only a junior physician. There's a lot I still don't know about physiology. I barely know anything about pathogens, which seemed to have played a part in what happened in Zeindorf."

"I trust your abilities even if you don't," I said. "I'm sure the Dipols will analyze the specimens themselves once we're able to send them some. While we're waiting, we should learn what we can before they degrade."

"Understood," Vena said.

"Any problems on your end?" I asked Levi.

His lips just barely turned at the corners.

"No," he said. "I was hoping you'd ask me to investigate them."

"It sounds like you two understand the situation. Do the best you can, and tell me what you learn once you have something for me."

They nodded, and Levi went to leave.

"Hold on," I said. "There's one more thing I want to talk with you about, Levi. But before that, Vena, I want my suit back on. Now."

"Oh, right, of course," she said, "let me find it."

She scurried around the jurte and, within a few seconds, came back to my side with the suit slung over her arm.

"Just as a warning," she said, "it won't be pleasant getting you back into it."

"I know."

"Well then, let me find another physician to help."

She draped the suit on top of my blankets.

"Why not Levi?" I asked. "He's already here."

Vena paused and looked at me, then him, and then back to me.

"He's not trained."

"To put clothing on? I'd have thought he did that at least once every sol."

I glanced at Levi and grinned. He still had that same half-smile.

"You're injured," Vena said. "It's dangerous to move you, even to get you back into your suit."

She was being obstinate, and I suspected the reason for

it. Every Stamm approached societal norms differently. They only had the Decrees in common after all. From my limited time in Vromdorf, I'd already picked up on how prudish the Reisende here were. Still, if a Reisender was subtle, certain behaviors were ignored. Sex outside of coupling seemed to be allowed so long as it was treated like a secret, however poorly kept, and most importantly, didn't result in any offspring. Homosexuality appeared to operate under some kind of don't-ask-don't-tell arrangement based on what Levi had said. Vena's current sticking point? Nudity. It was petty. I wanted to laugh in her face, to force her pursed lips to relax into a smile.

"You'll talk him through it," I said.

I wanted her to admit what the hesitation really stemmed from. It was a little mean-spirited of me, but I was in pain and impatient.

"It's also a matter of propriety," Vena said. "You aren't wearing anything other than bandages."

"I'm aware of that, but shouldn't that be my call to make? I don't care if he sees. My suit doesn't leave much to the imagination anyway. This is quicker and more efficient. We're wasting more time debating it than doing it."

Vena couldn't argue any more. She had to know I'd pull out the show-stopper of 'I'm an Itinerate and you have to do what I say.' And I would have if she hadn't backed down, but she did.

"Fine," she said. "If Levi is comfortable with it, then he can help with your suit."

He nodded and moved down beside Vena. If he was excited or eager, I couldn't tell.

"I'll move the blankets out of the way then lift her legs," Vena said to him. "You undo the zipper on the suit and guide her feet and legs in."

Levi waited. Vena peeled the blankets back. Even the

mild decrease in pressure from their removal made my body ache. I steeled myself and tried to think how this would help in the long run. A few moments of agony then more rapid healing. It was logical, but my nerves screamed at me for it. The moment Vena started to lift my leg, I gasped. She stopped. My eyes were squeezed shut and my teeth clenched.

"Keep going," I said. "Just get it over with."

They finished the second leg and moved on to the torso. Vena and Levi each lifted a side of my lower back to get the suit over my hips, and something about that movement was too much. I saw white even with my eyes still closed. The sound went off. I groaned. Then I was out.

***

By the time I woke up, Vena was gone. It was just Levi sitting on some pillows by my side looking down at his hands and humming that tune he'd played for me on his flute my first somn in Vromdorf.

"I didn't take you for the motherly type," I said. "Lullabies and everything. Did Vena task you with that?"

A wave of red washed over his face. I glanced down. Silver covered my arm. A braid of orange sat on my wrist.

"She actually told me I should leave you alone to rest," Levi said, "but I reminded her that you'd asked me to stay for something."

"I need a drop with proper supplies for my wounds. You know what I'm going to ask you for, don't you?"

"I have a feeling," he said.

"I give you express permission to retrieve my comms from my jurte," I said. "Just like I did for the landrover."

Levi's brow furrowed then relaxed.

"Just before you passed out?" he asked.

I smiled and my too-dry lips cracked and splintered. Licking them, I tasted blood.

"That's right," I said, "just before I passed out."

"Where is your comms?" he asked.

"In the silver box lying near the mat in my jurte."

"I'll go get it now."

Levi stood. I struggled to look at him from that angle and had to settle with gazing at his shins instead. They retreated and disappeared, and I was alone. Levi dropped off my comms gear not long after. I sent a message to the Dipols and got the coveted drop with medical supplies the next sol. They helped, but the damage was severe. I was mat-ridden for a week, and even if I could've done anything besides sleep, I didn't want to.

Even before this accident, my fatigue had been overtaking me. Bit by bit. Sol by sol. Stamm to Stamm, I got more and more exhausted. You're just overworked, I'd tell myself. You're ready for the tour to be over. But that wasn't it because the end of my tour would be the end of everything. The end of the me that I was, set to become some other version of me, some other Lynev. The one that had agreed to the whole twisted thing in the first place. Most of the time, I hated her for that. Other times, I pitied her. But either way, I didn't want to become her. I didn't want to lose myself.

My injuries meant my tour was delayed, and the situation with Zeindorf meant I didn't have a Stamm to go to, not directly. When I messaged the Dipols, they said to stay put. They instructed me to heal fully, finish my GenMapping and coupling work in Vromdorf, and send anything the Reisende found from the samples. They would decide on the best path forward. I was a good little soldier and followed their instructions to a tee. I healed to the point that I could move on my own then limped back to my jurte. I was giving myself one somn's sleep before diving back into the GenMappings.

When I entered my jurte, someone was sitting on my mat. Maybe it was wishful thinking, my subconscious telling me that I wanted it to be Levi. In any case, I assumed it was him.

"You're getting to be audacious," I said. "People will talk if you take to visiting my jurte too often."

He stood, and the light from the urn overtook and replaced the shadows that had obscured him. There was a moment of confusion. The face was Moray's, but he wore Reisender robes.

"The hope is they didn't notice me at all," he said.

He showed his wide grin. That face with that voice drove home the fact that it really was him.

"I thought something happened to you," I said. "You never responded to my message."

I didn't move any closer, despite the fact that my ribs and legs were both screaming at me to sit or, better yet, lie down.

His grin faded.

"My comms stopped working. Can't really ask the Dipols for help with a broken comms without a comms."

"Do you want me to request a new comms for you?" I asked.

"And tell them that we're interacting? No, I can get the thing working again once I get to my next stop. I've got to check on something to the north, but I figured I'd stop in Vromdorf on my way in case you were still here."

"So you did get my message?"

"Yeah, but I didn't respond before my comms went out. I'm glad I stopped in though. You got attacked? I overheard the Reisende when I was sneaking into the Stamm and trying to find which jurte was yours."

"Why the disguise?" I asked, pointing at the robes. "And why the secrecy? You could've just told the Reisende who you were and what happened."

"I didn't want to complicate things. This is your Lat. If I rolled into the Stamm, they'd be suspicious. Why are there two Itinerates on the same Lat at the same time? Too much is already going wrong. We don't want to set them off, right?"

He was right. The Reisende didn't do well with sudden changes or any kind of upset to their beloved routines.

"You mean Zeindorf?"

"It's all they're talking about," he said. "That and you."

Moray eyed me.

"You look pale," he said. "Want to sit?"

Before he clicked his tongue for the final 't,' I executed a poorly controlled fall onto my mat. The fact that only a groan sounded rather than a blood-curdling scream meant I was more healed that I'd realized.

"Got you good, huh?" Moray said.

He was down beside me in an instant, piling pillows behind my head and under my knees.

"Maybe even better than that one that got you," I said.

He was close now. Through his grin, I saw the worry nestled underneath. He looked worn and frazzled with circles under his eyes that hadn't been there before.

"When the Dipols sent me to Zeindorf," I said, "I knew something had happened to you."

Moray scowled.

"They shouldn't have sent you. It's not a good sign."

"Why? If they couldn't get a hold of you, it makes sense to send the next nearest Itinerate. I just don't know what they plan to do in the long run with a Stamm missing now."

"Why did they send you at all? Couldn't they tell from orbital data whether the Reisende were alive or not?"

"They wanted me to collect samples to send to them. I had to bring a few Reisende along."

Moray's mouth opened.

"That's bad," he said, "very bad."

"What? Why?"

I propped myself up with my elbow and regretted it. I had to settle with lying on my back instead, him sitting just beside.

"Isn't that what you did," I said, "when they sent you to the other Stämme that went missing? I figured we were just filling in for you."

"No," Moray said. "I never collected any samples and definitely didn't go with any Reisende. Sometimes, they would have me check on the platforms to make sure nothing would interfere with them during the Reisen."

"So, how did they analyze the bodies?"

Moray shrugged and looked lost in thought.

"I never went near any of the dead Reisende," he said. "They specifically told me to stay away. They sent bots and drones in to sweep the jurten and other stuff out of the way. I just kind of oversaw the process in case there were issues. I always assumed they sent in Dipoli specialists after the fact to investigate. This is why them sending you in, like they did for what they did, is bad news."

"How?"

Moray stared back at me and moistened his lips with a flash movement of his tongue. It was gone before I really saw it. He did that when he was nervous.

"If they sent you," he said, "it means they either couldn't or wouldn't send Dipoli in. It's not good, one way or the other."

My fingers migrated down to my wrist and played with the bracelet there. Unbraid. Braid. Unbraid. Braid. I was starting to piece things together, finally seeing through the haze of pain that had clouded my thoughts the past week. It had all been odd, and I'd known that, or rather felt it, but ignored it.

"Did you send them samples?" he asked.

"They wanted the Reisende to analyze them first."

As I said it, I saw what it meant.

"So," Moray said, shaking his head, "the Dipols couldn't send their own in. This thing is bigger than I thought it was. Maybe it's even gotten to them."

"What is it?" I asked.

My fingers moved faster, looping and looping fabric, over then under, repeat, repeat.

"I have no idea," he said. "They never told me anything. I was just the grunt they sent in to check the bot's work."

"How many Stämme did they send you to?"

Moray hesitated. He licked his lips again. I tried to steel myself for the answer.

"Eight," he said, "within the past six months. But two of those were in the last month alone. Whatever it is, it's picking up speed."

"I still need to find out what my Reisende found from the samples they collected. But from what they could make out while we were there, a plague seems most likely."

Moray stiffened.

"You wore protective gear?" he asked.

"Special rebreathers the Dipols dropped, goggles, hazmat suits, and gloves. We left everything in the drop box it came in once we were done in Zeindorf. We didn't stay in the Stamm any longer than the time it took us to collect specimens. A few hours maximum."

"That's good," he said. "But they didn't send in drones for the removing debris? You didn't help with that at all?"

I shook my head in what felt like slow motion. Everything was stretching out in time and space, except my braiding. That pace was quickening with each revelation.

"Not good," he said. "Correction. Bad. Really bad. One tier below catastrophic maybe?"

Everything vibrated, my own energy bled out to infect my surroundings.

"I get it," I said. "They didn't bother clearing Zeindorf because there's nothing left behind it. The Stämme to the east of us are all gone."

"It's the only thing that makes sense."

Moray moved in close, lying down on the mat next to me. The contact made the vibrations freeze out. His arms wrapping around my own grounded me. The panic subsided and left only a dead weight in my stomach.

"Let's hope your Reisende can tell us what the hell it is we're dealing with because either the Dipols know and don't want to share, or, more likely, they don't have any idea what it is we're up against."

It's strange how terror can affect you. This awful unknown that hung over us ought to have crowded everything else out. It ought to have consumed all our thoughts. But the other side was that it made us aware of the transient nature of existence. If this plague was coming for Vromdorf next, I wanted to make the most of every moment that was left. My injuries kept anything carnal off the table, so instead we just held one another.

Lying there, cradled against Moray's chest, watching it rise and fall, I felt odd. Or maybe it was the situation I was in that was off somehow. I stopped and analyzed it. I'd been glad to see that the person sitting on my mat was Moray, but I'd also been disappointed. Then I understood. Even if it hadn't been for my injuries, I don't know if I would have wanted anything to happen. Something stood between us now—Levi.

Maybe it was his daily visits when I was in the Medizin Jurte, playing his flute for me. I passed my convalescence by daydreaming about him. Played back our interactions. Pictured how he must have reacted on seeing me naked when he'd helped Vena put me back in my suit. I liked that he liked me, got high on the idea of it. I always assumed my little crush on the Reisender would evaporate if and when I saw Moray again. But it hadn't. Did Levi remind me of someone in Nord? Someone the other Lyn yearned for, someone waiting for her to return?

I sighed. Moray angled his chin downward to look at me.

"Did you ever get close like this with a Reisender?" I asked.

His breath caught then resumed. I pulled myself up and watched him.

"Do you really want me to answer that?" he said.

"You don't need to. You just admitted to it. How many times?"

He shook his head and knocked his curls loose. I tried to imagine the Reisende he'd chosen and pictured how they must have felt in this same moment. They must have looked at him and marveled that he'd settled on them. He was perfection, everything about him symmetric, every cell where it ought to be. He was their holy grail. GLEtch-free. Like me.

"More than once," he said.

"Two? Four? Twenty?"

I kept my tone ambiguous. Was I jealous? Curious? Turned on? He wouldn't be able to tell.

"I don't interact with them the same as you," he said. "I don't do a tour like you, Stamm to Stamm, Lat to Lat. Whenever I interact with Reisende, it's random and usually not a reason for celebration. I took what I could get when I could get it. If you don't understand that, I don't know what else to say."

"It didn't bother you that they were Reisende though?" I asked.

"Reisende, Dipoli, who cares?" he said.

"Their GLEtches didn't disgust you?"

He smiled.

"Sometimes, I liked them for their GLEtches," he said.

"I can't tell if you're being serious."

"Who did you think I was when you first came into your jurte?" he asked.

I'd hoped he hadn't picked up on what I'd said back then. I should've known better.

"A Reisender botanist who's smitten," I said with a smile.

Moray grinned wider.

"It's nice to be wanted, isn't it? Just be careful. You might get sucked in."

It was probably already too late by then.

Hybrids

Levi

When Lyn finally came hobbling into the jurte that served as my lab, I had to stifle my relief. I hadn't appreciated how worried I'd been until she was actually out of danger.

"Are you sure you're up for this?" I asked.

"Show me what you've found," Lyn said.

Between the research I'd been doing and the Reisen set to happen the next sol, everything in the lab was in a state of controlled chaos. Even so, I'd been careful to make sure nothing even remotely suspect was out. Even if there had been, I doubt she would have noticed. She was still in pain and distracted by it.

Lyn walked to my side and leaned against the table.

"First, the sapling," I said.

I showed her the specimen Vena and I had collected, the one that had been sprouting from a Reisender's chest. It was fading even after I'd transplanted it into proper soil, but it wasn't completely gone yet.

"You found it in a body?" she asked.

"In a Reisender. In close association with the black spots we noticed on the other victims' sternums. It's definitely a product of those. The plant's roots were coming from the spots."

Lyn leaned over to look at the example I had under the microscope.

"It's similar to luftors," I said, "but different in fundamental ways."

"Such as?"

I removed the sample and switched it with another. I positioned a seemingly empty glass slide and refocused for her. I moved out of the way and waved for her to take a look.

"Those are its reproductive cells. If it was a true luftor, you'd be looking at gametes like pollen, but that isn't pollen. At first, I thought it was a different species of luftor, but then I looked at the structures in detail. They're unicellular, which means they can't be pollen. They're spores."

"Like mold?"

"Yes, fungi produce spores, but some plants do too. It's not unheard of for plants to use spores rather than pollen."

She pulled away from the microscope's binoculars and looked at me.

"For luftors though?"

"I've never seen it."

"What does it mean?" she asked.

I switched out the slides under the microscope and pointed at the new one. She leaned forward and looked down the eyepieces. I knew what she saw because I'd spent years staring at the same thing. There were little rows of cells arranged in neat stacks with splashes of green.

"That's a typical luftor," I said. "Plant cells through and through. They're rectangular and regular. The chloroplasts show up nicely in that green and tell us these plants are autotrophs, that they get their own energy using photosynthesis."

I grabbed another slide and swapped it with the previous one. I'd studied this sample for hours trying to make sense of what I saw.

"That's from the sapling's stalk," I said. "It should look like the other one."

Lyn leaned in and gripped the binoculars.

"It doesn't," she said. "It's more irregular and tube-like. The cells branch out. No, that's not the right word. Bud out, maybe, from one another?"

"Do you see green anymore?"

Lyn spent a few seconds eyeing the field of view.

"Just a little here and there. Not like the other one."

She pulled back and looked at me.

"If someone showed me that sample without telling me what it was, I'd say it was a fungus. It has all the trademarks of it. Those little buds you mentioned are hyphae, which are basically how fungi eat. They don't chew their food. They absorb the nutrients from it, it usually being dead matter. They do that by infiltrating their food with those hyphae. One last sample."

I removed the slide and put another into place. It was covered in fine filaments that looked white to the naked eye.

"These were in the soil just below the body, beyond the roots of the sapling."

"More hyphae?" she asked.

"Not quite. We call these mycorrhizae. They're fungi that have a symbiotic relationship with plants. They help the plant with nutrient uptake from the soil. In exchange, the plant gives the fungi energy in the form of sugars."

"So those aren't that unusual then?"

"Well, I've never seen this much mycorrhizae associated with such an underdeveloped root structure. For a mature and massive tree? Yes. For a tiny little sapling? No. The fungus isn't really getting anything out of helping the sapling to this level. It's almost like the mycorrhizae are sacrificing themselves to help the sapling grow more rapidly. Or doing more than nutrient uptake."

Lyn leaned away from the microscope. She was at least partly supporting her weight with her arms based on the pressure in her hands.

"Let's sit down," I said.

I moved towards the cluster of excess burlap that served as seats. Lyn managed to make it to the pile and eased herself down.

"What does it all mean?" she asked.

"These aren't your typical luftors. They're some kind of plant-fungus hybrid. They use spores for reproduction, chitin in their cell walls, and hyphae for getting nutrients. Then again, they aren't all fungus. They look like plants, and they still have chlorophyll for photosynthesis. They can use different mechanisms, depending on their environment and what makes the most sense at the time."

"Photosynthesis if there's enough light or eating dead matter if not?"

"Exactly."

Lyn lifted her hands and laid the palms against her eyes. Her suit almost glowed in the dim lighting of the jurte. The stitches on them crosscut her stomach, where the labspawn had wounded her. Her chest rose and fell with each deeper-than-usual breath. I had a flash of her exposed breasts from when Vena and I had put her suit back on. It felt like weeks had passed since then. I'd been consumed with my work, in equal parts excited and terrified by what I'd found.

Lyn removed her hands from her eyes.

"This sounds like it was engineered, not evolved," she said.

"I don't really know what can and can't be done with GenEn," I said, "but I agree. This kind of leap is outside the realm of natural selection. Plants and fungi are in two different kingdoms. Actually, fungi are more similar to animals than plants in most ways. There's no path that would bring the two together, not on the timescales that we're talking about."

"Then someone made these, on purpose."

I nodded and looked away. My hands pinched my robes, and I forced them to be still.

"It wouldn't be the first time someone did this kind of thing with luftors," I said.

"What do you mean?"

"No one knows for sure if he used GenEn, but there was a botanist in Vromdorf who tried to make luftors more robust. He was named Rohn. From what I'm seeing, there are a lot of similarities to what he did."

"A Reisender who used GenEn? When was this?"

I held out my hands and smiled.

"Just to be clear, we don't know for sure if Rohn used GenEn. It was a while back, over twenty years ago."

"What happened? What did he do?"

"I'm not the best person to ask," I said. "I was still very young when it all happened, and no one likes to talk about it, even now. But from what I've heard, Rohn was too smart for his own good. He was brilliant. That, I can confirm. I've seen his work, read his notes."

I pointed to a small bookshelf on the side of the jurte opposite where we sat. There were over a dozen journals stacked in one long row.

"I didn't think Reisende kept books," she said.

"We usually don't, but the luftors are special. We need to know as much as possible about caring for them. Not everything can be passed down orally. Besides, Rohn did a lot of good work, work it would be irresponsible to throw away."

"Did he write about creating new luftors?"

"Not exactly. That's why I said I don't really know what he did. From what I've heard, he got ambitious. He kept trying to make the luftors better, more productive, more robust. Then he got fixated on the idea of creating a breed of luftors that were so resilient, they could survive the extremes outside of the Break."

"That's impossible," Lyn said.

She leaned towards me, eyes wide, one hand fidgeting with the bracelet on the wrist of the other.

"How did he plan to do it? And why even bother?"

"For the how, no one knows the specifics. I've looked over his notes, and it seems like he was trying to make them incredibly resilient. Rock-like exteriors, stomata that would seal off to keep from losing moisture, leaves that would shed themselves. Something about getting them to go into a dormant state when they weren't in the Break. It supposedly worked, but the luftors he made never came out of their dormancy. Like they were stuck somehow, and he left before he ever fixed the flaws."

"Left the Stamm?"

"Went Rogue, yes. As for why he created those luftors, why do any Reisende skirt the Decrees? Autonomy. I think Rohn saw the Lats as our leashes. We needed the Lats to move the platforms and the platforms for the luftors. If we could suddenly cut that connection, if the luftors would awake and produce ONi without us needing to pull them along, we'd be unburdened. Partly anyway. It was a small step towards freedom."

Lyn leaned back, and a spasm shot over her face. Her hand gripped her stomach where her wounds were hidden beneath her suit. I looked at her but didn't say anything. She got annoyed when I was fussy about her injuries. She wasn't used to being so helpless or reliant on Reisende.

"I don't know how the oberhaupt let him get away with his work," she said.

"Like I said, no one knows for sure if it was GenEn."

"What else could it be?"

I rose from my pile, headed to the bookshelf, and grabbed one of Rohn's journals. The hemp-linen cover was faded and smooth from both his hands and mine. I walked over to Lyn and flipped through the entries until I found the diagrams and text that I remembered. Then I knelt down and sat just beside her, our elbows touching. I tapped one drawing he'd done that showed two luftors with an inset of a pollen grain of one and the ovule of the other. Lines extended from each and met at a point with bulleted text below that outlined desirable features.

"He could have crossbred them like this shows," I said. "It's like GenEn but without the tech. It's not forbidden."

"Or he could have told everyone that's what he was doing even while he was actually using GenEn."

I closed the journal and placed it on my lap. I continued to sit beside her, crossing my legs, my knee brushing against her ankle.

"Maybe," I said. "It'd explain why he left."

It was hard to talk about Rohn in this way, hard to feed her what she needed to hear.

"You think he got caught and was trying to avoid punishment?"

Punishment. A euphemism. Any Reisende that committed GenEn would be killed without hesitation. Even exile from the Stamm, offered for less extreme offenses, wasn't an option for those who committed the ultimate taboo.

"I have no idea," I said. "Every time I asked, no one wanted to say anything. No one talks about Rohn."

"You said that was twenty years ago?" she asked.

"More or less."

"So Aarman would remember?"

"Aarman was oberhaupt when it all happened. If you can get him to tell you more than I've been able to, would you tell me what you find? I know it's not really need-to-know, but it wouldn't be against the Decrees since it was within Vromdorf."

"You almost sounded proud when you talked about Rohn's work. You look up to him."

"He was brilliant," I said. "His work motivated me to learn more about the luftors."

I stopped and stared at the journal.

"But it's more than that," I said. "Did I mention his family name? Zetmer. Rohn Zetmer."

"Your father."

After a few seconds, Lyn used her arms to push herself up. She had to hold onto my shoulder to stabilize herself. But even once she was standing, she stayed bent over, her hand still in contact with me.

"I'll let you know what I find out about him if anything," she said.

"And about these hybrids? You'll tell me what the Dipols say about my findings?"

"It depends," she said. "If they need more analyses, then yes. If not, I don't see how me conveying anything further is necessary."

"I want to know. I need to."

I stared at her and couldn't tell if I was demanding or pleading.

"Either way," she said, "it doesn't matter at the moment. Comms are down. I can't get anything out to them."

"Is that normal?"

"It's not abnormal. Probably interference from a storm coming off the Break. Nothing to worry about."

"If you say so."

"Thanks for your help, Levi."

Lyn hobbled out of the jurte.

It had all gone so well. I felt light as I packed the specimens away and placed Rohn's journal back on the shelf. Would he be proud of me? At least at what I'd learned, not so much what I may have done. But that was the lingering question. Were the hybrids really what I thought they were? I'd exhausted my own lines of research, and the picture still had holes punched all over it. I had to know the whole story. I needed to know what Vena had found.

***

It was hard getting Vena alone. If she wasn't in the Medizin Jurte helping with the GenMappings, she was either with Cade or Emyla. After trailing her on and off for a sol, I eventually gave in and left her the sign we'd used back when we'd been involved—a little square of red fabric hung near the entrance of the Essen Jurte. It was inconspicuous to everyone else but an obvious mark to the two of us. For a year, it'd been synonymous with sex. She'd see it.

The same sol I put it up, she found me in the luftor fields. Boots padded in the soft soil, and I looked up from my inspection of a budding ONi crystallite. She came within a meter of me and stopped. The distance she left between us told me just how dubious she felt about responding to my summons at all. I stood upright, letting the crystallite fall from my fingers, swinging like a pendulum on its branch.

"You saw my message?" I asked.

"I'm here, aren't I?"

I waved in the direction of my lab jurte, which we'd frequented on occasions like this. She shook her head slowly and crossed her arms.

"If you have something to say to me, let's do it out here. That place is..." She paused. "Dangerous."

"For who?"

"The both of us."

I crushed the surge of hope that leaped at the tail of her statement. I wasn't going to get distracted, wasn't letting my dead love rise from the ashes. It was pointless, and besides, I'd outgrown Vena.

"So you want to stand out in the luftor fields instead?" I asked. "I'd like to have a proper conversation, sans rebreathers."

"What's this about, Levi?"

I sighed and moved forward a step. She retreated.

"Not even a year goes by, and this is how you treat me?" I asked with a half-scoff and half-laugh. "You think I have so little inhibitions? I'd, what, jump on you the moment we're alone and unseen?"

She just looked back at me, and I cursed under my breath. She was getting under my skin. My emotions were going to undo everything if I didn't get them under control. The whole hybrid situation was too big for me to fumble. I steadied myself. I pictured Artur, imagined Lyn, and threw myself into fantasies with the both of them, alone, together. Any bygone yearning for Vena faded into nothingness.

I held out my hands and smiled behind my rebreather.

"Suit yourself," I said. "The last thing I want to do is make you uncomfortable."

"You shouldn't have used the red square then," she said. "Why not just tell me you needed to talk?"

I shrugged and turned back to the luftor nearest me. I cradled the uppermost ONi and rubbed the branch it held on to. Her eyes watched my movements.

"You're too popular to get a private audience with these days," I said. "The red square was a sure way to talk with you one-on-one."

Vena tilted her head back and sighed towards the sky.

"Please don't tell me you're going to make a grand

romantic gesture to try to win me over. A last-ditch effort to keep me from coupling with Cade?"

I barked out a laugh then snuffed it as soon as her eyes narrowed.

"Does that really sound anything like me? No, Vena, this is about Zeindorf. I've had time to study the samples and digest what I found, and it's got me worried."

Vena's eyes shifted left and right. She even went so far as looking over her shoulder.

"Well," she said, "Lynev will send our findings to the Dipols, and they'll take care of everything. You won't have to worry about it much longer."

"Did you meet with her yet?" I asked.

I knew she had based on my trailing of her. It had been the sol prior.

"Levi," Vena said, "please don't do this."

"What is it I'm doing?"

She was using her parental tone with me, chastising me already, which meant she wouldn't even begin to consider what I had to say.

"Lynev said we weren't to discuss anything about Zeindorf," Vena said, "so let's just stop the conversation right here."

I stepped towards her, and this time, she stood her ground. She could deal with this kind of defiance.

"I'd love to," I said. "I'd love to just hand off my data and findings to Lynev and trust that the Dipols will do what needs to be done to protect us, but I can't turn off my brain like that. There are too many bad signs."

"Levi," Vena said in a warning tone.

"I'm just venting my frustrations, looking for moral support. You won't even try to help me in that way?"

She wavered, and I pressed on.

"What if the hybrids are the product of GenEn, and

yet the Dipols don't know anything about GenEn?" I asked. "What if they pretend to but don't? What if it's all a black box to them, to be feared and hated and shunned?"

"Shouldn't it be?"

She didn't mean what she said. She didn't buy the lies that the Dipols told us, not deep down in her core. None of the Reisende really did. We'd had our wings clipped. There was vast potential lying in wait and going to waste all the while. We could be so much more if given the chance, if woken from our hibernation, shaken from our stasis. I saw what we could achieve, sol after sol, in the small, mundane acts of our nomadic purgatory. There was greatness. We just needed the collective push to become more.

I shook my head at Vena's hollow statement of regurgitated propaganda.

"Knowledge is never inherently dangerous," I said. "People are. And in the situation we find ourselves in, the Dipols not knowing a thing about GenEn, is bad for all of us. How can they stop it if they don't understand it?"

"Drop it, Levi, okay? I see exactly what you're trying to do, and it's not going to work."

She moved in until our faces were only a hand's width apart.

"Do you really think I'm so simple?" she asked. "Or did you forget how well I know you?"

I'd been caught, and there was no elegant way out. Instead, I grinned and shrugged. Vena stayed in close.

"This is why I couldn't be with you. This is exactly why I chose Cade."

She turned and went to walk away, but I grabbed her arm as a reflex. She looked back at me with wide eyes. I'd never done something like this before. Vena had always been right. When she'd had her say, I'd always backed down but not anymore. I wasn't the same old Levi she thought she knew so well. I'd learned too much. Done too much.

"You can't say something like that and not elaborate," I said.

She tugged her arm, but my fingers only squeezed tighter. Emotion was winning out again, but I couldn't force myself to be rational this time, not after what she'd said. A year of silence, of wondering why I hadn't been enough when Cade of all people had, and now this.

"Please, elaborate," I said.

"Let me go."

"I will once you do what I asked."

Her face started to get red behind her rebreather, but she stopped trying to wrest her arm free.

"Why did you choose Cade?" I asked.

"Because of this," she said. "You're too unpredictable. You always have been. One minute an angel. The next a labspawn. Always so rebellious, and always questioning everything. I just couldn't risk tying myself to someone like you. Cade was the safe option. You're too much of a wild card for the future I want."

I relaxed my grip, and she slipped her arm free. She stopped and watched me for signs of what I might do. I knew what needed to come next, but I was distracted by her last few words because they told me that Vena was priming herself to be the next oberhaupt. She was the perfect replacement for Aarman, and she couldn't link herself to someone like me. It made sense, was perfectly logical, but that didn't make it sting any less.

"I didn't want to do this," I said.

Vena narrowed her eyes and looked ready to bolt down the row of luftors. I folded my hands behind my back and rocked on my heels.

"I was hoping you'd see reason," I said, "but you're just as oblivious as you've always been. Wedded to the Dipols, worse than Aarman even."

"I'm not giving you anything on Zeindorf. This conversation is over."

Vena turned and took three steps in the soggy soil.

"Tell me what I want to know or I tell everyone about us," I said.

She froze.

"That was in the past," she said. "Why would they care?"

She turned around with a face that was hard to read, but I didn't need visual cues. She was shaken. If she hadn't been, she would have already left. She was panicking. Good, that's exactly what I needed.

"Cade would care."

"I wasn't with Cade when I was with you," she said.

"We both know Cade and how he'd react to learning you'd been with me time and time again."

"I chose him," she said, hands on hips. "That's more important than whatever happened in the past."

I walked up to Vena and towered over her. She stayed still and stiff. I could almost feel her shaking. I didn't relish terrifying her so much, but then again, I had tried to appeal to her reason. Since that hadn't worked, all I could use was fear to get what I needed.

"You know exactly how he'll react," I said. "Cade despises me, and you willingly laid with me over and over again. He'll never see you the same. He'll probably call the coupling off. Is that what you want, Vena? To implode your life just because you persist in following archaic rules that serve no purpose? Believe me, I don't want to do this, but I don't have a choice. This is so much bigger than you or me or even Vromdorf. I need to know what you found out about the luftors. Tell me, or I go directly to Cade."

She dropped her hands to her sides and sagged. I'd won. She shook her head and plodded in the direction of my lab jurte. It didn't even take her ten minutes to convey her findings, but they were chock-full of menace coupled with what I already knew. I saw the complete picture, and it was horrifying.

The hybrids had used living Reisende as hosts. The spores killed them then fed on the body to grow. So they hadn't just opportunistically used already dead Reisende. It was everything I'd feared and more. It wasn't something the Dipols could fix. We were running out of time. I knew what the next step had to be, but it was a massive leap bordering on fantasy. If I was going to do it, I'd need Lyn to trust me and see me as an ally and partner. The survival of the Stamm, of many Stämme even, depended on it. It was time to show her what I really was.

GLEtch-free

Lyn

I pushed the mush that was meant to be my dinner around on my plate. First into one pile then two. The grain didn't taste like a thing, but I should have been grateful for it. It could be one of the last meals I'd get for a while. Without Zeindorf, Vromdorf was wholly reliant on the Dipols for food drops, and there had been comms silence with them for three sols now.

The timing was awful. I finally had data from both Levi and Vena on the Zeindorf samples. All that was left was for the Dipols to digest the findings and make a plan for what to do to mitigate the threat. But here I was waiting and waiting to even tell them what we'd found.

A shadow fell over my plate, and I glanced up. Levi smiled and looked down at the spot opposite me. It was his approximation of asking for permission to join me. The Essen Jurte was only a quarter full, meaning he had his choice of seats, but I was thankful for the company. I nodded, inviting him to sit, then pushed my plate aside.

"The food not to your liking?" Levi asked.

"It's terrible, as usual, but don't worry, I wouldn't dare waste it. I'm just taking a break."

Levi scooped some of the mush from his plate and took a bite. He licked the spoon as he pulled it out of his mouth. That sensuality yet again.

"I heard you finished the last GenMap," Levi said.

"This sol, yes. I just have to upload it to the network."

For some strange reason, my connection to the network was intact despite the comms being down. There was probably a tech explanation as to why the one could work when the other didn't, but it was one of the many things that I knew next to nothing about. Another chunk of information that took up residence in that big blank in my mind.

He took another bite and chewed. I was envious of his ability to stomach nourishment that tasted of nothing. It was a useful trait, especially for anyone stuck living in the Break with all its hardy but painfully bland fare. Of course, the only thing I had to compare it to was the food at the Wilkommen dinners. Maybe my taste buds were being so sensitive because, in the back of my mind, I knew I might be stuck in Vromdorf for a long while yet. No more Wilkommen dinners for the foreseeable future. Stuck living like a Reisender.

"On to the couplings tomorrow then?" Levi asked.

"Yes," I said, "after I announce the results of the GenMapping. But don't worry, your name and Emyla's were removed from the pool, just like you asked."

"I would hope so."

Levi's smile faded, replaced by a flicker that could've been a wince. He swallowed then put his spoon down on the table and pushed his plate to the side, the same as mine. He leaned forward and spoke in a whisper.

"I need to ask you favor," he said.

"I'm listening."

Levi glanced over his shoulder. No one else was within earshot, but he tried leaning in closer before giving up and relocating to the bench just next to me. He scooted in closer than he needed to until his leg grazed mine. I didn't pull it away.

"You can use your GenMapper to get anyone's GenMap, right?" he asked.

"It's a GenMapper," I said, "so yes, it can retrieve a GenMap."

"Run a new one, I mean, for me?"

"Yours? Why? Your physicians have the results somewhere in their piles and piles of scrolls, and if it's a more detailed version you want, I can pull that from the network directly. Although you wouldn't understand what it says if I showed you."

Levi shifted his leg so that it was flush with mine all down our thighs. Again, I didn't pull away.

"I want to run a new one," he said. "I don't trust the old one. So, will you do it? This somn?"

I didn't understand what he was getting at, but this wasn't the place to press him for answers.

"I have to upload the last child's GenMap," I said. "It takes about three hours, as long as the signal is good."

"And if you ran mine right after that, it'd be done by next sol?"

I nodded. Levi was nervous or giddy. I couldn't tell which.

"I'll come to your jurte later then," he said.

Levi rose, and I grabbed his arm and pulled him back down to the bench with a jolt.

"You can't just invite yourself to my jurte like that, Reisender."

He was getting too comfortable and cocky. This level of familiarity wasn't something I'd had to deal with before, and

I didn't know how best to approach the situation. My default was to be harsh and stern. An Itinerate.

Levi looked back at me and just waited, waited for me to say something else. He called my bluff. I couldn't even pretend to be annoyed with him. It was hard enough not letting my excitement show. I wanted him in my jurte. I relished the thought of him stealing in in the middle of the somn.

"I'm not promising to run your GenMap, to be clear," I said. "I need you to explain more before I agree to it. But yes, you can come to my jurte two hours before midsomn. The GenMapper should be done and cooled down by then."

I pulled my leg away, shoveled the remainder of the mush into my mouth, and pushed my now-empty plate towards Levi. Then I left the Essen Jurte and headed back to my own. As soon as I got in, I connected the GenMapper to the network and started offloading the data.

While I waited, I alternated between pacing the small space and tidying it up. The latter didn't involve much work given the few things I had, but I wanted to keep busy. I wanted to move my hands and have my mind focus on something tangible.

As instructed, Levi patted on the inner flap of my jurte two hours before midsomn. The GenMap had long been still and quiet. I was lying on my mat, braiding and unbraiding the bracelet, staring up at the ceiling. At the sound, I got up and walked over to the entry. I pulled the fabric aside and ushered him in.

The air was full from fresh ONi and smelled slightly sweet courtesy of a powdered herb I'd picked up a few Stämme back. Levi stood in the middle of my jurte and looked around. It was the first time he'd been here with me in it.

"Stark and soulless," I said, throwing my hand at the environs.

"You're an Itinerate. Why would you have any keepsakes or decorations?"

I moved over to the urn and sat on one of the two pillows beside it. I angled my head at the other one. Levi threw the robes shrouding his legs out of the way and took up the seat. He didn't bother to drape the robes back over his limbs like the Reisende usually did. It wasn't as though I could see any actual flesh. He wore beige pants under the robes, but in this way, I could make out his form better.

"The GenMapper is ready," I said. It sat on my lockbox, waiting. "But before I agree to run your GenMap, tell me why you think your current one is faulty."

Levi crossed his legs and rested his forearms on his knees. He stared at the ONi.

"I've known for a long time that I was different, beyond just having minimal GLEtches. I don't know how I knew, but I did."

"What are you saying, exactly?"

He was still looking at the ONi, maybe even staring at them harder.

"I'd like my GenMap to speak for itself."

I shifted on my pillow. This wasn't how I'd thought the conversation would run. He was being evasive, and I was getting impatient.

"Levi, I'm not going to run your GenMap unless you tell me more."

He finally pulled his eyes away from the ONi and looked back at me.

"My mother and father had GLEtches. You saw what Kelica has to wear just to be able to see. So tell me, how do two Reisende with a moderate or worse GLEtch count produce an offspring with minimal GLEtches? And how does their other child have moderate GLEtches, like them? And what's more, tell me what my GLEtches are because, for the life of me, I couldn't tell you."

"You think you're GLEtch-free?"

"Suspect I'm GLEtch-free."

"Reisende aren't GLEtch-free. The only way that could happen is from GenEn. GLEtch-free for your kind is a misnomer. GLEtch-filled would be more accurate."

"Labspawn."

I shook my head and scooted closer to him.

"Anyway, it's impossible," I said. "Reisende don't have the tech, let alone the knowledge to do GenEn."

"What about Rohn's luftors? And he was my father. Connect the dots for yourself."

There wasn't any reason to keep arguing with Levi, and he did have a point. He was physically indistinguishable from an Itinerate. Whether that meant he was really GLEtch-free, only the GenMapper could say. I rose and moved over to my lockbox. I grabbed the GenMapper then opened the box with my free hand. It wasn't very large, maybe a quarter meter by a quarter meter, but it was crammed full of supplies.

I dug around until I found a satchel and, in that, a needle. I went to the urn, put the needle between the pinchers of the fire-stoker, and shoved it deep into the embers. I let it sit for about half a minute before pulling it free. Levi watched each of my movements. When I had the needle, freshly disinfected, in between my thumb and forefinger, I waved him over.

"Will you need my heel?" he asked.

I'd never done a GenMap on an adult before, but the sampling location didn't matter. Only the blood did. I held out my hand for his. Levi placed his palm in mine. I turned it over then pricked his middle finger with the needle. He didn't react beyond watching the bead of crimson growing and growing. When it was large enough to threaten spilling over, I positioned a vial below his finger. The droplet of blood plunged down and splashed right where it needed to.

I repeated this a few times until I had enough sample. Then I mixed the solvent into the vial, stirred the solution, and deposited the sample into the GenMapper. The sequencing started, and the device whirred away. I cleaned the supplies and stowed them back in my lockbox, all except the GenMapper. That got to sit on top while it ran through its rounds. It would be hours yet until we got the results. Now, there was nothing to do but wait.

"If you're right," I said, "it means an Itinerate falsified the records. It's a serious crime."

"That was twenty-five years ago," Levi said.

"If they're still alive, they'll be punished. Them and whoever worked with them."

I avoided saying Rohn. This was all hypotheticals still.

"It'll be another few hours," I said. "You can leave and come back if you'd like to get some sleep."

Levi shifted and pulled his flute from his robes.

"To pass the time," he said. "Only if you'd like me to play, though. I'd rather not leave and come back if that's alright by you. Me going in and out of your jurte so late in the somn is likely to be noticed."

"And you not leaving my jurte all somn isn't?"

Levi smiled and looked down at the flute laying in his palms.

"I don't mind those kinds of rumors, but if you do…"

He left the last part of his sentence hang in the thick air.

"I don't care what Reisende think of me," I said. "Besides, I wouldn't mind the company or a tune."

Levi nodded, repositioned his legs, then lifted the flute to his lips. He breathed out, and the instrument sang. So soft at first. Barely audible over the GenMapper's whirrings. I almost had to lean in to pick it up. Slowly, though, the music rose and rose until it swelled.

Maybe it was the stress of the situation with the Dipols and Zeindorf. Or maybe it was the draw I felt towards him, but for the first time in my life, visions came to mind in tandem with the sounds. Landscapes, alien and austere, rose up before me. Cliffs of white were topped with tuffs of green. Endless water slammed into the rock, crashing and breaking and doing so over and over again.

I didn't know where the images came from. It wasn't Neuen. It was another world, maybe an ancestral memory tucked away in my genome. Where humans had come from, perhaps? A place both violent and majestic in its beauty and strength.

Then the sound faded. Levi pulled his lips away from the mouthpiece and lowered the flute. He glanced at me, and I don't know what he saw. I was so out of myself that I didn't even bother to present a version I wanted him to see. Whatever he glimpsed must have pleased him because he was beaming.

"Where do you get those emotions?" I asked. "How do you infuse them into the music like that?"

"I just take all my hopes and wants and channel them. It comes out like that because of who I am. Remember what I said the first time I played for you? Outsized ambition."

It was a tragedy, him having the skills he did and wasting them living in a Stamm. It was too small for him, too simple. Sitting there, with the urn casting flickering flames on our faces, I saw it. The yearning, his angst. But at the time, I mistook the source of his desires. In my egotism, I thought it was all directed at me. I made the mistake of imaging myself as the axis of Levi's world. The nexus of his desires.

I stoked the embers then glanced at my mat. Levi's eyes followed mine.

"I'm going to try to get some sleep," I said. "I need to be alert when I announce the GenMap results."

"Go ahead. I'll keep an eye on the GenMapper and let you know when it's done."

I pushed myself off my pillow and moved to my mat. It

was big enough for two. It had accommodated Moray and me. I removed my boots and sat on it. Levi's back was to me. I took the moment to parse through my thoughts. I weighed the pros and cons, of what was best for me and him, and what it could mean if I was stuck in Vromdorf for a long while yet. I couldn't come to any conclusions. I was evenly split, cleaved down the middle, a human-take on the Break.

"You should get some rest too," I said.

Levi peeked over his shoulder at me. I started undoing my braid. I never went amongst the Reisende with my hair flowing freely. Even during our trip to Zeindorf, I'd kept my braid in, even if it was less comfortable to sleep that way.

"There's room enough for two on here," I added.

He'd been waiting for the invitation. He came over and removed his boots before sitting down beside me. I tossed my hair over my shoulder, leaned back, and laid with my hands folded on my stomach. Levi did the same. We both stared up at the ceiling, studying the shadows writ there, looking for signs of what might come next. I toyed with my bracelet, and his eyes watched my fingers work.

"Where did you get that?" he asked. "From Nord or a Stamm?"

My hands stilled. I held the fabric taunt.

"A Stamm," I said. "My first one, actually. It was a gift from two Reisende I approved for coupling."

"And you kept it all this time?"

I was so used to seeing the bracelet that it had become almost invisible, its finer details lost to familiarity. But Levi's question forced me to see it with fresh eyes. Nearly three years it had sat on my wrist, been undone and redone. Time and circumstance had taken a toll that I was only now seeing. The orange, once vivid and deep, had faded to a muted facsimile. The thread was worn and frayed. It was old beyond its years, tired, ready to be finished with its duties.

"It's calming," I said, "to braid and unbraid it. But more than that, it's a reminder of why I do what I do."

"To cleanse us of our GLEtches," he said.

"To help you."

Levi winced and shook his head. He was struggling with something, debating if he could unburden it on me.

"I really am here to help," I said.

Levi looked away, eyes trained forward.

"Gerald died because of me," Levi said. "He was only out in the fields because I'd asked, not the other way around."

"I know," I said.

Now it was Levi's turn to look at me and for me to look straight ahead. Our heads tied by strings. One movement an inverse of the other.

"I'm a plague to this Stamm," he said.

At the time, I thought Levi was referring to Gerald's death or else his potential for being the product of GenEn, but now I know that he was hinting at the awful truth. He wanted to tell me everything then and there, but he didn't. And maybe it was for the best that he hadn't. I don't know how I would've reacted. Or if things would have played out as they had.

"You're the only Reisender that I've ever gravitated towards," I said. "You're different from them, GenMap aside."

Levi turned to face me and held his head up with his arm.

"That's why I'm a plague," he said. "I infect you Itinerates too."

"Do you mean Artur?" I asked.

"He was already jaded by the time he got to Vromdorf," Levi said. "Like most Itinerates. But maybe he would have managed to finish his tour if it hadn't been for me."

"He didn't finish his tour?"

I turned on my side too and faced Levi head on. Our

lips couldn't have been more than a hand's length apart. His warm breath met mine. The vibrations from his body traveled through the mat.

"He went Rogue," Levi said.

That was a caustic word to an Itinerate, and I had to fight the bile that rose up.

"Artur stayed in Vromdorf for four weeks," Levi said. "Then he went north into the Break. He asked me to go with him, but I refused. I can't help but think I pushed him down that path. Without me, he would have been left alone with his own worse thoughts. Maybe they would have mastered him anyway, or maybe he would have learned not to listen to them."

"Any Itinerate that goes Rogue has something innately wrong with them. You didn't push him down that path. He was always going to go that way."

Levi heard my words, but they just skimmed right off of him. He had an armor up against me, in that of all moments. If he hadn't, maybe things would've gone differently. Instead, I rolled onto my back and faced the ceiling again. The moment was lost. Levi moved onto his back too, and within a few minutes, his breath came louder and more rhythmically. I sighed and tried to find some sleep myself.

The beeping from the GenMapper woke us both. Levi jumped up and leaned over the device. He didn't dare touch it. I grabbed the GenMapper and scrolled through the results. There wasn't much to see though. The GenMap highlighted the defects that the Stämme were working towards erasing. The more information displayed, the more work they had to do to cleanse their genome.

Levi's was blank expect for the GLEtch count listed at the top of the output. GLEtch-free. Just as he'd predicted. I held the device out to him, and his eyes scanned over the display, widened then narrowed. He rose from the crouch we'd both been in and paced the room, occasionally rubbing his hand over his face.

"You were right," I said.

"GenEn. Labspawn."

If it had been any other Reisender, I would have flown into action. Informed the oberhaupt and lead physician. Made preparations for quarantining his genome. Notified the Dipols.

But this was Levi, and I couldn't see him as just another Reisender. The shock he must have felt, it infected me, stole into my soul and blackened it. A pit sagged in my gut. My breath came short. It wasn't fair. It had been out of his control, and yet the punishment would be the same, regardless.

I didn't let any of my inner turmoil show. I acted the part of an Itinerate. Stoic. Distant. I waited for Levi to notice me again. After a few minutes, his pacing slowed, and he looked at me.

"What happens next?" he asked.

"I tell the oberhaupt. We ensure that your genome isn't passed on."

"Can't have me infecting the Stamm. See, I told you. So sterilization then?"

I nodded, my voice suddenly caught in my throat like it had swelled to twice its size. Without thinking, I moved to Levi and embraced him. One hand to his neck, the other on his back. I pulled him in and held tight. He was stiff at first but then softened and melted into me. Being so close, it made me hunger for more, but Levi was grieving. I couldn't take advantage of him like that. Instead, after too little time, I released him. We looked at one another, suddenly shy and sad.

"Why did you do this?" I asked. "If you really thought you could be GenEn, you had to know what that would mean."

"Like I said, we can't have me infecting the Stamm. If I ever coupled, it would have meant passing my genome on and polluting the collective genome of the Stamm. It'd be undoing everything the Stamm has worked towards for generations. How couldn't I do this?"

I didn't know what to say in response to that. It was selfless and tragic and just another one of the countless sacrifices that the Dipols demanded of us all.

"You'll get through this," I said.

Levi nodded, slipped his boots and rebreather on, and left my jurte. It was in the early hours of the sol, but I needed to make preparations for Levi's sterilization as soon as possible. The Decrees were blindingly clear on that front. Twenty-five years had gone by since the unthinkable had happened, since some Reisender had repeated the taboo, but now that I knew, I couldn't waste a second to rectify the breach. To do otherwise was to be complicit in the gravest of crimes.

The conversation with Aarman was boilerplate—me telling him what had happened, what Levi and I had found, him in a daze from still being half-asleep or from the news or both. Talking with him was a formality. The more critical conversation was the one I needed to have with Kelica.

I found her in the Medizin Jurte, and when she spotted me, she brightened. Her mind was on the GenMap announcement, and I almost debated putting this off until after I'd gone through that ritual. Almost. The worst of all the taboos had been committed. Nothing could stand in the way of remedying it.

"The GenMaps will have to wait," I said.

Kelica's smile faded, and that characteristic hardness settled on her again. Somehow, that made what I had to do next easier. I didn't like her. I found her critical, harsh, and demanding. I winced at some of the things she said to her physicians. She liked to find fault in their work and even went so far as belittling the ones that weren't as skilled as the others.

Despite all of that, I didn't relish telling her the news. Levi wasn't just some Reisender in her Stamm. This was her son, from what I could tell her favorite one, and I was going to make her sterilize him.

"A serious infraction of the Decrees has come to my attention this sol."

I paused, not sure what to say next. Her shoulders were higher than usual, and her breath barely came at all.

"There's evidence that a Reisender in Vromdorf committed GenEn," I said. "One of you has a genome with all the markers for it."

"One of the children?" she asked.

I shook my head and forced myself to say everything I needed to. The start and stop of these punctuated exchanges weren't making things any easier. It needed to come out all in one go. Like ripping briars out of the flesh they'd embedded themselves in.

"Levi. I ran his GenMap, and it presents as GLEtch-free. That's ridiculous, of course, and can only mean that someone tampered with his genome back before he was sired. It's so long ago at this point, I'm not sure if the culprit is even still around, but once the Dipols hear about this, they'll make the decision on punitive measures. For now, we have to isolate Levi's genome. He has to be sterilized. There can't be any delay. He already knows and is ready. You, Kelica, will have to be the one to do it as the lead physician."

I broke off and waited for the turmoil to hit. But it didn't. Kelica's eyes were wider than usual, her lips more tightly pursed, but other than that, she didn't show much of a reaction at all. I waited. She blinked a few times and cleared her throat.

"I have to do it?" she asked.

"Yes."

Kelica blinked again and again like her sight was blurred by her upturned reality.

"We'll hold off announcing the children's GenMap results until the next sol," I said. "How about you go back to your jurte and rest? We can do the sterilization this somn. That will give you and him time to prepare yourselves. I can't give you more than that. The Decrees are very clear when it comes to GenEn. Delaying even this much could get me in trouble."

Kelica shook her head and mumbled a vague acknowledgment of my offer before leaving. I'd give her until just after the somn meal to come back. If she didn't, then I'd have to go and find her. It'd be my duty to force her to perform the sterilization. I shivered at the thought of it.

In all fifty-six Stämme that I'd been in prior, there hadn't been a single case of GenEn. And that made sense. GenEn was the enemy. GenEn was the Reisende's curse. So who in the world had decided to set them back so much? I hadn't wanted to mention Rohn to Kelica. She was already reeling. And if anyone could put those pieces together, it would be the woman who'd been married to the man. I'd done my duty. Now, I just had to make sure the sterilization happened, and that the Dipols learned about all of this as soon as I could reach them.

Sterilization

Levi

I lit the brazier and heated the urn in my family's jurte then flopped down on my mat. I turned onto my back and stared up at the ceiling. I didn't know when my sterilization would take place, but it had to be soon. My mind was empty. I was calm.

I'd done what I had for a concrete reason, but I hadn't expected this kind of reaction in myself. It was like an unburdening I hadn't even known I needed. A warmth and wholeness flooded me, and I had to find an outlet for it. I grabbed my flute and sat with my legs crossed and back straight. I pressed the opening to my lips then let my fingers fall where they wanted.

It was a new song, nothing I'd ever played or heard, but somehow it was fully formed. The melody came out of the ether and transformed into something winding and wandering and impossibly sad. It was me. The song was my journey to this moment.

All the pain and struggle that had tried to smother me. My loneliness and otherness first from being too perfect, the envy of the Stamm, and later from my secret shame at knowing the truth. I was special in all the worst ways, but it was what I wanted. It kept me apart. It drove me to achieve greatness at a break-neck pace. All those hours poring over Rohn's scribblings. All those lonely somns in the jurte out in the luftor fields studying the plants. It had all led to this moment, this horrible, awful, but pivotal moment.

Then the song cut off. There wasn't an ending for it yet. It built and built, but I didn't know where it would go. An explosive, violent finale? Or a fading into obscurity? It felt sacrilege to preemptively force the song to a conclusion that hadn't come. No, better to leave it in that uneasy state. Indecisive and incomplete but honest.

I pulled the flute from my lips and let it drop to my thighs. The room resolved again. Back in reality, Kelica stood at the entrance, transfixed. My instinctive reaction was to hide the flute. She hated the thing; it had been Rohn's.

"That was moving," she said.

She crept further into the jurte and came to my mat. I eyed her warily. She never gave compliments, especially about my flute playing.

"I've got a lot on my mind," I said. "This helps me process it."

I cradled the flute in my hands.

"Yes," she said, "this somn will be difficult."

She crumpled down onto the floor. The look on her face was something I'd only ever seen brief glimpses of over the years when Rohn's name was mentioned. Grief. But this time, she didn't bother to hide it. She was drowning in it and grasping for me. I held her hand and wrapped an arm over her shoulders.

She didn't deserve this from me. I ought to have left

her huddled on the ground and marched out of the jurte. Then again, I couldn't blame this on her. Besides, she was a Reisender too, just as manipulated as the rest of us, another victim of the Dipols.

"Did you come to get me for the sterilization?" I asked.

She winced at the last word then hardened and shrugged my arm off her shoulders. She was hurt but also angry.

"We'll do the procedure later," she said. "I needed to tell you some things before then. Things maybe I ought to have told you before you decided to unburden your soul on the Itinerate."

Kelica glared at me, but I held her harsh gaze.

"Rohn and I had a shared vision," she said.

I held my breath. Kelica never talked about Rohn. He was a borderline forbidden topic in our jurte.

"That's why we gravitated towards one another," Kelica said. "We were both so certain that GenEn would save the Reisende."

I pulled back. Kelica watched me from the corners of her glasses, the curvature of the lens distorting her eyes.

"We'd befriend and seduce Itinerates. They were so fragile and raw by the time they got to Vromdorf, it wasn't hard to do, but then I suppose you know that too, seeing how you latch on to them. From our forays with the Itinerates, we learned about GenEn, bit by bit. It took us years to gather the knowledge and equipment to do it ourselves, but we did manage it.

"Things were good for a while. Rohn focused on his luftors, and I focused on the Reisende. Then Rohn lost the vision. He pulled away. He became more and more of a maverick to the point where he openly defied the Decrees. He didn't believe in conforming to the Dipols's ideals anymore. He wanted to break free."

Kelica stopped and turned to face me. I didn't shrink

from her stare like I had when I was younger. I didn't judge her or Rohn.

"And that was his undoing," she added. "That belief is incompatible with the Stamm. Aarman didn't have a choice. Either Rohn had to mend his ways or leave, and he chose the latter."

"Aarman let him leave?" I asked.

"He didn't stop him, but I didn't bring this up because I wanted to talk about Rohn. I brought this up because you should know the truth about what you are and why. I know you think that Rohn made you GenEn, but he didn't. I did."

How had I not seen it? In all the years I'd lived with Kelica, how had I never sensed the defiance? Behind her unassuming ways, she'd been the single greatest threat to the Stamm, until the hybrid luftors and their creator.

"Why?" I asked.

"You were my masterpiece, Levi. The culmination of my life's work. Your genome is pure, and it was meant to slowly trickle down into the collective genome over the ages, but everything is ruined now. Your sterilization marks the end of everything I strived for. My dream dies with it."

"I always thought you treated me differently from Cade for a reason, and now I know why. Not your favorite son. Just your favorite science project."

"You're wrong," she said. "I love you more than you could ever know or understand. You're me in so many ways. The similarities shock me sometimes. You're the apple of my eye. You always have been."

This wasn't like Kelica at all. The praise, the love, the pride. I wanted to shout at her, unload the anguish at this truth that only made everything all the more tragic. But I didn't. She was right. This situation had been like lifting a mirror to my eyes. I wasn't so different from her after all.

"How did you know?" she asked. "About the GenEn.

That Itinerate didn't just randomly decide to check your GenMap. You asked her to, didn't you?"

"Yes," I said.

"Why?"

I let a smile peel back.

"Like mother, like son," I said.

"Elaborate. I'm being honest with you. It's only fair that you do the same."

"Fair? Fair is you not performing GenEn on me in the first place. Fair is you having told me all of these things years ago."

Kelica leaned forward and stared down at her hands. Her fingers were interlaced and locked.

"There never would've been a good time to tell you," she said. "And as for performing the GenEn, it was a gift. It still is a gift, no matter what anyone else says. Your GenMap is indistinguishable from a Dipoli's, which tells you everything you need to know. They only decide to label you as flawed because it helps them maintain their control."

These were my own words. All this time, defiance was lying in wait in my own Stamm, right in my same jurte. How many others thought as we did? How many were waiting for the moment to hit back and take their freedom?

"When I first tested my GenMap, I thought I was poison," I said. "But now? I don't care that I'm GenEn, but I do disagree with the whole system, which puts me more in line with Rohn than you. We ought to be forging our own path, not conforming to the Dipols's vision."

Kelica stuttered, her eyes shifting left and right. She didn't understand.

"Then why did you have the Itinerate run your GenMap?" she asked.

"I need her to trust me. I wanted her to know I was GenEn because sympathy is the fastest way to achieve that.

I'm sorry that means your work was all for naught, but it's a small price to pay. This GenMap nonsense is a distraction. The hybrids are all that matter, and to stop them, I need Lyn to be on my side."

Kelica shook her head over and over again. I'd smashed her dream to pieces in pursuit of something she didn't understand. She didn't know about the hybrids. And even if she had, they would have been a problem for the Dipols to solve, even for Kelica. She was stuck in the past, embedded into the very fabric of the Dipols's elaborate tapestry, and she didn't even know it. But she would, soon enough. They all would.

I rose from the mat and left the jurte. I needed to take a walk. There were too many revelations to digest, and I couldn't think straight with Kelica hovering. I wandered the weaving corridors between jurten. It was midsol, and Vromdorf was bustling, despite the looming threat.

Of course, these Reisende knew nothing about what exactly had happened in Zeindorf. They didn't even know the hybrids existed. To them, the situation in their neighboring Stamm was a distant tragedy. One Stamm apart or Stämme on the opposite end of the Break, it didn't mean much to them. We never interacted with the other Reisende. They were more alien even than the Itinerates, who we saw at least once every year. The only contact with other Stämme was done by traders, and even then, it was only trader-to-trader. We had no bonds to other Reisende except that they shared in our exile and lived the same nomadic existence.

But the lack of concern about Zeindorf wasn't because the Reisende in Vromdorf didn't care. It was because they were incapable of it. To them, something unfortunate had happened to Zeindorf, but Zeindorf was not Vromdorf. The Dipols were investigating. The Dipols would fix whatever problems there were. That's how my fellow Reisende viewed the situation.

Ninety-nine times out of one hundred, they would be right. The Dipols would solve everything. Except, this time I knew the cause—the hybrids. And I knew what they were—GenEn. This wasn't something the Dipols were equipped to solve.

The Reisende I passed couldn't know this, of course. So why did I glare at them? Did I want them to feel the same terror that was gripping my own heart? Did I really want them to know the truth? No, but I envied them and their obliviousness. I wanted to feel safe and secure in the chokehold of the Dipols. I knew too much though, done too much.

"Is it true?" someone called after me.

I was near the luftor fields. I turned and glanced over my shoulder. There was Emyla, picking at her fingers and fidgeting. I hadn't tried to avoid her since returning from Zeindorf, but I also hadn't made a point to talk with her. She, on the other hand, had stayed out of my way. I'd taken it as a sign that my harsh words had done what they needed to. Had the sting worn off?

"Is what true?" I asked.

She stepped closer then hesitated.

"Well? You called out to me, Emyla."

"Lynev spoke with my father not too long ago."

Emyla lowered her head and came in close. I let her because I knew what she'd say next. I was ready to deal with the fallout of the sterilization but not to have people gossip about it before it even happened. Just a few hours was all we needed. A few hours of tight lips for the secret to stay secret. Once it was over and done with, then the Stamm could know. Then I could face whatever looks they threw my way. Shame, disgust, pity, but I had to be solid going in. Emyla wasn't about to undo that. I grabbed her elbow and pulled her into the luftor fields. Once we had only plants on one side and empty plains on the other, I let Emlya go.

"You shouldn't be listening in on Aarman's conversations," I said.

"I was sleeping," she said. "I haven't been well. Ever since the sol you left for Zeindorf."

I smothered a sigh.

"What did you hear?"

She leaned in close despite the fact that no one was nearby. I wanted to back away, but the luftors brushed up against me. I didn't want to damage their ONi.

"She said you were GenEn."

Emyla's voice cut off.

"The Itinerates know their business, don't they?" I asked. "If Lynev said I was GenEn, it must be true."

"No," Emyla shouted.

She was seething, hands clenched, back arched.

"You're perfect, Levi. How could you be GenEn? It doesn't make any sense."

"I'm GenEn. My genome is GLEtch-free. And do you know how we found that out? After all this talk of coupling, I knew something was wrong with me, but I had to be sure. We ran my GenMap. See, Emyla, you didn't want to couple with me after all."

I brushed past her and strode straight down a row of luftors. In that moment, I didn't know why I'd said that to her. Had it been to spare her? To make her more accepting of the reality? But I'd lied and said her trying to force the coupling on me had essentially led us to that moment. Why had I said that if not to hurt her?

I couldn't deal with her, couldn't deal with anything. I wasn't relishing the thought of what had to come next, and talking with Emyla, seeing her rage and fear, it wasn't going to help prepare me. The sterilization had to happen, and I needed to be ready for it.

I found refuge in my lab jurte and spent the rest of the

sol checking and rechecking my findings on the hybrids. The last piece of the puzzle stared at me. White text set on that black screen of my GenMapper, the GenMapper I'd found buried in my mother's chest years ago, the one I now knew had been Kelica's and not Rohn's. The hybrid's genome stared back at me. It was so achingly familiar that I couldn't not see the truth. I had to fix this. What was losing my fertility in the face of righting my wrong?

***

My mother was strong if nothing else. I was sure that Kelica wouldn't be able to do the procedure given everything she'd told me. It would be undoing her life's work, and yet when I entered the Medizin Jurte, just as the rest of the Stamm was heading to the somn meal, Kelica was there waiting.

Lyn stood to the side and nodded at me. Two junior physicians were preparing a mat. I was relieved that Vena wasn't one of them. I'd managed to avoid her ever since my blackmailing and was hoping to keep it that way for as long as possible. Putting my life in her hands seemed too tempting after what I'd done. One less thing to worry about.

"Get changed into a gown," Kelica said.

She pointed to a bundle of clothing on a stool near a screen. I walked over, grabbed the beige fabric, and switched it out for my robes. It took me a few tries to unlace my boots. My fingers kept dropping the strings. By the time I came around the side of the changing screen, everyone was standing in a line beside the raised mat serving as the operating table. I came up next to it and looked at them. Lyn gave me a weak smile. The others wore masks over the lower halves of their faces. One of the junior physicians waved down at the mat, and I laid on it.

Kelica slipped gloves on her hands, looked me in the eye for several seconds, then pretended I was any other patient. She lifted the front of my gown to expose my genitals. As

Kelica worked, she spoke out each step, either for my benefit or for the junior physicians. Lyn hung back, but even though she was the furthest away, I made the effort to look at her most often. I was doing my duty and sacrificing a part of myself for it. I needed her to see that and believe it, otherwise, this was all for nothing.

"Removing hair in the surgical area," Kelica said.

This part I could have been asked to do myself and was the most embarrassing for me. Knowing that my mother was the one doing it, only made my face burn worse. I gritted my teeth and stared up at the ceiling of the jurte. By the time she was done, my whole body ached from unconsciously tensing my muscles.

"Applying a local numbing agent to the scrotum," Kelica said.

Two pricks from a needle, first on the left side then the right. After that, I didn't feel a thing anywhere near my groin.

"Making two small incisions into the scrotum," Kelica said.

I half-wished she wouldn't talk out the steps anymore. I looked at Lyn, her mouth opened slightly. Her eyes met mine, and she gave me a nod.

"I see the vas deferens," Kelica said. "Cutting a small section out and removing it."

I tried to block out Kelica's words because, in that moment of all moments, the reality of what was happening hit me. I didn't want children, didn't want to couple, but I also believed that nothing was wrong with my genome. I locked my eyes on Lyn and focused on why I was doing this. I needed the sacrifice in order to save the Stamm. A cut here and a snip there were a small price to pay after the part I'd played in unleashing chaos.

"Vas deferens is removed. Cauterizing and stitching the ends."

My eyes shot up to the ceiling and stayed fixed there.

There was a sizzling sound followed by a strange smell, reminiscent of meat but with a tartness to it. I was smelling myself burning. It was a scent I hoped I'd never be exposed to again. Then there was some tugging, and finally the physicians moved back. I angled my eyes down and watched them.

"Now, the other side," Kelica said.

I clenched my jaw. There were the same tuggings, same sounds, same odors, then Kelica and the junior physicians were moving away, helping me change back into my robes, guiding me to another mat.

"You have to rest the next few days," one of the junior physicians said. "Nothing strenuous. Avoid heavy lifting. You can walk and move around, but be mindful of your condition."

He looked away at the last word. Kelica's back was to me as she cleaned and stowed supplies. I waited for her to turn around, but her back was all I got. Maybe she'd been unable to meet my eye because of what she'd done, both in the present and in the past. I may have outed myself to Lyn, forcing the sterilization to take place, but Kelica had been the one to use GenEn on me in the first place.

But I couldn't dwell on Kelica. I'd gone through what I had for someone else. The look Lyn gave me said everything I needed it to. My gamble had paid off, and I was in her good book.

Still, I needed to be sure and test the waters, and for that, I had to be alone with her. I waited for the physicians to file out of the jurte, but as the last was leaving, Cade came in. He was subdued which meant he knew what had just happened. The whole of the Stamm had to by now.

"Courtesy of Aarman," Cade said.

He thrust a basket at Lyn and struggled to make eye contact with me. He glanced at Lyn then me then the basket then the scrolls on the tables. Nothing remained from the operation except that burnt smell, lingering in the vapors from the ONi.

Lyn put the basket down on the mat just beside me. She lifted the cloth covering the contents. Rolls, jars of jams, chunks of butter, delicacies reserved only for a Wilkommen dinner, and that despite the food rationing.

"I appreciate it," I said.

I angled my head at the basket. Cade crossed his arms and nodded. His eyes skittered around the jurte again, while Lyn and I waited for him to say whatever it was he was struggling to.

"Did you want some?" I asked.

He started. His arms fell to his sides, and he stared at me for five full seconds before clearing his throat.

"No, thanks," he said. "I'm not really hungry."

He gritted his teeth and clenched his hands into fists.

"I just want to say that this is shit," he said. "This thing that happened to you."

Cade shook his head and forced a smile that shifted into a grimace.

"You get under my skin sol and somn," he said, "but you didn't deserve this."

I nodded slowly and watched him. His eyes jumped around the room again.

"I appreciate you saying that," I said.

Cade grunted, turned on his heel, and marched out of the jurte. Then it was just Lyn and me and my terrible sacrifice.

Strings

Lyn

I was going to stay with Levi for the somn. After everything that had happened to him, it was the least I could do. I ruffled through the basket Cade had brought and pulled out rolls and buns and jars of jams and savory spreads. Levi grabbed a knife and split a roll open with it. He lathered on butter and jam then took a big bite and chewed away. Almost content.

"You seem in good spirits," I said.

"I got through the procedure," he said. "And now my genome won't wreak havoc. I did my part."

He motioned at the bag, and I took a roll out. I didn't have much of an appetite though. The smell of his charred flesh still lingered in the too-close air of the jurte. I'd never seen a sterilization before. It hadn't been pleasant.

I picked off pieces of my roll with my fingers and dipped them into jam. My mind was all over the place. One second, it settled on Levi. The next, it jumped to the GenEn. But the worst was when it veered towards the Dipols. I didn't want to think about them. They were still silent. I was still aimless without their instruction. This sol marked the fourth since the comms had gone down. Too long. With too much of significance happening all the while. I focused back on Levi. He was something concrete, something that could be an anchor.

"Maybe I ought to get a bracelet like that," Levi said.

He pointed at mine. It sat in my hands. I'd been toying with it without even realizing it. It was a bad sign. The frequency that I relied on it. It meant I was panicking. I needed to get a hold of myself. Be calm. Stoic. Unmoved. An Itinerate. But with those ochre eyes staring at me, how could I even hope to be any of that?

I held the bracelet out to him.

"Take it," I said.

Levi shook his head and waved a hand.

"You need it more than me," I said.

"Are you sure?" he asked.

I thrust it at him. He grasped the bracelet, and it slipped out of my fingers.

"I don't need it anymore," I said. "I don't need to be reminded of why I do what I do."

"Because you believe in your mission or because you don't anymore?"

I didn't know the answer to his question. I didn't want to lie or scold him, do what my Itinerate instincts whispered that I ought to do. Instead, I pivoted.

"My first Stamm was very difficult," I said. "I struggled to adapt."

"But you've adapted now?"

I threw up my hands and laughed.

"I thought I had," I said. "I had a routine, I did my work, I kept my eyes trained ahead, but everything is falling apart. Zeindorf. The hybrids. You."

I dropped off. There was a bubbling in my chest.

"I know how you're feeling," he said. "About your tour. About going home."

"Oh?" I asked.

Levi held the bracelet in his hands and stroked it.

"You're terrified," he said.

I went still.

"Artur was too," he said. "It's why he went Rogue. It's the same reason every Itinerate that passes through is so haunted."

"And what reason is that? Since you know us so well."

He leaned in and spoke softly, despite the fact that no one else was in the Medizin Jurte.

"Because you have no idea what comes next. You have no memories from before your tour."

All the chaos of my internal dialogue, all the panicked chatter, shut off with that statement. It was reduced down to one focal point. I didn't know what to do. Deny it? But what did it matter? That was the whole problem to begin with. It made no difference if the Reisende knew that I didn't know anything about myself. That was probably why they'd done it to us in the first place.

Even if I wanted to divulge secrets about the Dipols, about Neuen, about the whole sorry system, I couldn't. I was as clueless as the Reisende. Just a good little soldier following my orders not because I believed in them but because I didn't have an alternative. I had to finish my tour to find out who I even was.

"You could have been a murderer, and this is your punishment," Levi said. "Or you could have been a fanatic, and this is your holy quest. That bothered Artur, the not knowing who he was, but what terrified him was the thought of his tour ending. To Artur, it would be dying. He was convinced that when he got back to the Dipols, they would restore his memories, but then the version of him that I knew, the Itinerate Artur, would cease to exist. Even if they let him keep the memories from his tour, which Artur was almost positive they wouldn't, he'd become a different person. It would be a kind of death, and he didn't want to die."

I didn't know what to say or how I wanted to move forward. It was an inflection point, and I knew it. The consequences were looming. I couldn't see the best path forward. Levi saw through me. Maybe he'd always been able to. Every word he said about Artur mirrored my own struggles for the past few years. I knew exactly what that horror was. It had been creeping up on me in time with my footfalls. Every step along my tour brought me closer to my end.

I didn't want to become that other Lyn. She'd done this to me. She'd agreed to go on the tour knowing that her memory would be wiped probably on both ends. She hadn't cared what it would mean for me. She hadn't thought about how I might feel about it because, to her, I was the imposter. I hadn't asked to be forced into existence, but now that I was here, I wasn't going to let her take control back so easily.

"Are you worried about dying when you get to Nord?" he asked.

There he went again, seeing through me. It was an invasion, a prying, a snooping that I hadn't condoned. I made myself hard and cold.

"That's none of your business," I said.

"You don't have to pretend with me. You don't have to hide the real you."

"And what do you think the real me is? You said it yourself, Itinerates have no memories. I don't know a thing about myself. The real me is a mystery and will stay a mystery until she kills this Lyn."

I was fuming. Not at him but at the circumstances. I'd never talked about this with anyone, not even Moray. All my angst and rage and terror were coming out in a torrent. Levi stood in the face of the storm, pelted by the elements but patient and open.

"I don't know the real you either," he said, "but I see something lurking like a fire that's quelled before it takes or a depth of feeling that can't bubble through to the surface. You can feel them too, can't you? The strings?"

"Strings?"

Levi laid the bracelet on his knee and put his wrist on top. He tried to knot the fabric.

"That's where the anger comes from and the frustration and exhaustion," he said. "You feel the strings tugging at you, trying to control you."

Was he right? I didn't know.

"The puppet masters in the Dipols," he said. "We play by the rules, people like you and me. We do our duty even if it costs us everything. You gave up who you were to serve them. I gave up the future of my genome to be in line with their vision. Don't people like us deserve to know what we're a part of? Haven't we earned the truth?"

"What truth? What are you talking about?"

He was failing to knot the bracelet, his fingers slipping and dropping the orange threads.

"The hybrids," he said. "They're a threat, and yet the Dipols aren't doing anything to stop them. Lucky for us, I know how to neutralize them."

I had a thousand questions in the face of that answer, but the foremost among them was how, in the span of eleven sols, this Reisender botanist had learned enough about the hybrids to claim he could put an end to them.

"How?" I asked.

"It's too difficult to explain, and you wouldn't like it if I told you. Better for you to be in the dark because, in order to do it, I'm going to need access to tech only the Dipols have."

"GenEn?"

Levi stared at me. That toxic word. The reason we were sitting in the Medizin Jurte in the first place. If it had been any other time, if Zeindorf hadn't happened, if the comms weren't down—but there was no point thinking about the outlandishness of the proposed solution. The question was, how desperate was I?

"What makes you think the Dipols can't do whatever you have planned?" I asked.

Levi dropped the fabric again, and I leaned in and tied the pieces around his wrist for him. He turned his arm and inspected the adornment. My gift to him.

"Somehow, I doubt that Zeindorf was the first Stamm that got hit by this," he said. "If the Dipols could have stopped it, they would have. The only solution is to go to Nord."

***

After Levi's sterilization the prior sol, I almost didn't expect Kelica to show up for the GenMapping results announcement, but she was a professional. The physicians had the scrolls laid out in a line, evenly spaced. The ink well was there with a pen just next to it. I nodded at them as I entered and made my way over to the table. Their chanting and humming started.

I had to wait for the parents to arrive before making the announcements, but in the meantime, I got to work transcribing the results from the GenMapper to the scrolls. It was a tedious and delicate process. The paper was brittle and prone to cracking. The ink wasn't viscous enough and ran too freely along any bends in the sheets. I had to write slowly. Wait for each line to dry before moving on to the next. It took me a few hours to copy over the necessary data. I got lost in the process, blind to what it was I was etching into permanency.

During the whole of it, Kelica was still, so much so that I

forgot she was even there. Then the first of the eight couples arrived, and she moved. She migrated over to them and murmured empty nothings. Near midsol, my hand aching, my legs stiff from standing too long, I leaned back and sighed. Then, the soft murmur of the Reisende's chantings and hums ramped up into near shouts. I turned around and stood in front of the table. The jurte was crowded. Time to take part in the little show they all expected.

I turned back towards the table and gave myself a moment to take in the broad strokes of what I'd done. These children would be defined by the symbols I'd just set to parchment. Who they could couple with. What kind of future they could expect.

I was sick to death of GenMaps. Stamm after Stamm of them. This same ritual set on repeat with the looks on the parents' faces just different degrees of despair. And yet, too little GLEtches was worse in some ways. Look at what it had meant for Levi. The falsification of his GenMap that had necessitated his mutilation.

And all of this was a distraction, as Levi had reminded me last somn. The hybrids were what we ought to be thinking about, but thinking wasn't the same as doing. And what could I do about them? It was easier to follow the path of least resistance. To do what the Dipols had conditioned me to. I was an Itinerate. I ran GenMaps. I assessed couplings.

I grabbed the first child's scroll then faced the hoard within the jurte. Dozens of others would be amassed outside, waiting for a message to cascade out. I cleared my throat, defocused my eyes, and looked away from the formless faces. The shouts cut off in an instant. The jurte was still. I honed in on the text in my hands and read off the contents.

Child's name, parents' names, birth date, a series of nonsensical alphanumerics meant to act as a shorthand for the more comprehensive GenMap, then the coup de grâce—the GLEtch count. I'm not sure if there was a way to actually quantify just how flawed the genome was, but if so, the Reisende were spared that at least. The GenMap kept it vague by using broad categories—minimal, minor, moderate, major, and maximal GLEtches—which, I assumed, followed some kind of Gaussian distribution.

I went through the first scroll.

"Tann Brome, sired by Lilya and Thoms Brome, birthed sol four-two-four of year ten of era three. Dominant abnormalities P1C1R5S3N7, P2C1R3S9N2, P2C1R8S4N6, P5C2R9S1N3, P11C1R4S4N8, P15C2R9S7N1, P21C1R6S1N5, P23C2R7S3N9. Moderate GLEtches."

I rolled the parchment up, bound it with a twist of hemp, and moved on to the next. Then, the next and next and next, until I'd announced the results of all eight children. Overall, a typical result for the Stamm, most of the newly born with moderate or major GLEtches. It was news everyone had expected and yet no one wanted to hear. The looks on the faces in the crowd ranged from bitter to resigned. Vromdorf was every Stamm. I was beyond exhausted with the slog, and despite that, I felt a compulsion to continue the song and dance. Strings perhaps? Tugging me along even while my heart and mind were elsewhere.

"We begin on the couplings next sol," I said.

The Reisende filed out. I stood by the scrolls, nodding or murmuring nothings to those who passed by. Aarman came up beside me.

"Another year of GenMappings complete," he said. "I wonder if you could stop by my jurte for a private discussion."

"Right now?"

"Yes."

"Lead the way," I said.

We were silent while waiting for the Medizin Jurte to clear

out. Walking to his own, we didn't exchange any words either. Once inside, we sat down on pillows.

"Have you decided how you'll inform the Stamm of Levi's sterilization?" I asked.

"Inform them? Most have already heard from each other. Do you expect me to make an announcement?"

"I expect you to use this as a teaching moment. GenEn happened in your Stamm, oberhaupt."

Aarman tapped his forefinger on his knee in time with his words.

"But not on my watch," he said. "My predecessor's. Besides, the Stamm has enough to worry about without vilifying one of our best and brightest."

There was a bite to his words and a snarl hovering on his lip.

"You're annoyed with me," I said. "Why?"

Aarman leaned forward. He interlaced his hands and rested them on his crossed legs.

"If we're being candid," he said, "do you really need to ask me that?"

"Don't answer my question with a question," I said. "Would you rather have had Levi's GenEn be passed on?"

Aarman rose from his pile of pillows, one slipping with its newfound freedom.

"What I'd rather have is for things to go back to normal," he said. "I'd rather have the food security we enjoyed when trade with Zeindorf was possible. I'd rather know what happened to them and what the Dipols plan to do about it."

I looked away and immediately regretted it. He pounced.

"Have they said anything?" he asked. "They need to tell us what's going on. I have to do what's best for my Stamm, and I can't without all the information."

"The Dipols have all the information," I said. "They'll decide what's best."

Aarman frowned and stepped closer to me. I rose from my pillow. He was taller but not by much. Still, he managed to exude something that made the proximity akin to towering.

"And when will that be, Lynev?" he asked. "Before or after my Stamm has run out of food? We're low on supplies. It's already been eleven sols since the last drop. We need another one."

Aarman didn't know that the comms were down. This was the fifth sol since I'd last heard from the Dipols. Levi's words from the previous somn rang in my ears.

"How much longer can you last?" I asked.

"I just told you we're running low," he said.

I shook my head, lowered my chin, and glared.

"Answer my question, oberhaupt. If another drop doesn't come, how long?"

He finally understood.

"Did they say why?" he asked.

"They haven't said anything, and if it stays that way, I'm asking you how long can the Stamm last?"

Aarman stepped back then wandered around his jurte, murmuring to himself. I let him go on for a space before calling him back to reality.

"How long, Aarman?"

My voice startled him, like he'd forgotten I was there. The fragility of the Reisende hit me. Their lives were normally so predictable, maintained, controlled, but once the strings went slack, they fell limp to the stage. Well, some of them did. Kelica, Aarman, Cade, Vena. But not Levi because he always felt the strings and despised them. Until he'd put a name to the feeling though, I'd been just as clueless as the Reisende. Did that mean I'd crumble too without that invisible support? I hadn't yet, but then again, I was immobilized. Wasn't that basically the same thing?

"If we stretched the rations out, maybe a week?" Aarman said. "Has this happened before? Losing contact with them?"

"Not for this long. I'm going to have to make a decision soon."

***

I waited and waited and still the comms stayed silent. I pushed on and did the coupling assessments. Pretended everything was in order. Tried to smother the rising panic bubbling from deep within. Two sols after my conversation with Aarman, Moray came back to the Stamm.

I was lying on my mat staring at the ceiling when the entry flap of my jurte swooshed. Some of the air rushed out, and a chill came in to take its place. I didn't bother to move, and only knew it was Moray when his head popped into view, eclipsing the jurte's ceiling. He was wearing his Reisender disguise again, but it looked more frayed and worn.

"Did another labspawn get you?" he asked.

"Sometimes I wish the one had got me better," I said.

I patted the mat, and he moved down and scooted in beside me. We propped up our heads with our elbows and hands, him on his right side, me on my left.

"You're sounding down and out," he said.

"The comms are down and out, pretty much since the sol you left. And a lot has happened here since then. I need to get in touch with the Dipols."

With Moray's return, a weight lifted. I wasn't alone in the struggle anymore. The decision wasn't only mine to make, and yet, at the same time, I didn't like my reaction. I didn't want to rely on him, or anyone for that matter.

"Since I left?" he asked. "That's what, seven sols?"

"Seven long and hard sols. I had to order my first sterilization. GenEn, decades past, but still. I need their guidance on that, but more importantly, I need confirmation they got my report on Zeindorf. Also, the Stamm is running low on provisions."

Moray hummed a bit then went silent. I let him mull my words. I'd been agonizing over the dead ends for sols now. The least I could do was give him a few minutes to think. Eventually, he focused back on me. He smiled and stroked my arm.

"The way I see it," he said, "you've only got one option—travel to Nord."

I sucked in a breath and held it.

"I know," he said. "That's a big no-no, right? We'd be 'abandoning our tour,' except they abandoned us first. The comms can't be down for so long without something having gone very wrong."

"What did you find?" I asked. "Where you went to check on something?"

"More questions than answers," he said. "Even before you said anything, I was already considering going to Nord myself."

"You can't reach them by comms either then?"

He shook his head.

"I repaired my comms, but when it didn't work, I figured it was a problem on my end. If you're having issues too, it means it's not just me."

Moray sat up, and I instinctively followed. We sat cross-legged, facing each other head on.

"What do we do?" I asked.

"You already know the answer to that."

I pulled back and looked at him. He was different somehow, unrelated to the Reisender robes. There was a hardness in him that I hadn't noticed before.

"What did your Reisende find out about Zeindorf?" he asked.

I'd forgotten that he didn't know. The last time we'd talked, I hadn't yet gone over Vena and Levi's findings.

"Nothing good," I said. "Something's wrong. GenEn most likely. Luftors becoming something hostile, using human flesh as a nutrient substrate. They're hybrids now— half plant, half fungi."

"GenEn? By who?"

"Probably a Reisender in Vromdorf that went Rogue years ago. The same one that did the GenEn on the one we had to sterilize."

"They were a busy one, weren't they? You told the Dipols?"

"This was all after the comms went down," I said. "There's no knowing if they received anything I sent."

Moray nodded slowly, over and over again, more to himself than me.

"Maybe they didn't get it, but don't you think it's odd that they haven't noticed the comms issues or, better yet, haven't fixed them? I'm not convinced the comms really are down. I think the Dipols got your messages, and either they don't know how to stop these hybrids or they don't want to. Either way, we need answers. We deserve answers. We've done our time. This isn't us going Rogue. This is us truly fulfilling our duties. We're here to help the Reisende, and they're dying off like flies."

"You both said the same thing," I said.

"What do you mean both?"

Rogue

Levi

From the moment I met him, I didn't like Moray. He kept eyeing me when he didn't need to, looking me over, evaluating me. More than that though, he was too sure of himself. And of course, I could tell there was something between him and Lyn.

"Another Itinerate?" I asked.

Lyn nodded then moved to the urn in her jurte to refresh the air and lighting. I didn't like how Moray left this up to her.

"Don't let the Reisender robes fool you," Moray said. "It's just a disguise."

He and I faced one another and were nearly at eye level. I couldn't tell who was taller, but I suspected he was by about a centimeter. I didn't like how that annoyed me.

"I didn't think Itinerates were ever on the same Lat," I said.

"It's complicated," Lyn said.

She spoke over her shoulder as she stoked the embers and ONi.

"Lyn saved me," Moray said. "She patched me up after a nasty run-in with a labspawn. We decided to keep in touch."

"Were you lost?" I asked.

I wasn't willing to let the prying drop. Lyn tossed three pillows around the urn and beckoned us over. Moray waved his hand to the side.

"After you, Levi Zetmer," he said.

He had a disarming grin. His teeth were perfect in shape and color, and his lips weren't overly broad like mine. I moved to the pillow on Lyn's left. Moray followed and took up the one on her right. We sat as a triad.

"Moray isn't a typical Itinerate," Lyn said. "He doesn't do a tour in the same way as the rest of us."

"I'm a jack-of-all-trades," he said.

"I don't know what that means," I said.

"It's not important," Lyn said. "What is important is how we deal with the hybrids."

I nodded and waited.

"I'm not sure why you brought Levi here, Lyn," Moray said.

"He knows more about the hybrids than I do, and apparently, he might know how to stop them."

Moray frowned and hummed for three seconds too long. I had to force myself not to tap my fingers on my knees.

"He said the same thing as you," she added.

"What's that?" Moray asked.

"The Dipols can't or won't help us," she said.

Moray drummed his fingers on his lips.

"He needs to go to Nord," Lyn said. "He needs their tech."

Moray laughed then darkened when he realized she was serious.

"You want us to bring a Reisender with us to Nord?" he asked. "Look, it's bad enough we're ending our tours prematurely. They won't like that, but maybe, just maybe, they'll forgive us for it, given the circumstances. But bringing a Reisender along? To the Dipols? That's beyond forbidden. They won't stand for it."

"I can stop this whole thing," I said.

"Right," Moray said, dragging out the word. "Some random Reisender miraculously knows how to stop a plague when even the Dipols can't."

"Or won't," Lyn said.

"Which would only be worse," Moray said. "They wouldn't want any of us there in that case, which I'm willing to risk with the two of us. Him? Not so much."

"If they're choosing not to step in to help, then it won't matter who goes," Lyn said. "We'll all be imprisoned or killed. But if they really aren't able to figure out how to stop the hybrids, then maybe Levi can help."

"How would he help? He's a Reisender."

"I'm sitting right here," I said through gritted teeth. "If you want details, then ask, but I doubt you'd understand what I have to say."

"He's the son of the man who likely created the hybrids," Lyn said.

Moray's head whipped from me to her.

"Come again?"

"We think the hybrids were created a few decades ago by a Reisender botanist who later went Rogue," she said. "The hybrids were meant to survive the day-night cycles of Neuen, but at some point, they must have mutated and became deadly to us. It's like they use human bodies as nutrient substrates when there isn't another viable source."

"And Levi is the son of this botanist?"

"Rohn Zetmer," I said.

Moray's face did something between a spasm and a smile.

"How does you being this Rohn's son factor in?" he asked.

"I've studied his work for years," I said. "I know what he did better than anyone else. I'm probably the only one that can undo it."

Moray looked at me to the point of awkwardness, but I didn't back down.

"You're talking about GenEn, I take it?" Moray asked.

I shrugged.

"Which begs the question," he said, "how does Levi Zetmer know how to perform GenEn?"

I sighed and shifted on my pillow. This was always going to come out, sooner or later.

"I don't know for sure," I said, "but I've been taught a bit about it. Between that and reading my father's notes, I think I can exploit a weakness in the genome. A kill switch."

They both looked at me blankly, and the reality of just how little they knew sunk in. I'd run into it with Artur too, but then again, Artur had made a conscious effort to learn about GenEn during his tour. These two were clearly not as rebellious as he'd been.

"There's always a kill switch with GenEn," I said.

"But the hybrids have mutated," Lyn said.

"It'll still be there in one form or another. It's tacked onto junk code, usually the telomeres."

Again, blank stares. I had to fight my disgust at the forced ignorance. Here the Dipols were lording over us Reisende, and they didn't even have the decency to properly educate their soldiers on the weapons they were meant to be nullifying. If they stole their memories, why not give them that forbidden knowledge for the duration of their tour? I knew the answer already. They couldn't risk us squeezing the information from our jailors.

"How do you know all this?" Moray asked.

"An Itinerate taught me some of it," I said. "And before you ask, yes, he went Rogue."

When I said 'Rogue,' a look passed between Lyn and Moray. They tried to play it off, but that only piqued my interest.

"What?" I asked.

"When did this Itinerate go Rogue?" Moray asked.

Lyn's eyes were telling him something, but I couldn't decipher their code born of familiarity.

"Last year," I said. "Why?"

"We're getting off track," Lyn said. "The bottom line is we have to bring Levi with us to Nord. If we do, and he isn't needed, then fine. But if we don't bring him, and the Dipols don't know what to do, that could be a mistake that wipes out what's left of the Reisende."

"They won't let us do this without there being consequences," Moray said.

He leaned over and grasped Lyn's hands. I clenched my jaw.

"It's on me," she said. "My call. My burden."

Moray went to say something but stopped himself. He just gripped her hands tighter and shook his head. I didn't like how Moray let her sacrifice herself so readily.

***

"I think Aarman should know," I said.

I repositioned my bag on my shoulder. Lyn, Moray, and I were packed and ready to leave the Stamm. We'd waited until the next sol to reconvene in her jurte.

"Aarman's reasonable," I added. "He'll probably even agree with us."

"We can't risk it," Lyn said. "If he's against you going, what then?"

Moray was holding some piece of tech over Lyn's wrist, and they both stared down at the display.

"Is it working?" she asked.

"Give it a second," Moray said.

"You could just say you're ordering me to go," I said to Lyn.

Moray made a clicking sound with his tongue that grated on my ears, and I tried not to glare at him. I hadn't warmed up to him with more exposure. It was going to be a long two weeks traveling to Nord.

"Your oberhaupt would know the risks we're taking bringing you," Moray said, "and I doubt he'd go along with it. Just in case this isn't clear to you yet, Levi, there's a high probability that the Dipols will have you executed."

"Levi knows what he's getting into," Lyn said.

The prior somn, Moray had left Lyn's jurte to prep their gliders. While he was out, she had explained the plan, including what I was agreeing to. She hadn't needed to though; I knew what going to the Dipols meant.

"I'm just making sure he's committed," Moray said. "There's no turning back once we set out."

"I'm committed," I said. "Me sitting in Vromdorf isn't helping anyone. I have to do what I can to protect it."

"You're a brave one," Moray said.

His tech gave off a few beeps, and some of the tension in the Itinerates' faces faded.

"Does that mean it worked?" Lyn asked him.

"Your tracker's off," Moray said. "The Dipols won't see us coming."

"Are you sure this is a good idea?" she asked. "Won't they think it means we went Rogue?"

"Trust me, this is how we get close enough to even stand a chance of getting into Nord. Besides, with all the comms system weirdness, they'll think it's just another malfunction."

A horn sounded outside indicating that the Reisen was starting. We were going to take advantage of the general disorder and confusion it bred since it gave us our best chance of leaving the Stamm undetected. We were lucky the

Reisen was occurring so conveniently for us. If I'd been more superstitious, I would have seen it as a sign.

"Perfect timing," Moray said.

"Are we ready?" Lyn asked.

Moray and I nodded and gave different flavors of yes. The three of us donned our rebreathers attached to almost overflowing ONi satchels. I'd grabbed an ample supply of them from the fields earlier in the sol. I'd calculated and recalculated how much we would need for our journey even factoring in potential slowdowns. I just hoped it would be enough. If I was wrong, we might never reach Nord or else be stuck slowly suffocating while we banged on their pearly gates.

"Lead the way, Moray," Lyn said.

He knew where the gliders were waiting for us.

"Here goes," he said.

He ducked through the flaps, which slapped shut with a thick sound, and Lyn counted out the seconds. We were staggering our escape to avoid unwanted attention.

"Okay, good luck," she said then slipped out.

The reality of the situation hit me with a thud to the gut. I kept questioning myself, wondering if this was the best path, doubting my ability to pull it all off. Then, I reminded myself there was no other option. This was the only way to stop the hybrids, and if we didn't kill them first, they would kill us off. That thought alone spurred me on.

Once a minute had passed, I went out into the Stamm. I couldn't help but think how this might be the last time I'd walk through these corridors, past these jurten, among these Reisende. They were my people, even if their stubbornness and forced ignorance kept them from soaring. I wanted to stay to see what would unfold, see if they would manage to wake from their long slumber, but I didn't have that luxury. I was doing what I was doing for them and would just have to satisfy myself with conjured visions of what-could-be's.

I regretted not giving proper goodbyes. I'd said what must have felt like overly-emotional good-somns and good-sols to Cade. I half-wished I'd made an effort to see Vena and Emyla, but I'd already burnt bridges with them. There was no point dragging it out.

But there was one person I had to see before I left, and Lyn and Moray would just have to bear with me. Maybe they were right about Aarman, but someone needed to know we were trying to save the Stamm. The Reisende deserved to know the alternative if we failed.

I weaved through the labyrinthine gaps between jurten in various stages of dismantling. Reisende looked after me as I flew by, avoiding collisions by centimeters. I caught glimpses of faces I'd known my whole life, and memories came flooding in. I had to push them aside and focus. I couldn't afford to get sentimental. I was going to save them and all Reisende, first from the hybrid threat then from the chokehold of the Dipols. This was too big a thing to fail, years in the making, not quite what I'd envisioned but so it was.

When I got to our jurte, Kelica was struggling to dislodge a post. I knelt down by her side, my movement drawing her attention.

"Let me help," I said.

She kept her hands on the post. It had been five sols since my sterilization, and she still wasn't talking to me. She could barely stand to look at me. I didn't know if it was disappointment in the decision I'd made or with herself for causing it all to begin with, but either way, she was doing what she did—bottling up her emotions, forcing them inward, making herself ill from the effort. She looked like she'd aged a few years. I couldn't leave her like this, in this state or with the uncertainty of my disappearance. She, at least, would know where I'd gone. And why.

I grabbed ahold of the post a bit above her own grip.

She shook her head then we tugged on my count of three. It came free, and we sighed in relief.

"We need to grease that slot," I said.

She rose from her crouch and moved to the next post. I moved between her and it.

"I don't have time to go into the details," I said, "but I wanted to tell you that I'm leaving for Nord. The Dipols don't know what they're doing. What happened to Zeindorf will happen to Vromdorf if I don't do something. I have to go to them. I'm leaving with Lynev."

Kelica's eyes widened then glazed over. She didn't want to hear it, me telling her about what was as good as my suicide.

"You'll do no such thing," she said. "You'll let the Itinerate go. You'll stay here with your people, where you belong. GenEn or not."

She pushed me aside to get to the post. I stood next to her, watching her struggle to pry it free from the ground.

"I can't explain everything," I said. "I don't have time, and you don't know what's happening, but believe me when I tell you that it's bad. I have to go. Lyn can't solve this without me. I'm going to fix it, but if I don't, if I don't make it back, stay as close to the Break's frost line as you can. It's your best chance to avoid the same fate as Zeindorf."

Kelica stopped and looked at me, long and full. I tried to spell out my crimes to her using the anguish in my eyes alone. I don't know if she understood, if she saw what I wanted to show her, but there was a kind of acknowledgment because she gasped and slumped. We weren't all that dissimilar. She at least recognized that. There wasn't time for more. I nodded then sprinted away at full speed.

When I got to the edge of the Stamm, I slowed to a walk and scanned my surroundings for any protectors. Cade was a few jurten over, helping an older couple load their belongings onto the tracks. I waited to see if he'd glance my way, but he kept his focus on them. I couldn't linger. I headed out into the Break towards the distant figures I knew were the Itinerates. No one stopped me.

When I finally caught up to Moray and Lyn, they looked at me for answers about my delay.

"I got waylaid," I said.

"No protectors following you though," Moray said, "which means we must be in the clear."

He'd removed the Reisender robes that had been covering his Itinerate suit, and his true status sunk in for me. He was just as perfect as Lyn. They were made for each other, and I was the interloper. I pushed the thoughts aside and glanced back at Vromdorf. I tried to make out which speck was which Reisender, but they were reduced to an anonymous blend of indistinct shapes.

Moray and Lyn's rummaging brought me back. They were strapping down components on their gliders and double-checking the hold. I moved closer, handed off my pack, and waited for them to be ready.

"You'll ride with me," Lyn said. "You and Moray would be too heavy together. My glider can just handle our combined weight, as long as we stow all the equipment on Moray's."

"Here I was so looking forward to having Levi as my co-pilot," Moray said.

I gave him a too-hard pat on the shoulder before moving to Lyn's glider. She hopped on and extended her arm to help me up. The gliders were designed to only hold one person, forcing me to sit close.

"Put your arms around my torso," she said. "Otherwise, you'll fall off."

I wrapped my arms around her stomach.

"Is this too tight?" I asked.

"That's fine," she said. "Just to warn you, the glider can be rough. We have to ride the gales rather than fight them, which doesn't make for a smooth ride. Hold on, and you'll get used to it after a while. We can stop and take breaks if you need it."

"Got it," I said.

"All set?" Lyn asked.

Moray gave her a thumbs up, and I said a "yes" to her ear. Then, Lyn engaged the glider's drive. There was a spinning sound. It started with a low pitch that increased in frequency until it became a continuous buzz. Once the rate had settled, Lyn kicked up a metal stand that went flush with the glider's cylindrical body. The whole object hovered a half meter from the ground. Little clouds of dust moved skyward in what looked like steady columns before dissipating in a fan-like shape. Once both gliders hovered, the Itinerates turned something on the handlebars, and we shot up.

My breath caught. My stomach jumped. I squeezed Lyn too tightly, a puff of air coming from her mouth.

"Sorry," I said.

I doubted she could hear it over the buzz and through the rebreather. As we moved further upward and headed deeper into the nightside of the Break, the winds lashed us. Just when it felt like it was too chaotic to surf, Lyn relaxed her forward hold on the handlebars, unfurled the glider's wings, and caught a gust. We sailed. With the buzzing quieted and the wind gentler, the exhilaration washed over me. I laughed and shouted.

"Quiet," Lyn said. "Labspawn."

In the thrill, I'd forgotten about that ever-present danger.

"Keep a lookout for them," she said. "Tell me if you see anything odd. They strike hard and fast."

"Understood," I said.

I turned my face to the side and watched Moray. He was to our left and slightly forward, scanning the horizon, no doubt for the labspawn lurking. We stayed on alert for hours and only caught glimpses of them a few times. Eventually, the adrenaline wore off, and exhaustion kicked in. I held on for as long as I could, but when I realized I'd be the weak link anyway, I tapped Lyn's waist with the hand gripping it.

"Can we take a break?" I asked.

She nodded then inched forward. Once we were abreast with Moray, Lyn gave him a kind of toss of her head and moved towards the ground. The gales were more manageable on the way down, and within minutes, we were there. The muscles in my arms and back ached. I only realized how tense I'd been when I let go of Lyn and slid off her glider.

"We'll rest for several hours," she said.

Moray was already unloading and unrolling a jurte. I moved to help him, but he shooed me away.

"Focus on loosening up," he said. "You're all shakes."

I held out my hands and stared at their vibrations.

"Ten hours?" Lyn said to him.

Moray nodded. She removed the other jurte on his glider and started to assemble it. I sat on the dirt cross-legged and stared at the Break. It was the deepest I'd ever been in it, the perpetual twilight closer to true night here. The sky a navy blue, the stars more distinct, the ground encrusted with ice. The cold leeched in through my robes and invaded. By the time the jurten were up and connected, I was shivering.

"You shouldn't sit on the ground," Lyn said.

She extended a hand to help me up, and I grabbed it and pulled myself to my feet. She angled her head towards the jurte Moray was ducking into. I followed. The interior was crammed, clearly only meant for two, but we didn't have much of a choice. We would have to make it work over the coming weeks. Nearly two of them in this bitter cold and deep dark, constantly on edge. I didn't know how they could stand it, but then again, it was the only life an Itinerate knew.

"Get some sleep," Lyn said. "I'll take the first watch and Moray the second."

She dropped off some blankets before slipping back into the Break. I looked around for space to stretch out. Moray was already curling up. I laid flat then shifted on my side with my back to him. I was out within seconds.

When Lyn and Moray switched out, their movements woke me. I cracked my eyes open, stayed still, and watched as they came together then apart. The embrace was quick, but it told me everything I'd been anxious to know. I hadn't imagined the bond between them. I waited for Moray to leave and for Lyn to settle on the mat that he'd occupied. Only then did I shift and draw her attention to me. I sat up and looked around. Her eyes were on me, and I smiled back at her and pretended to rub the sleep away.

"What time is it?" I asked.

"Too soon to set out. I only just switched watch with Moray. Get some sleep."

She laid back on her mat, but I stayed upright. Her eyes drifted back to mine, sucked in by them. Moray or not, we had a connection of our own, and even if it was only tenuous and bred partly of sympathy for my sacrifice, I was emboldened by it. I scooted closer to her until we were hip to hip.

"I'm beyond exhaustion," I said, "but I can't sleep or stop thinking about Nord."

"Try not to think," Lyn said.

That was asking too much of me. My mind was a constant murmur, a buzz, an endless chain of cause and effect, action and reaction. She was asking me to fight my very nature.

"It's just, we don't know anything about the Dipols," I said. "Either of us, or any of us." I tossed my head towards the jurte flap to indicate Moray. "Everything could be a lie, and we wouldn't even know it, would we?"

Lyn was watching me closely, hoisted up on her elbows. I

waited for her to reply because I could see her desperate to let something out, but she only stared at me like she needed me to verbalize what she felt. Maybe it was a part of that block they all had, that buffer choking off the emotions trying in vain to surface.

"Sometimes, I get this overwhelming feeling it's all a lie," I said. "Like a fog covers everything, but for a fraction of a second, it lifts, and I see the truth. But then it's gone before I can soak it in and understand what it all means."

"If there's something to know, we'll know soon enough," Lyn said. "For now, try not to think about it. Focus on now. Focus on the present."

I should have taken her advice to heart, should have leaned down and touched my lips to hers. I thought I still had time, thought maybe she'd look at me that way for a little while longer. But we always think we have more time than we do, don't we?

***

This journey was different than the trip to Zeindorf. That had been a mystery to solve. There was a heaviness to this one because of where we were going and why, but also because of the distance between me and them, a distance that only became more pronounced as time passed. I was an outsider. A Reisender deep in the Break, transiting Lats.

I sat behind Lyn and clasped my arms around her torso for hours at a time, but once we landed, she gravitated to Moray. There was little overt physicality between them, but there didn't need to be for me to feel the connection. Whatever might have passed between me and her was voided so long as he was around. It made the sols stretch and the somns teem with wild fantasies. I wanted to get to Nord even knowing that it might mean imprisonment or worse.

The trip featured the occasional labspawn sighting, but

Moray and Lyn always managed to keep their distance. It helped that the vast majority of the creatures were land-bound, although Moray told a story one somn about a labspawn that had shot up some kind of acidic projectiles when he got too close. We only glimpsed flyers a couple of times during the first four sols. Of course, the longer we went without an attack, the less vigilant we were.

They came on the fifth sol. I only noticed the one when I was glancing down at the ground to give my eyes a break from the wind. It had a massive wingspan. Even still, I almost didn't see it owing to how the colors that faced us matched that of the dirt below. It was a kind of countershading. The prey for them was above, in the form of Itinerates, and below, in the form of Reisende. I watched it for a few seconds to see if it had spotted us. The lidless eye set on the top of its flat head stared up at me. It was black with a white speck in the middle. A tremor ran through me, and I squeezed Lyn's shoulder.

"Labspawn below."

She looked around but couldn't seem to find it. I reached my arm forward and pointed it out. It was hiding in her blind spot. I glanced over at Moray and saw another in his. They were hunting in a pair.

Lyn migrated towards Moray. She was trying not to key the labspawn into the fact that we'd spotted them. When Moray noticed her, Lyn signaled to him with her free hand. I couldn't tell what she said to him, but there was a finger pointing up then down.

"There's another below him," I said. "They're in your blind spots."

She stiffened and signaled to Moray again with two fingers. His eyes widened, and he nodded.

"Hold on tight and keep your head low," she said.

I ducked down and interlocked my fingers around her

stomach. She reached her free hand back and pulled at a rod attached to her glider. Moray did the same, their movements slow and smooth. Then, we dove.

The plunge was almost vertical, and I buried my face in Lyn's braid. The gliders screamed. The sound was matched by a reverberating wailing that got louder and louder until it was all around us. I couldn't stand it. It was too much. My ears were going to rupture.

I let go. I was in freefall.

I tore my eyes open, terrified by the mistake I'd made. Lyn was gone. I was falling through the sky, crashing towards the ground. I screamed. Nothing made sense. There was a brown blur then a dark blue streak then a silver sliver. My stomach told me I was tumbling, but I didn't know how to stop it. Without knowing where the thought came from, I threw my arms and legs wide to catch as much of the wind as I could. Somehow, it helped me stabilize. The brown stayed below and the dark blue above, but the ground was coming closer fast. I didn't know what else I could do.

I looked around frantically, trying to find Lyn and Moray. Then, I saw them—Moray off to my left, and Lyn straight ahead. They wielded their metal rods, electricity arcing from each. The labspawn were all around them, their wingspan nearly twice the size of the gliders. One of the labspawn's tails lashed Lyn's glider, and she started to circle before reversing the spin. It was the chance she needed. The creature thought she wasn't a threat for the moment, but she was already back in control. She shot up, and her rod discharged. The bolt hit the labspawn's head. Lyn didn't wait. She charged the rod again and struck a second time.

She flew over to me as the creature fell. I didn't know if she'd make it. The ground was impossibly close now, and she seemed so distant. She was good though, the glider like an extension of her. She moved flush with me, dove a few meters, then inched upward until I was able to clamber back behind her. I held her tightly and kept my eyes shut.

"We're here, Levi," she said.

The wind was quiet and still, the gliders mute. I peeked out, and she looked back at me from her seat. The dirt stretched out around us. Moray stood nearby.

"We should make sure they're finished off," he said.

He spun his rod and marched off, little clouds of dust erupting from each of his footfalls.

"He's right," Lyn said. "Wait here."

I let go of her waist and slumped back. Lyn trotted after Moray. I was embarrassed but grateful for the chance to sulk unobserved. How had I done something so stupid? Why had I let go of her to shield my ears? The experience drilled home just how wrong it was for me to be in the Break. I didn't belong. I was out of my element.

I glanced in the direction Lyn had moved. She stood about thirty meters away beside Moray, their suits catching the faint light and making them glow. The ruins of the labspawn were crumpled on the ground. The Itinerates' rods zapped, and a long reverberating wail sounded. It was the exact same as the one that had almost gotten me killed. So, it had come from them then. My shame faded as curiosity took hold. I slid off the glider and jogged over to Lyn and Moray.

"What was that sound?" I asked.

"Some kind of auditory attack," Moray said.

"How did you two stand it?"

"Conditioning, most likely," Lyn said.

Moray inspected the labspawn, and Lyn looked at me.

"I'm sorry about that," I said. "I shouldn't have—"

"It's okay," Lyn said. "Just don't be so eager to let go of me next time."

I was shaken but determined to continue. Things went back to the way they had been before for a little while, but then three sols later, there was a shift in Moray. He became doubly focused and vigilant with a nervousness or restlessness to him.

Even Lyn seemed to pick up on it. She watched him when she didn't need to. Sometimes, she looked at me to see if I saw it, and I told her I did with my eyes. We waited for whatever was going to happen to happen. On the next sol, it did.

"I know of a bunker we can stop at this somn," Moray said.

We were packing up the jurte to set out for the sol. Lyn froze.

"A bunker? What's that?" I asked.

"A permanent structure," he said. "This close to Nord, you can actually have those."

I'd noticed the gradual lessening of the deep dark of the Break as we'd inched poleward. Now, we were mostly bathed in a perpetual dawn or dusk. Because the extremes of day and night didn't exist here, the ground could be dug into, foundations laid, permanent buildings erected.

"It's abandoned?" Lyn asked.

Moray nodded as he secured items on his glider. He spoke casually but avoided eye contact.

"What was it used for?" she asked.

Lyn mimicked Moray by focusing on what her hands were doing rather than staring at him.

"There's some old tech in it," he said, "but I can't tell what it was. Maybe something to do with servicing the drones that do drops?"

"How did you find it?" Lyn asked.

She was retying a knot she'd already gone over twice now.

"Why were you this far north?" I asked. "There aren't Stämme here."

Moray glanced at me and smirked.

"But sometimes Rogue Reisende or Itinerates wander this way."

"So that's what you do," I said. "That's how you're different from Lyn, and why you were on our Lat."

I switched my focus from him to her.

"And you knew too, Lyn," I said.

She stopped playing with the knot, dusted her gloves against her thighs, and rose from the crouch she'd been in.

"Yes, I knew," she said, "but it wasn't necessary for you to know. I didn't want us to get distracted."

"Distracted?" Moray asked.

He followed Lyn's eyes over to me. I clenched my hands into fists and set my jaw. The intensity of my reaction surprised even me, and by the way the Itinerates looked at me, the tumult I felt on the inside wasn't diluted much by the time it got to the surface.

"So you hunt them down?" I asked.

I already knew the answer to the question, but I wanted to see understanding dawn on him. He opened his mouth, made a small "o," and gave up putting any sound to it.

"I wouldn't call it that," Moray said.

"About a year ago," I said, "an Itinerate left Vromdorf and didn't continue his tour. Name of Artur. Remember him?"

Moray's face stayed still. He didn't give anything away.

"Artur," I said, moving closer to Moray. "He was about as tall as you. His hair was straighter though and a lighter brown. His eyes were too big for his face and sunken in a little too much. He had a huge smile and a kind of halting laugh, although I guess you wouldn't have seen him do either of those last two, would you? Less joy. More terror and fear."

I stood in front of Moray. Lyn crept closer, angling to intervene if the heat got any more scalding.

"I can't say," Moray said. "I've got no way of knowing time with how my routes go."

"Did you kill him?" I asked.

Again, that stony look that I couldn't see through.

"Don't answer that," Lyn said to him then turned to me. "What does it matter if Moray or labspawn or the elements got Artur, Levi? We need to stay focused. Whatever happened is done."

She faced Moray.

"Let's go to your bunker."

Moray nodded, gave me one quick glance, then moved to the other side of his glider to finish securing it. I was so fixated on him that I jumped when Lyn sighed beside me.

"You're better off not knowing," she said. "It wouldn't change anything. Moray is the same as me. He doesn't have any control over his life. He woke up in the Break with no memories. No one to tell him anything. Just a set of tasks running through his head on repeat as the only thing to keep him grounded."

I tore my eyes away from Moray and looked at Lyn.

"You knew Artur was going to die when you told him you wouldn't go with him," she said. "So don't be angry with Moray over it. Be angry with the ones that put us all in this sad situation to begin with."

Lyn had a point. Artur was gone, and I hadn't done anything to stop him. Besides, his going had helped me, in a way. Had that been why I hadn't stopped him? Because I needed him to go where I couldn't? All so I could get one step closer to the endgame? If so, I'd used him, which would make me infinitely worse than Moray. Who was I to feign shock and rage towards the Itinerate who was just doing what he was told?

***

We surfed the wind for several hours, but by the end of the trip, the air was noticeably calmer. We managed to make it to the bunker that Moray had mentioned. He pointed to a small black smudge that, on descending, resolved into a door set into a sloping roof. We landed about a hundred meters from it and approached on foot. The structure was pale gray except for the rust-encased hinges and wheel centered on the door. There were no signs, no markings, no way of knowing what was lurking below.

"Let me go and check that it's safe," Moray said.

He gripped the wheel on the door and gave it a few forceful turns until metal scraped and something thudded within the wall.

"Be careful," Lyn said.

He nodded then pushed in, hard. The door was heavy, and I moved to help him with it just as it gave way. He waved me back, grabbed his gun leaning beside the door, and slipped through the crack that he'd made. Lyn and I couldn't see in, but slightly warmer air wafted out.

"We'll give him a few minutes," Lyn said. "After that, we go in."

I didn't have a weapon on me and didn't like the prospect of diving into those dark depths defenseless.

"I won't be much use if it comes to a fight," I said.

Lyn moved to her glider and detached the rod from it. She pressed a button, and it buzzed to life. I walked to her side and peered down at the piece of tech resting in her hands. She held it out to me. I hesitated. Even then, even after everything that had happened, all that I'd done, I was still dancing on my strings.

"I give you express permission," she said.

I took hold. Lyn pointed to a chrome rectangle that stuck out.

"That button," she said. "Use your thumb, like this."

She gripped it and tapped her thumb to the button without depressing it. She held it out to me.

"You try," she said.

I took the rod. She let go and stepped back. I repositioned my hands and pushed against the rectangle. The buzzing shifted to a snapping. Streams of light sprang from one of the tips and curved back on themselves. Little arcs of death.

"Touch that electrode near someone or something to fry them."

I released the button. The arcs disappeared, but the rod continued to vibrate and hum with latent energy.

"Turn it off with the other button, the smaller round one."

I searched for the raised circle and pressed it. The buzzing wound down, and the rod went silent and inert.

"Better?" she asked.

"Let's just hope he comes back."

A scrapping and screeching came from the depths of the bunker. We both froze and kept our eyes trained on the crack. Lyn hoisted her gun in both hands, and I squeezed the rod in both of mine. We didn't hear anything else and just stayed fixed in our poses. The same sound issued again then there were footfalls. Moray peeked his head through the crack.

"All clear," he said. "Come on."

Lyn moved in, and I followed. We slipped through the threshold. While Moray waited for us to acclimatize to the dark, he gave us an update.

"It's still abandoned," he said. "We should be safe to stay here for the somn."

"How's the air?" Lyn asked.

"Once we get through the airlock, we can take our rebreathers off."

Lyn shifted, a vague outline of her moving. The surroundings were finally starting to resolve.

"How is the air any good if it's abandoned?" she asked.

"Some kind of tech we don't know about?" Moray said. "Anyway, at least we'll be able to save ONi."

My own satchel was alarmingly light, and we still had at least two sols until we got to Nord.

"We're getting low," I said. "We don't have a lot of leeway."

"All the more reason to stay here to get some rest," Moray said.

He glanced at the rod in my hand.

"Arming the Reisender now?" he said to Lyn.

"We're already breaking so many Decrees," she said.

My vision was finally settled. The light filtering through the crack behind gave me enough to work with.

"Ready?" Moray asked.

Lyn and I both nodded and mumbled our yeses. Moray vocalized something I didn't catch, and a faint glow came off the tip of his gun. Lyn did the same. Moray headed towards a set of stairs that descended below ground level. At the time, it was the first staircase I'd seen, and I didn't know what to make of it.

I watched Moray and Lyn go down then carefully mimicked their movements. As we got to the bottom, the temperature stabilized. Outside, the air wasn't so biting this close to the poles, but it was still perpetually chilled. Down here though, surrounded by massive rock, it was almost comfortable.

There was something else to the air, a kind of sweet smell I caught even through the thin air and my rebreather. It had to be intense, whatever it was. It was familiar too, but I couldn't place it. I ran through the herbs Emyla would surround herself with while working, tried to link them to the fumes the powders would emit when volatilizing, but this wasn't those. It had an earthy and acidic quality.

"Are you sure the air is safe?" I asked.

"I checked," he said.

"It smells strange," I said.

"Tobacco," Lyn said. "Not a favorite of most Reisende seeing how there are more important crops to grow and more efficient ones for the herbalists to use with their fumes."

I knew that name and could place it now. It was something I hadn't smelled in years, something from childhood.

"It's always smelled like this," Moray said. "It's okay. Probably just a remnant from the Dipoli that used this place before they abandoned it."

We reached a landing at the foot of the stairs. Moray moved towards a metal wheel set in the center of a large door. Lyn and I stood by. The light was faint even coming from both of their guns, but I could make out some details. This door was metal, like the one above, but less worn. Here too, there were no markings to hint at what was inside.

Moray braced himself, sucked in air, and strained against the wheel before it gave. This was the source of the screeching we'd heard earlier. It took a couple of full turns then the door popped out. Moray opened it enough for each of us to slide through.

The room on the other side was small, no more than three meters in each direction, a perfect square enclosed by metal. Moray closed the door using the same kind of wheel mechanism on this side then went to the door opposite. On the far right, there was a rectangle with buttons set in it, which he pressed in a rapid sequence. They beeped when he touched them then gave a set of three quick beeps once he was done. A low and deep thud sounded in the door then a hissing. Once it stopped, Moray grabbed hold of a handle on a long strip of metal that was barred across the door. He huffed and pulled it all the way to the left.

"We're in," he said.

Only he hadn't said it over his shoulder to us but in the direction of the button pad beside the door. He turned back to us.

"Just push it and head in while I fix something," he said.

Moray moved to the door we'd come through. Lyn went forward and pressed a palm to the smooth metal. The door groaned on its hinges and just barely swung inwards. She stopped and slung her gun over her shoulder before pushing with both hands. I leaned the rod I had against the wall and helped her while Moray fiddled with something on the outer door.

Without warning, our door swung with too much ease, and we both lunged forward. When I glanced up, the door was fully open. A row of people stood in front of us, guns drawn.

"We only have these as a precaution," someone with a gravelly and somehow familiar voice said. "The hope is, we don't have to use them."

I glanced over my shoulder to where I'd left the rod. The muzzle of a gun was pointing at me from behind with Moray peering down the sights.

"Don't even think about it," he said.

I looked at Lyn. She was frozen, her hand hovering over the barrel of her gun, ready to sling it off her shoulder if only she wasn't the object of ten other such weapons.

"What's going on?" I asked.

"We're going to have a talk," the gravelly voice said.

I searched to see who it belonged to. None of them wore rebreathers. A man stepped forward, and I suddenly understood why I knew the voice and where that familiar scent came from.

"Who are you?" Lyn asked the man.

"Rohn," I answered for him.

Rohn

Lyn

Levi said Rohn, and the man didn't argue. In fact, he snapped his head to look at Levi then squinted. They stared at each other. I tried to spot the similarities in father and son, but I couldn't. Where Levi was tall and lean, Rohn was swarthy. The son looked Dipoli, and the father a Reisender through and through. Pale blue eyes. Remnants of blond hairs set in gray. I couldn't see the connection. To Cade? Yes. But Levi? Not at all.

"Moray mentioned that you came," Rohn said to Levi. "I don't know that I would've recognized you if he hadn't though. Makes me feel ancient just looking at you. You're all grown up."

I glanced back. Moray was pointing his gun at us. We were flanked and grossly outnumbered, but fighting them was the last thing on my mind. It had been in the forefront until Rohn's name had sounded out. Now, I just wanted to understand what was happening.

"How are you here?" Levi said to Rohn.

"I found this place a long time ago and made it my home," Rohn said, "but you don't mean that. You want to ask, 'how are you still alive,' right?"

Levi nodded.

"Follow me," Rohn said.

He waved his hand and turned. His people kept their guns fixed on us but parted to let us move through. Levi advanced. I stayed put.

"Come on, Lyn," Moray said. "You too."

He snatched my gun and tossed it over his right shoulder where his own now hung. He grabbed my arm and nudged me to follow. I lumbered after Levi in a daze. Moray kept a hold on me as we moved further into the bunker. We were in a small entryway with only two features—the massive door that led to the airlock and an opening that led into a hallway.

The hall cut to the left and right. The left was lit and the right dark. Rohn, Levi, and the little train of Rohn's cohort all turned to the left and headed down a nondescript tunnel. The walls were smooth and gray. They joined the ceiling to form an elongated arch. The lighting was yellow and came from fixtures attached above and covered by cages. A hum came from each as we passed below. Our footfalls echoed. No one spoke.

As we advanced deeper, the tobacco scent grew more potent until it overpowered the general mustiness of the place. We passed five doors on alternating sides of the hallway. Then Rohn stopped. I couldn't see past the heads of his nine-odd followers. Metal groaned, and a gush of air rushed past us. The tobacco smell cascaded out.

"Here we are," Rohn said.

Rohn's people filed into a large and brightly lit space. It was a series of rooms but with no walls, just their contents delineating them. There was a sitting area with cushions on the ground and the odd bench made from the pallets used for drops. Another space had a table with four sets of short, mismatched legs. There was the sleeping area with mats laid out haphazard and people's belongings heaped into piles.

Then I spotted the plants through sheets of foggy, translucent material. I couldn't make out what they were, but the differences in shapes and colors implied dozens of crops. A cornucopia of vegetation, each in its own microenvironment, encased in plastic. Lights were set in the ceiling and trailed off into the distance. Rohn's plants dominated the bunker. I'd never seen such a massive space. It was like ten Essen Jurte in any given direction.

Moray let go of my arm then shut the door behind us. He slid a long metal rod across it, and I finally understood that Levi and I were prisoners. Moray moved to stand beside Rohn, and his betrayal finally hit me. I gravitated to Levi's side. The others surrounded us in a semi-circle. Rohn picked up a pipe from a crate serving as a table and took a few puffs. Levi nodded at the pipe.

"I forgot you used to do that," he said. "I'm surprised you were able to keep up the habit out here."

"It might look like we're living rough," Rohn said, "but it only looks that way. This place is home. It doesn't move with the Break. It doesn't shake with the gales. It's stationary. You can't even imagine what that means until you've lived it."

Rohn took another couple of puffs from his pipe then put it down. I looked again at our surroundings and saw what he meant. There were signs of care and comfort that I hadn't seen in any Stamm. These people could have possessions just because they wanted to. Weight wasn't a precious commodity. Space wasn't so painfully limited. Even so, there was the wear, agedness, and desperation to use and reuse everything. There were no drops or Stämme to trade with in this place.

"You can take your rebreathers off in here," Rohn said.

Levi removed his, and I did likewise.

"Why are we here?" I asked.

Rohn came to the front of the group. His robes had that same threadbare aura as the environs. I looked over the others behind him. All Reisende.

"It was only supposed to be you," Rohn said to me.

Then he glanced at Moray.

"She was set on bringing him along," Moray said. "I didn't want to raise suspicion by refusing."

"So you said," Rohn replied.

He looked at me and smiled.

"The short answer?" he said. "We need your help, Lynev. More specifically, we need it to get access to Nord."

"It's not all that different from what you had planned," Moray said. "It's just, I lost access to Nord when I went Rogue. We need an Itinerate who's still in their good graces."

I refused to even look at him. I kept my eyes trained on Rohn.

"Let's sit," Rohn said.

He waved Levi and me to a set of cushions. Some of his cohort lingered. Others wandered off and busied themselves with tasks. Moray hovered nearby. Rohn sat cross-legged, facing both Levi and me, leaning forward with eager eyes.

"Vromdorf may be one of the only Stämme left," he said. "I've been tracking the hostile luftors."

"You created them," I said.

Rohn nodded stiffly.

"But not like they are now," he said. "Not on purpose."

"You were trying to make the luftors resistant to the day and night," Levi said.

Rohn gazed at Levi. His pursed lips transformed into the barest hint of a grin.

"Something like that," Rohn said.

Levi leaned forward on his pillow. A manic light came into his eyes.

"I've studied your notebooks," he said. "I'm a botanist too."

"Are you now?" Rohn asked.

His hands rested on his jawline. He tapped his index finger against his cheekbone. There was curiosity in his expression but not the pride I might have expected.

"You were frustrated," Levi said. "You made the hybrids, the hostile luftors, with the hope that they would eventually spread across Neuen."

"Very good," Rohn said. "But do you know why I did it?"

They were tilted towards one another on their cushions. Cross-legged, hands on knees, necks craning. I was an afterthought to their reunion.

"You wanted the Reisende to be independent of the Lats," Levi said. "To break free from the Dipols."

Rohn's eyes widened, and a bark of a laugh came out. The noise startled me.

"Exactly," Rohn said. "I got this idea stuck in my head when I was still just a kid. A theory about why the Reisende wander. Yes, it's partly to keep us separate from the Dipoli so their precious genome doesn't get corrupted."

Rohn looked over at me and grinned. He shifted on his cushion to free a part of his flowing robes. He lifted the fabric to expose his back to us. There were splotches of blue-gray clustered near his ribs and on his spine.

"This GLEtch is harmless," he said over his shoulder, "but it's still a GLEtch."

He let the robe fall and faced us again.

"That's not the real reason they exile us though," he said. "Our expulsion from the Dipols was also meant to exile us intellectually. If we're constantly on the move, we don't have the time to grow roots and just learn. The Dipols made us dependent on them for a reason."

Rohn stopped and let us mull over his words. I didn't disagree with him, but I wanted to know where this was going and why he needed to go to the Dipols.

"Why the luftors though?" I asked. "It seems a roundabout way to break free. One that would take generations to work."

"True," Rohn said. "But it was also the thing I knew best. Got to start somewhere, right? Unfortunately, Aarman didn't see it that way. He said I was going too far, flirting with GenEn, and he wasn't wrong. I did use it but only minimally."

"What does minimally mean?" I asked.

"A very small amount," he said.

I narrowed my eyes, and he sighed.

"I didn't create these luftors like they are now, okay?" Rohn said. "I couldn't have, even if I'd wanted to. I didn't have that kind of skill or knowledge of GenEn."

I had him in the lie, although I couldn't quite grasp why he was bothering to lie at all.

"Don't sell yourself short, Rohn," I said. "We know how skilled you are with GenEn. The proof is sitting right here beside us."

I glanced at Levi, who was staring at his father. Rohn looked from me to him and back.

"I don't understand," he said.

"Levi's the product of GenEn, thanks to you," I said.

"Me?" Rohn asked. "I had nothing to do with that. It was all Kelica."

Levi pursed his lips but didn't have the shock I would've expected. Then the truth sank in—Levi had known. He'd known that the GenEn was Kelica's doing, and he hadn't told me. Why? But of course. It was a son protecting his mother. He didn't want her death on his head.

"I know it's easy to make me out to be this big bad GenEn'er," Rohn said, "but you were her idea, Levi. I didn't even know about it until after you'd been born."

"How would Kelica even have the knowledge for GenEn?" I asked. "And why would she do something like that? It doesn't make any sense."

"It's not so hard to learn about it," he said. "If you're persistent and know where to look. Besides, she's a physician. If anyone could do GenEn on a person, it'd be her, not me. As for the why, there was ample reason."

Rohn paused again and looked at Levi.

"I was her greatest achievement," Levi said. "I was meant to purify the Stamm, my genome passed down over the ages."

"So she told you?" Rohn asked.

"Only after we found out I was GenEn," Levi said. "Then she admitted the truth."

"All of it?" Rohn asked.

Now Levi looked confused and waited for more.

"You still think I'm your father?" Rohn asked.

"Aren't you?" Levi said.

"Kelica was skilled, but she had her limits. She couldn't have made your genome what it is using her own and mine. No, she had to start with something a bit purer."

Rohn stopped and let us make the connection for ourselves.

"An Itinerate?" I asked.

I didn't believe it even while I said it. We were sent on our tour without the ability to reproduce. The last thing the Dipols wanted was for their female Itinerates to come home with a GLEtch-riddled child in the womb. Equally distasteful was the very idea that Rohn was hinting at. A male Itinerate diluting the GLEtch count of a Stamm. That was the Reisende's burden to bear. How dare an Itinerate lessen their suffering even an iota? Male or female, it didn't matter. We couldn't impregnate or be impregnated. At least, that's what I had believed.

"It's not possible," I said.

"Kelica found a way," Rohn said. "She got the seed of a male Itinerate and used it in combination with her own egg to create Levi here."

We both glanced at the object of our conversation. Now Levi showed the shock I had expected earlier. Kelica hadn't told him this part of his twisted heritage.

"I'm half Itinerate?" he asked.

"Kelica's idea, not mine."

"It doesn't matter," Levi said. "None of this matters. The hybrids are the only thing we should be talking about right now."

Rohn smiled and patted Levi on the shoulder.

"A Reisender after my own heart," Rohn said. "And my thoughts exactly. Lynev, I need your help to stop the hostile luftors. I need the tech that's in the Dipols to have any hope though."

"Like I said," Moray added, "not so different from what you had planned, except it'll be Rohn going with you instead of Levi."

"No," Levi said. "We go with the original plan."

I looked at him, but he stared at Rohn.

"I have to be the one to go to the Dipols," Levi said. "I know how to stop the hybrids, how to actually stop them. It's not some hypothetical like it is for you. I know exactly what needs to be done."

"And that is?" Rohn asked.

"GenEn," Levi said.

No talking around the point now. Truth after truth was being exposed, but the biggest one hadn't come out just yet. Moray's betrayal. Rohn being alive. Levi the son of an Itinerate. All of that paled in comparison to what came next.

"I know exactly how to stop the hybrids," Levi said, "because I created them. Not you, Rohn, me. This wasn't an uncontrolled mutation of something you did years ago. This was a deliberate act by me, one that back-fired, and one that it's my responsibility to clean up."

I don't know which word was the one where my brain made the connection. A compression of air. My ear processing those fluctuations in pressure into an electric signal. My brain discerning what those signals meant. From a sound in a string of sounds to the meaning behind it. At some point in that cluster of words, I understood what Levi had done. Then the various strands resolved into finite links. The hints. The suggestions. The ache of him trying to tell me what he'd done without words. It had all flown right by. Not anymore though. As soon as I heard it, I didn't doubt the validity of it. I knew Levi had created the hybrids, and maybe I'd always known.

I didn't need to hear any more. I didn't want to. Lies and lies and lies. Half-truths. Omissions. Concealments. Manipulations. Toying with my feelings to get what he needed from me. Him. Moray. The ones I should've felt safest with had used that security against me in the worst way. I looked through Levi. I looked through Moray. I rose, turned, and walked to an unoccupied corner of the bunker. I sat on a lumpy cushion, my hands in my lap, my eyes defocused.

All the while, I heard Levi's voice and Rohn's and occasionally Moray's. Plans and actions and next steps. No thought of consequences. Rush, rush, hurry, do, achieve, correct, repair, save. Two of them had done the unthinkable— GenEn. And now they were going to go into the wolves' den and demand the Dipols let them use forbidden tech to correct their mistakes. And I knew, knew, they would get what they wanted because the Dipols didn't have a grip on the situation. The world ripped apart by one ambitious and dangerously intelligent man. The only hope of salvation by the same one that had doomed us in the first place.

I should've been angry, bitter, filled with hot, searing rage, but all I could find was a creeping numbness. That deep, dark well where the emotions would bubble from was closed off. I'd let myself get to this point because of my fascination with the promise of that well. Of what it could mean. I'd wanted to plumb its depths, find a part of myself that was stymied away, but at what cost? Better to feel nothing than to be used. I wasn't going to let it happen again. I would help Levi save Neuen, but beyond that?

GenEn

Levi

"What happened exactly?" Rohn asked. "Give me all the gory details. It's important."

I glanced in the direction where Lyn strayed after my revelation. I didn't like how she'd reacted. I was ready for a scolding or, at the very least, a death stare, but the blankness that took hold of her, the coldness and stiffness, it was somehow worse. I admitted to creating the hybrids, and she'd just walked away and sat down in seclusion with her back to us. I needed her to hear the rest of my story. I needed her to understand why I'd done the ultimate taboo, but she wouldn't even give me that. No, I was dead to her.

"Levi," Rohn said, snapping his fingers at my face. "Focus."

My attention shifted and locked in. He was right. This was important, and I needed to remember what my priorities were. This was about Neuen, not Lyn.

"What do you mean?" I asked. "What happened as in how did the hybrids get to be this way?"

Rohn frowned and nodded. It was impossible to tell what he felt towards me. Disgust? Horror? Relief? Envy? Probably all of them at once.

"I designed them to be different," I said. "More akin to your luftors actually, a continuation of your work or maybe a successor. Anyway, I knew making them robust enough to survive Neuen's day and night wasn't going to work. The conditions are just too extreme for any kind of complex life. Maybe prokaryotes but not luftors. The ONi alone are so fragile and delicate. There was no way to design them to survive and be of any use to the Reisende after coming out of hibernation."

Rohn let his frown flicker into a smile. He knew exactly what I meant. I was lecturing a master, and time was a luxury we didn't have.

"I wanted them to be mobile like the Reisende, but free of the Lats. Instead of making it so any given plant would survive, I wanted them to survive long enough to bear ONi then pass the baton on to the next generation of luftors. I made them short-lived but prolific in reproductive capability. I gave them qualities to thrive for that."

Rohn rose from his seat and waved for me to follow. He headed for a wall of translucent fabric towards the rear of the room. Blobs of vegetation were only just visible beyond. I followed until we stood at the barrier, the lights hazed out into dim circular spheres. The tobacco's scent was even stronger, bordering on oppressive. The air was full and damp. Moray came up to my side, and Rohn eyed him before shaking his head.

"Not you, Moray," he said. "You stay here and watch the Itinerate. Levi and I are going to talk shop."

Moray paused then laughed.

"Wait," he said, "you're serious?"

Rohn waited.

"I can talk shop too," Moray said. "Who's been the one helping you track the hybrids? Who's been the one to bring you samples?"

"That's not talking shop," Rohn said. "I mean genetics. GenEn. We don't have time for distractions, and you've got a job to do. Lynev needs to be on board with this, or the plan is dead before it even starts. Convince her that this is the right call. She trusts you."

"Probably not anymore," Moray said.

I didn't wait for Moray to do as he was told. I pushed my way through the sheets, and they parted in my wake. I inspected Rohn's lab while the two of them argued. There were rows of plants stretching into the distance—corn, tobacco, tomatoes, bean stalks, leafy greens, squashes, cucumbers, peppers, carrots, potatoes, more.

But the thing that I honed in on were the luftors. They lorded over the other vegetation. Their smooth, black, vine-like stalks. Their round, gray dots of leaves. And of course, those beautiful, gem-like glowing blue crystals. ONi. More than I'd ever seen on a single plant. The plants were more ONi than leaves, sagging under the weight of the crystallites, almost difficult to see beyond the diffuse blue light refracting.

Rohn's luftors were different even from his previous generation. He had obviously continued his work even after leaving Vromdorf, and the lack of a Stamm hadn't hindered him in the least. In fact, he was thriving.

"Impressive, no?" Rohn asked.

He came to my side. No Moray, which meant Rohn had won their argument. Now, it was just me and the man who I'd always believed was my father. The truth still hadn't sunk in. I didn't know if it ever would. I was his son in spirit. I had weaved an invisible bond between us through our shared love of botany, and for years, that had sustained me. It had made the sting of his abandonment less sharp. It had given me succor in my own otherness. Rohn was a black sheep, and so of course I was too.

"How did you improve their yield so much?" I asked.

Rohn crossed his arms, and he became Cade, the likeness jarring.

"How do you think?" Rohn asked. "GenEn, which brings me back to my question. What happened to your luftors? What made them become the hybrids you call them now?"

"I don't know," I said. "I fused plant with fungi which created the hybrids' precursor. It was the easiest way to give them the traits I needed."

"Easiest? Really? I wouldn't call combining two organisms in different taxonomic kingdoms easy. I'd call it a nigh impossibility. Turning the evolutionary clock way way way back. I don't even think I'd have that skill nowadays, let alone when I was your age. How did you learn GenEn? From Kelica?"

I moved to the nearest luftor and just barely held an ONi.

"No, I didn't even know Kelica did GenEn until recently," I said. "I taught myself from your notes and the equipment I found in Kelica's things. I also learned from Itinerates over the years. I don't know how to explain it, but the work just came to me. I understood it without too much effort, almost like a silent compulsion. If I didn't know any better, I'd say I was a puppet dancing on strings, but the Dipols are the puppet masters. Why would they want me to know anything about GenEn?"

"Maybe the Dipols aren't the ones doing it."

"Who else is there?" I asked.

Rohn shrugged and took ahold of an ONi near the one I held.

"We know a fraction of a sliver of anything," Rohn said. "I've been living here, near Nord, for ages now, and I don't have a clue what's beyond those city walls. There are so many secrets, so many lies. I learned to stop worrying about all the things I don't know and can't control. I've devoted myself to digging into what I do have a grasp on instead."

He tossed his hands out to indicate the bounty encircling us.

"I thought you left Vromdorf to keep doing your science without any obstructions."

"I did," Rohn said. "And I have. See for yourself. If you look closely at my creations, you'll understand just what I've managed to achieve even in this sad little hovel I call home."

"But the luftors," I said. "Your luftors. The ones that would survive off of the Lats?"

Rohn smiled and patted my arm. For over two decades, I'd thought the man was my father and was long dead. Here he was grinning at me and talking shop, and yet it had lost all meaning. I wasn't his progeny, and for some reason, that made all the difference. He was a stranger. A brilliant botanist, but one who had no part in my genesis. Besides, he'd already said it himself; I'd surpassed him.

"My luftors would have never worked for all the reasons you already said," Rohn replied. "For a while, I tried. I spent so much time refining them, on making them viable, but it was a wasted effort. Isobel, the Itinerate I left with, she was fading away, and I couldn't stand to pull myself from my work. When she died, it was the wake-up call I needed. I gave up on those luftors. I refocused my efforts on things that mattered."

"Corn?" I asked, eyeing the stalks nearby.

"Sustenance, yes, for me and the others that came later. We found this place, Isobel and me."

"Did you leave to be with her?" I asked.

"Isobel? No. I mean, I cared for her, sure, but I left because I had to. Aarman gave me an ultimatum. Stop my work or get out of the Stamm."

I didn't know much about the Itinerate that Rohn had gone Rogue with except the rumors that he'd been involved with the woman. When I was younger, it had pained me to think how my mother must have felt about the whole affair, but as I got older and had my own dilemmas of the heart, I'd understood that Rohn was just a man in a difficult position.

"So, I left," Rohn said, "and Isobel was kind enough to guide me through the Break. We survived in the rough for a while. Living in her jurte. Constantly on edge over labspawn. Terrified that we would starve or suffocate if we didn't find a way to get food and ONi. Then we found this bunker. We settled in and made it our home. Others trickled in over the years."

My thoughts strayed to Artur. He'd gone north and spread my luftor spores. He'd kickstarted the whole thing. Had he found this place too?

"Did an Itinerate come here around a year ago?"

Rohn cocked his head slightly and shook it.

"Moray's the only Itinerate we've had here in a while."

"But you've had some come?"

Rohn nodded.

"Where did they go? Everyone here looks Reisende."

"They died," Rohn said. "They just kind of faded and failed. Physically. Mentally. Most lasted less than a year."

"That's very strange," I said.

"It's just one of the many mysteries tied to the Dipols. The Itinerates have no memories of life in Nord. They go into their tours like a blank slate. The Dipols are a nameless, faceless entity that the Itinerates follow without question, despite the lack of actual contact. Even Moray, who's a special kind of Itinerate, has never talked with anyone from the Dipols. The communications are always text-based. The drops are always manned by drones.

"Even Nord itself isn't what it seems. We have our

Reisender folklore, but besides that? It's supposed to be a glass city nestled safely in the temperateness of the north pole, but it's not like the city that we all wax on about—sharp spires reflecting the sunlight, bustling streets filled with Dipoli, a utopia that we don't get to be a part of. Except, I spent a long time watching Nord and studying it from afar, and there was never any movement. Just the occasional drone heading south for some drop. If it was Süd? Sure, that would make perfect sense. It's not really a city at all, just a base, somewhere for the Itinerates to start their tour, another option for drops to come from. But Nord?"

Something about what Rohn said caused my hands to start vibrating. I jammed them into my robe's pockets, and they brushed against a wooden rod. I pulled it out, and my flute, Rohn's one-time flute, sat in my hands. I glanced up. Rohn knew it was his.

"I brought it with me without even thinking about it," I said. "Not much chance to play it in the Break considering the labspawn and everything, but it's like my good luck charm."

I held it out to Rohn. He put his hands below mine, and I released my hold. The flute dropped into his palms. He pulled it towards him and inspected it like he was reacquainting himself with an old friend. He rolled the flute over and over, eyeing it from all sides and angles, running his fingers along the body, pressing them to the holes. Then, he stopped.

"Play something," I said.

He shook his head and placed the flute back in my hands.

"No," he said. "I used that thing as a way to vent, but I've got no angst now. I left it in Vromdorf for a reason. It's yours. Besides, if it's a good luck charm, you'll be needing it more than me. You're right, Levi. You created the hybrids and know the most about them. You should be the one to clean up your mess. You'll be the one going to Nord."

It was what I wanted, the whole reason I'd left Vromdorf

and traveled the Break with Lyn and Moray, so why was I suddenly hesitant? Part of it was what Rohn had said about Nord, the creeping unease that gripped me with every revelation he gave. But it was more than that. We were close. Just a couple of sols, and we would be in Nord.

I wasn't ready for my story to be over because going to Nord meant the end, one way or another. Even if the Dipols let me do what I needed to do to stop the hybrids, there would be nothing after that. I'd performed GenEn. I'd endangered the entire planet with my recklessness. There was only one punishment for a Reisender like me.

"Before you go," Rohn said. "I need to know everything that you do about the hybrids."

He brushed past me, waving for me to follow. We came to a table set against one of the translucent sheets. A microscope sat on it, but the rest of the surface was covered by papers. He shuffled through the pages until he found a fresh one and a writing tool. Rohn pulled a stool from underneath the table and dropped onto it. He looked up at me and waited.

"Everything?" I asked.

"Everything. You have to understand, if you don't make it to Nord or the Dipols don't let you in and you can't make it back here or they let you in but don't let you do the GenEn, I have to be able to carry on your work. We can't trust the Dipols to do it. I'm your plan B."

I glanced around for a chair but had to settle on a bucket. Rohn stared at me, pen in hand.

"I'm going to stop the hybrids," I said. "I'm going to use the kill switch I built into them. It's true that the tech in Nord is important, but we might be able to do it without it. If I don't come back, if you don't know what happens to me, you can probably do what needs to be done from here."

Rohn's eyes widened.

"Then we should do it now," he said.

"I said probably. I'm not sure, and besides, it would be difficult, time-consuming. It's the plan B, Rohn. You can't do anything until you're sure I'm not coming back, until you're sure the Dipols either imprisoned or killed me. Got it?"

"No, I don't have it, Levi. What the hell are you talking about? If we can stop this thing, we should do it now."

"No," I said.

I slammed my fists on the table and rose from the bucket.

"Doing the GenEn is only part of the reason I need to go to Nord."

Rohn glared at me. That was the death stare I wanted from Lyn.

"Go on," he said. "Because you know you're going to have to say more to get me to agree with whatever it is you're trying to do."

Here it was. The moment I knew would come. He'd been trying and failing to do what I was going to do, and because of that, Rohn would be the one most likely to understand me. And he did. Even if he was furious with me, even if he cursed under his breath and called me insane, he relented. Bit by bit. With each sentence I let out, he softened, because he started to see the whole picture. It was one last chance to achieve what he'd given up on achieving. We could free our kind and save them all in one go.

"You really are Kelica's son," Rohn said. "Arrogant to a fault with ambition that will be the end of you. I'd tell you to temper those demons of yours, but I think it's too late for all that."

"Does that mean you'll do it?"

"Yeah, I'll be your plan B. Let's just hope it doesn't come to that."

Chrysalis

Lyn

Moray sat beside me, waiting for me to acknowledge his existence, but I wasn't going to give him anything. Not after what he'd done. The numbness from Levi's revelation was still there. It had covered up and stoppered the well to my emotions. This reaction to Moray wasn't anger though. It was more rational than that. There were consequences for betrayal. Cause and effect. Action and reaction.

"I'm sorry, okay?" Moray said. "But it had to be done."

"Did it?" I asked, finally looking at him.

"It's the same plan—"

"That's not the issue, Moray," I said. "You lied to me because you thought what? You couldn't trust me?"

He leaned away and shook his head. Black curls tossed with the movement.

"I went Rogue a few months ago. If you found that out, who knows what you would've done."

I rose from my cushion.

"You could've told me before we left Vromdorf," I said. "I was already convinced we had to go to Nord with the comms being down."

Moray winced. His eyes darted away.

"What?" I asked.

He smiled and held his hands out.

"I might have played a part in that," he said.

"The comms?"

"They aren't down. Blocked, actually. By me, but for good reason."

I crossed my arms. I waited for him to elaborate.

"They wouldn't have said anything useful to you," he said. "Believe me, I was in your position for months. Lots of vague instructions and hollow responses. No details or explanations. I saved you the frustration."

"And replaced it with uncertainty and anxiety," I said. "I was waiting and waiting for them to give me something, anything to work off of."

"And you wouldn't have gotten it," he said.

"I had samples, data, things they needed."

"You think I didn't?" he asked. "Trust me, they weren't doing anything about the hybrids. I got fed up with it."

"And joined Rohn? When exactly did you run across him and this bunker? Before you went Rogue?"

"It doesn't matter, and you're going to be angry with me either way. The point is, Rohn is actually trying to do something to stop the hybrids, and the Dipols aren't. If it meant lying to you, that was a small sacrifice."

"You know that Vromdorf is running low on supplies thanks to your comms blackout?"

"It won't be much longer," he said. "Once we go to Nord, I'll remove the block. Besides, you should be thinking about the bigger picture. Vromdorf is one Stamm. The hybrids threaten them all."

"And if Vromdorf is the only Stamm left?"

"Sit back down," he said, patting my cushion. "I'm trying to explain myself here."

I sat and watched everything from afar. This had been how I'd felt when he'd first pulled the gun on me. Maybe, by now, the numbness would have given way to that spark of rage that hovered just out of reach, but then Levi had said his truth. The moment the fire was quenched, I knew it was gone for good. That same old exhaustion came in its place.

"I know why you did it," I said. "But just because I understand the rationale behind your decision doesn't mean I'm okay with the betrayal. You lied to me, Moray. You didn't trust me. That stings. I don't want to forgive you. Not right now, maybe not ever."

It was what he needed to hear. Moray didn't even bother to argue. He just sat in silence waiting for Rohn and Levi to finish their discussion. And he must have waited a long time because, despite everything that was happening, my exhaustion won out. I drifted off.

Then something woke me. I snapped my eyes open and scanned my surroundings. It was my Itinerate instincts. So used to living on edge in the Break. Watching and waiting for any sign of labspawn. And it was a kind of labspawn that woke me.

Levi stood nearby. The hand that must have tapped me moved back to his side. For a fraction of a second, I forgot what he'd done, what he'd admitted to. I almost smiled at him before the memories rushed in to buffer me and shield me from his manipulations.

"I just finished talking with Rohn," he said.

I turned on my cushion and glanced towards the transparent sheets they'd been cloistered behind. It was empty fog now. Rohn was elsewhere and Moray too. Most of the people in the bunker were sleeping, which told me it was well into the somn.

"You two must have had a lot to talk about."

I brought my knees up to my chest. I squeezed them with my arms. I thought maybe a physical sensation would counteract the creeping numbness that had fallen over me. It didn't.

"I had to tell him everything I know about the hybrids," he said, "in case the Dipols don't let me stop them."

I leaned forward. The stuffing in the cushion beneath me was all lumps and space, and I sank down. The effort to hoist myself was too much though. That nagging fatigue that had gripped me long before I'd arrived in Vromdorf was back and taking its vengeance. In all the tumult of Zeindorf and the hybrids, I'd gotten a surge of energy, but it had passed now. I was spent. Sleep hadn't brought any relief. This lethargy went deep, beyond the physical.

"It's suicide going to Nord," I said. "You know that, right? It was always going to be risky bringing a Reisender, and I was willing to do it when you were just some Reisender. But knowing what I know about you now? You broke the most fundamental Decree, Levi, and I'll be the Itinerate to bring you to Nord. There's only one punishment for the both of us."

"That's why I didn't tell you. I wanted to. I had to actively hold myself back from unloading everything to you that somn you ran my GenMap."

He wasn't lying. I'd sensed it back then and hadn't known what it meant.

"Why didn't you?" I asked. "Let me guess, you couldn't be sure how I'd react. Moray already said as much for why he lied to me."

"Moray's an idiot. He doesn't understand you. No, Lyn, you know this is too big to ignore. You aren't afraid to do what's necessary, but I didn't want you to pay for my mistakes. I wanted us to go into Nord without you aware of what I'd done because then maybe, just maybe, the Dipols would look past your infractions. If they could tell you really were in the dark about the part I'd played, then maybe the punishment would fall solely on me."

Levi watched and waited. His legs were locked at the knee. His lips pursed. I was the polar opposite. Slouched in the cushions. Barely able to raise my head. Listless. Drained. I wanted to believe him, but I was done being tricked. I'd opened myself up to two men, and both had used me for their own purposes. I was already thickening the callouses overtaking the softness.

"Is that it?" I asked.

"Is what it?"

"Your explanation. Is that all there is to it? Or was there another reason why you kept the truth from me?"

"What are you getting at?" he asked.

"Maybe you liked how I looked at you before and didn't want me to look at you like I do now."

Levi's eyes twitched.

"And how do you look at me now?" he asked.

He sat down on the floor in front of me. Legs crossed. Hands on ankles.

"You tell me," I said. "What do you see?"

"There's something in the way. I can't see the real you anymore."

I wasn't going to get sucked in by him. No talk of strings and puppets. Of knowing me and us being similar. None of it was going to sway me. I wasn't even going to give him my rage anymore. I was a wall. Impenetrable. Solid.

I leaned forward, and my knees got lost in the sea of foam held together by threadbare cloth, itchy and coarse.

"Maybe you never could see the real me," I said. "But you're right. You definitely can't now. You lost that privilege."

I braced myself and pushed free from the cushions that threatened to consume me. I brushed off my suit. Levi stood.

"Maybe you don't have to go to Nord," he said. "What if we put your tracker in me? I could take your glider and go by myself. Then no one else would have to put themselves at risk."

"Don't be naïve. We both know that would never work. You wouldn't even get to Nord's walls before they'd know you weren't me. Besides, I've seen how you operate on a glider. It doesn't give me a lot of hope for you making it there in one piece. I'm going to Nord. Not for you but for all the people you put in harm's way."

Levi stepped forward and reached for my hand. I jerked it away.

"I'm sorry," he said, "for everything, but you have to know that I was only trying to free my people."

I crossed my arms.

"That must sting," I said.

"What?"

"Realizing you doomed them instead."

***

Rohn held a black block identical to the one Moray had used to disable my tracker. He ran his fingers over the buttons and explained which I needed to press and what should happen after each.

"Just make sure it's working before you even get within a sol of Nord," he said. "Otherwise, the gates won't open for you."

I held out my palm and waited for him to hand the device over. He grimaced and shook his head.

"I told Moray this wouldn't work," he said. "I told him you couldn't be forced to help."

"I'm taking Levi to Nord like you asked. What more am I supposed to do?"

Rohn laughed before slapping the device in my hand. I tugged on it, but he didn't release it.

"You're angry and bitter, which doesn't make for an ideal ally," he said. "But beggars can't be choosers."

He shot his hand open, and the device almost slammed into my chest from the force I'd been exerting. I shoved it in my bag and glared at him.

"This isn't anger or bitterness," I said. "This is skepticism. The whole plan is flawed. Moray blocked the comms, which means I don't even have an excuse to be going to Nord. There was no radio silence. He did it, not them, not something else."

Based on his lack of a reaction, Rohn had been involved in that decision.

"But they don't know that," he said. "The excuse still holds. Besides, even if you heard from them, their responses would be as good as silence. Would you like to see for yourself?"

I opened my mouth and closed it. I stared him down then gave a curt nod.

"Moray," Rohn shouted.

His cohort were clustered together on mounds of bedding eating their morning meal. Black curls popped up, and Moray trotted over. He shot quick glances at me.

"Show Lynev the response we intercepted from the Dipols," Rohn said. "From the last message she got out."

Moray hesitated but relented when Rohn and I stayed motionless and silent. He moved over to a pile of tech, dug through the contents, and came back with his comms in hand.

"Give me a second to find it," he said.

Rohn and I waited.

"Here," Moray said.

He handed me the device, and I scrolled through the lines of text.

<Begin. Dipols received update re: Zeindorf investigation.

Findings from in-person assessment congruent with orbital optics. Findings from samples congruent with plague of new origin. Dipols will continue the investigation. If additional analyses are required, Dipols will inform. Itinerate Lynev instructed to remain in Vromdorf. Tour is delayed until further notice. Supply drops will be scheduled for Vromdorf when requested. End.>

My reaction was muted, but ghosts of emotions flitted through. A shade of shock. A whisp of wrath. But they faded just as quickly as they presented.

"You're just a tool to them like I was," Moray said. "They don't include us in the conversation because they don't see us as equals."

"What happens if we don't come back?" I said to Rohn. "If they end up shooting us down before we get there or lock us up?"

Rohn gave a barking laugh.

"We try again," he said, "with less advantages. Levi shared as much as he could with me about the hybrids. I'll do what I can from here, but truth be told, we need Levi to not fail. He's our best chance at turning this thing around."

"Speaking of," Moray said.

Levi was walking towards us, running his hand through his hair as he yawned.

"I've got something for you," Moray said to Levi. "Follow me."

The two of them moved to a shelf nearby. I focused on packing my bags for the journey. It would only take two sols to get to Nord from the bunker, but it was better to plan for the worst. We could get waylaid by labspawn or stuck at gates that refused to open. I unlatched my satchel and checked the ONi contents. Too low. I glanced up and found Rohn watching me.

"I need more ONi," I said.

"There's more than you'll ever need over in my fields. Take as much as you can."

He nodded in the direction of the transparent sheets that shrouded their contents in fog. I grabbed my satchel and headed towards the luftors. As I passed Moray and Levi, a glint of silver caught my eye. Moray held an Itinerate suit at the shoulders and moved it to hang in front of Levi. It was too short. He tossed it aside and grabbed a folded stack of silver. He unrolled it and held the next suit up to Levi. This one was a better match. I was close enough now to catch a trace of their conversation.

"I'd say that's a pretty decent fit," Moray said.

"What's it for?" Levi asked.

"To help keep you safe on the journey," Moray said. "Hide you from the labspawn. Maybe keep the Dipols from shooting you down the moment they'd otherwise spot your Reisender robes."

"You have a nice stash of Itinerate suits here," Levi said.

I slowed my pace and passed closer than I needed to.

"Rohn said there were a lot of Itinerates here at one point or another," Moray said.

"Did he mention why you're the only one now?" Levi asked.

"They all died," Moray said.

"He said they faded," Levi said. "All of them within a year. Aren't you worried that might happen to you too?"

The shelf cut off my view. It gave me the advantage of cover though because Levi's words caught my attention. I crouched on the other side of the shelf and listened.

"It's strange, sure," Moray said, "but I don't have many options when it comes to where I go at this point. Anyway, we've got enough to worry about with the hybrids. You should focus on your journey."

There were a few seconds of silence. I was almost ready to continue to the luftors when Moray followed up.

"Just do me a favor," he said. "Not that you owe me for anything, but just make sure to watch over Lyn. Keep her safe."

"She doesn't need me looking after her," Levi said. "She's perfectly capable."

"All I'm saying is if you can find a way to get the Dipols to spare her, then do it. She deserves it, especially after everything we put her through."

"Don't equate our situations," Levi said. "You had a choice. I didn't. I kept the truth from her to spare her, but your little stunt here upended everything. If it wasn't for you, Lyn would have a chance at survival. But now? What hope do you think there is in the face of all the taboos we've committed? Say your goodbyes because neither of us is leaving Nord."

A death. Returning home was always going to be one. Like the Itinerate Artur had said to Levi, returning to Nord meant getting our memories back but that in and of itself was a death. One Lyn would be reborn at the expense of this Lyn. Not anymore though. There would be no flood of memories for me. Just shame and punishment and eventually an execution. Well, this way I got my revenge on the Lyn that had put me through this whole ordeal. I was going down, but at least I'd take her with me.

***

Our sendoff was a muted affair. Only Rohn and Moray came out of the bunker. Gentle breezes ruffled our hair with only the occasional gust. It reminded me of my earliest days. When I'd set out from Süd at the start of my tour almost three years ago.

It hadn't been all that long, but even so, the memories were hazy. The further back I tried to peer, the foggier it got. Like trying to look through Rohn's translucent sheets. Murkier and murkier until the haze got so thick it became opaque. I had always been riding my glider, heading from Stamm to Stamm, running the GenMaps. What came before? What would come after?

"If you're able to do it," Rohn said to Levi, "I'd like to know, somehow."

"If we can find a way to get a message to you, we will," Levi said.

"I'll keep an eye on the hybrids," Rohn said. "If they don't start dying off in waves, I'll know you failed."

Moray crouched beside my glider, making the finishing touches on upgrades to the thrusters. He'd been working on it since the start of the sol. The tech needed to be able to hold the combined weight of me, Levi, and our supplies. Moray slammed a panel shut and patted the metal hull. Each slap reverberated and sent a hollow thud to my gut.

"All done," Moray said.

He rose, tools in hand, and moved towards the rest of us. Levi and I stood on one side. Rohn and Moray on the other. Levi held out his hand, and Rohn gripped it. They shook one, two times, and released. Moray didn't move, but he watched me closely. I nodded to Rohn and only looked at Moray. He winced, his pain apparent even with the rebreather covering half of his face.

I jumped onto the glider, and Levi settled in behind me. Then we were flying. Surfing the winds like a leaf caught on their gusts, entirely at its mercy. It took me nearly an hour to reach a good altitude given how calm the air was this close to the pole. But once we finished the ascent, there was nothing left to do except let the wind take us. I kept an eye out for labspawn. Even if we were both wearing Itinerate suits, there was always the threat. For the first time on my tour, I didn't catch sight of a single one all sol.

We only had one somn between us and Nord. We landed, erected the jurte, and settled in. I set proximity detectors, but the Itinerate suits at least made a full watch unnecessary. Even so, we were both tense. Because of what had happened. Because of what was going to happen. Because, even if I'd walled myself off, Levi still managed to pull at me.

While we sat in silence, eating our rations, I let the numbness creep over. From my sternum into my abdomen, seeping into my limbs, arms to fingers, thighs to toes, then up, up my throat, suffusing my neck, catching at my jaw, tugging on my tongue, bleeding into my eyes. Choking me. Blinding me. Blocking out the sounds and smells. I was inert. Enclosed in my chrysalis. Shielded and safe. I could take what I wanted without it reaching me.

I waited for Levi to lie down on his mat. The minutes slipped by. Once his breath came out rhythmically, I crawled across the jurte and nestled against his side. He shifted in his sleep but didn't wake. I brought my face close to his and looked at him, really took him in, without anyone else there, without him looking back. I reached out but didn't let my hand touch his face. The face was a sacred thing, the window of the soul, and his was cursed. This wasn't meant to be his triumph. It was mine.

I pushed my body against his. Thigh to thigh, breast to chest. I rubbed my hand from his leg to his groin. His breath caught. Eyelids fluttered. He looked back at me. Confused. Then brimming with want. Hungry.

He grabbed the back of my neck and tried to pull me to his lips, but I ripped his fingers free and bent them back. He gasped. I pushed away and rested on my knees. He rose to his elbows, watchful, eager. I unzipped my suit. Climbed out of it. Tossed it aside. He fumbled with his, free of it by the time I came back in.

Again, his lips sought mine. I pushed his face to the side and breathed in his ear while I stroked him. He sighed then reached for me. Fingers to skin. I let him take hold and explore, but anytime my walls would give in, I lashed out. Palm to cheek. Nails to chest. Teeth to ear. He suffered the punishment.

I wouldn't let him lead. When he attempted to, I struck back. He acquiesced. I straddled him, toyed with him. Pulled out the moment so it was torturous. His eyes begged and pleaded. My part swallowed his, and he groaned in relief. But the punishment wasn't over. Even then, I played with him, giving him only half of what he wanted. Dangling paradise on a string in front of his nose. Keeping it forever out of reach.

He saw what I did and bore it for a while, but eventually his true, gluttonous self emerged. He grabbed my arms and tried to force my back to the mat. I fought with a strength I didn't know I had. He would never have the privilege of lording over me. Not in that moment. Not ever.

I rocked and swayed him into submission. I brought him to the brink of ecstasy. Then, I stopped. Pulled free. Spat him out. Moved to my suit. Donned it. Crawled back to my mat and laid down, my back to him. He didn't dare come near me, but I heard him giving himself what I had denied him. Then I drifted into the nothingness of sleep.

Only it wasn't a nothingness. This time, I dreamed.

A golden city, spires of glass that reflected and refracted the light from a dim star, dust and dirt whipping through the derelict streets. Empty. Silent. Still. The buildings crumbled and shifted. The glass turned to steel to flesh. Throbbing, pulsing, humming. They were veins now. Soft masses, moaning and groaning and screaming. Blood rushed then halted within them. Without the constant movement, it started to congeal. Thickening and hardening, turning into concrete, into lead, into some form of matter so dense it shrank under its own mass. It was pulled in by a gravitational well that became impossible to escape. A black hole but a red-black of darkened blood. Spires turned to singularities. A glass city holding a secret.

I jolted awake and was shivering. Levi's breath, regular and constant, brought me back. I told myself that it was just a dream. I ignored the nagging thoughts reminding me I never dreamed.

The next morning, I rechecked the map that Moray had gone over with us to seal the route in my mind. Levi sat in silence, staring at his silver gloves. I glanced at him and got caught up tracing the curves of his muscle along the reflective fabric. But it was more of an idle curiosity than longing anymore. My domination had sated my bodily hunger, and my protective shell kept the more vulnerable feelings at bay.

"Are we not going to talk about last somn?" he asked.

"What's there to say?"

"For me? Plenty. I thought you hated me after knowing what I did."

"Lying together doesn't always mean love and respect."

"What did it mean then?"

I leaned in close. Put my hands to his knees and stared him down.

"I didn't give myself to you. I took you."

His eyes quivered. He knew it was true.

"A taste of heaven forever denied," I said. "You'll never have that again."

He looked at me hard then his frown shifted to a grin.

"Never say never," he said.

I pushed away from him. Irritated by his defiance. I wasn't going to let him sully my moment of triumph. I had wounded him, deeply. He could pretend it was otherwise, but I knew.

"We should go," I said.

I started to move towards the jurte's flap.

"Before we get to Nord," he said, "there's something you should know."

I sat back down. Levi's grin altered and now screamed of guilt.

"I didn't tell you about what I'd done to protect you," he said, "but there's no point hiding things from you anymore. You should know everything. It's only fair."

I waited. My hands folded one in the other. My face stern.

"We need to be on the same page when we face them," he said. "The Dipols, I mean."

Levi had a manic light in his eyes. He talked too fast, and his hand combed through his hair too many times. My stomach dropped. Maybe my triumph would be short-lived. I braced myself for whatever was coming.

"We'll already be at such a disadvantage with them," he said. "We've got to be solid, you and me. A united front. I can't have you shocked and angry with me in front of them, so let's get that over with now."

"Let's," I said.

I narrowed my eyes. He wavered then hardened.

"You know what I did," he said, "but not why. Not really."

"Does it matter?" I asked.

"It's all that matters—the why. I was trying to make the luftors robust, to free the Reisende from the Lats. It was going to be a bargaining chip, but it didn't work out the way I'd hoped."

"GenEn rarely does."

"I underestimated how unpredictable it could be," he said. "It's a cautionary tale, sure, but not in the way the Dipols would say it is."

"You used GenEn to create something that's killing off your people. It seems like all our warnings about it were spot on."

Levi shook his head almost violently.

"No, that's not what we should take away from this," he said. "The problem isn't the GenEn. It's the loss of the knowledge about it. We don't understand it anymore because they made it taboo. But outlawing something doesn't mean we suddenly unlearn it. Once the knowledge exists, it can't be taken back. It's a point of no return. Except the Dipols want to pretend they can just hide it from us, which will make it cease to exist. But that's not how it works. We were always going to find a way back to it, but it's the ignorance surrounding it that made it dangerous and got us to this point."

I let him finish his rant and waited for more because I knew something else was coming. Something bigger. The thing that was making him tremble, causing his words to catch and jumble, forcing his eyes to jump around and refuse to settle on any one thing.

"Can't you understand why I did it?" he asked.

"What are you trying to do here, Levi? Do you want me to tell you that you were right? That what you did was acceptable? Because it's not."

He'd tried to breach my wall, force it to crumble, but it was unscathed. Not even a chip in the stones. And I was leagues away. His cannons a distant boom, barely perceptible over the whisper of the wind.

He saw it. Levi couldn't win, not after what had happened last night. He slumped then planted his palms on his knees. He pushed himself to a stand, as much as he could in the jurte. His brown waves brushed against the cream-colored burlap while he craned over me.

"I'm not going to let this be a wasted opportunity," he said. "That's what you need to know. When we get to Nord, I'm going to finish what I started."

I stood and locked my hands on my hips. Our faces were a hand's width apart.

"What does that mean?" I asked.

"I'm going to get the Reisende's freedom. I'm going to demand it, and if the Dipols refuse, I'll let the hybrids kill them too."

"You'd be willing to let everyone die? The Reisende's freedom or no one's?"

"That's what I'm going to tell them. There's still Rohn. He can try to stop the hybrids, but the Dipols don't know that. And that's exactly how it needs to be."

"If you make that kind of threat, they'll definitely execute us."

Levi met my eyes and let his lips peel back into a smile with all the hallmarks of anguish. It was the kind of grin the dying give when they dare some higher power to let them off. Just a little more time to see what kind of havoc they can wreak.

"They were always going to murder us, Lyn. Reisender or Itinerate, we mean less than nothing to them. We're disposable, which is why I have to make my threat real."

Levi glanced at his bag. It was supposed to be filled with specimens to show the Dipols. It was meant to be proof of the danger. Now, I saw it for what it was. It was the danger brought right to them. No more waiting for the hybrids to make it to Nord by chance. No, Levi was the Trojan horse. He was the harbinger of their doom, and I was the one getting him admittance.

"Why are you telling me this?" I asked.

"Because I want you to know what you're a part of. You need to know that you aren't dying for nothing. This is bigger than the two of us."

If the numbness hadn't been all I was anymore, if my chrysalis had had a crack or any sign of weakness, maybe I would've been dumbstruck. Maybe I would've felt the horror I should have. But the screaming was cut off before it even hit my vocal cords. I wasn't the one making the decisions. I never had been. I was just along for the ride.

"Then let's go. Time to end my tour and see what kind of dying I'll be doing."

Levi went to say something then stopped. That mania he'd been exuding evaporated. A shell was all that was left in its wake. We'd make a fine pair now, two hollow bodies knocking on Nord's golden gates. Two puppets who'd managed to cut themselves free, only to fall limp to the ground. We were united alright, just not in the way that either of us would have hoped for.

Nord

Levi

I finally got my first glimpse of the sun, blood red and bloated, just hanging in the cloudless sky. I stared at it then looked away. It left a stain on my eyes that took minutes to fade. Eventually, Nord appeared in the distance as a faint speck on the horizon. A series of spires resolved, and as we neared, what looked like golden towers showed themselves to be cold glass and metal that reflected the perpetual glow from the sun. There were less than I'd imagined. Only five spires plus several others made only of a metal mesh.

Everything was surrounded by a dark gray wall that reached about halfway as high as the towers themselves. Either the wall was massively tall or the spires were deceptively short. There was nothing nearby to provide a sense of scale. No drones crowding the airspace or drops leaving or arriving or Dipoli appearing as little motes floating through the streets. Lyn tensed. We both waited to be hailed or shot down, but here was only stillness and silence.

When we got within a kilometer of the wall, Lyn descended. We were just able to glimpse the whole of Nord. We circled the city twice and found the same quiet and motionlessness. The details we spied didn't make sense. I'd never seen images of the Dipols, but I'd heard all the countless stories passed down from generation to generation of our home from the distant past. I knew those descriptions would be inaccurate, bastardized into something almost unrecognizable, but what we found was disorienting.

The towers looked more industrial than domestic with pipes and gratings where doors or windows ought to have been. The shine that reflected the golden sunlight wasn't from massive panes of glass that let the inhabitants gaze out. It was from some kind of protective cladding with a purpose I didn't understand.

Looking down towards the ground was equally confusing. There should have been streets paved smooth. Instead, there were just narrow corridors with a dirt cover, the same as a Stamm. I didn't know what a permanent city ought to look like, but I instinctively knew that this wasn't it. Something was off.

I tapped Lyn's waist and spoke into her ear.

"Should we go over the wall?" I asked.

She shook her head and spoke over her shoulder.

"I'm sure they have some kind of protective enclosure. Labspawn and all. We need to find a gate. Do this the right way—knock and wait to be invited in."

We dove and skirted about halfway around the wall until we found a kind of irregularity. We landed and investigated, but it wasn't a gate in the sense Lyn had meant. There was just an outline of a narrow opening plugged by the same material that made the wall itself. It looked like stone but would catch light and throw out an iridescence.

"I always assumed Dipoli didn't leave the city," I said. "Why would they need gates?"

"Itinerates," she said.

"Does any of this feel familiar to you?"

She shook her head, her braid hanging limp in the stagnant air. She reached out a gloved hand and touched the wall. A faint illumination appeared. She pulled her hand back, and it faded.

"How would you have gotten in if you had finished your tour?" I asked.

"I don't know. Maybe I would've known what to do if I was supposed to come here. Or they would've told me."

"We could keep circling the wall until we find something more promising?"

"Hold on, I'll ping them with my comms."

Lyn went back to her glider and rummaged through her bag until she pulled the device out. She touched her finger to it and traced patterns.

"There," she said.

"You told them we were here?"

She nodded then looked back at the wall. We waited, but nothing happened. About a minute later, her comms emitted a chime. We both snapped our heads in its direction. She read the response, her eyes flying over text I couldn't see. Her brow furrowed, her lips silently mouthed the words, then her eyes widened.

"They're letting us in," she said.

As if in response to her words, the plug shimmered, jerked, and dissolved into a faint transparency.

"They said to enter and go to the tallest tower," she said.

We both looked at the opening then back at one another. I waved my hand for her to go first and watched her pass through the threshold without issue. Her image was there on the other side, distorted and undulating, beckoning me. I hesitated and glanced back at the horizon. I took one final look at Neuen then stepped through. It was the same on the other side. The air equally thin, the light equally faint, but a thrill ran through me. I was in the Dipols.

"Where to?" I asked.

Lyn pointed to a spire.

"They said the highest tower, which is that one."

She set off. I jogged to catch up and walk abreast.

"Doesn't this place seem off?" I asked.

"It's the Dipols. Of course it'd seem strange to you."

"Where are the Dipoli?"

"Probably in the towers. The air is thin here too. Why would they go outside when they have everything they need inside?"

She was aloof and cold towards me, and I couldn't blame her. I was lucky she spoke to me at all after what I'd done. Our little dance of the flesh last somn hadn't softened her towards me. In fact, it seemed to have done the opposite.

"Is this what it's always like?" I asked.

She shrugged.

"You still don't remember?" I asked.

She glared at me then walked on faster.

"Let's just get this over with," she said.

We went the rest of the way in silence, and the stillness of the place got to me. I kept checking over my shoulder and watching darkened corners as we passed. It wasn't exactly sinister, but there was something disconcerting about it. The lack of wind, the pale-yellow glow, the cold, gleaming monoliths. Everything was silent, still, reflective. It was so alien. Walking in the spaces between the structures, my boots sank into a fine powdered sand. Glancing behind, our footprints alone meandered through the corridors. No one else walked these paths.

After a quarter hour or so, we made it to the spire that Lyn had pointed out. This close, it was even more dizzying, its peak stretching into the sky, the mirroring of its glass and metal making it almost an extension of that expanse. I was frozen, mesmerized.

People had built this, this colossal, bulking but also elegant thing. Such a far cry from the jurten. No wonder the Dipoli viewed us Reisende as savages. Then again, they were the ones who had clipped our wings. If we were able to stay in one place, a less hostile place, who's to say we too couldn't construct this? Or something even grander.

I stared at the top of the spire, leaned back to try to take it all in. There was movement on the edge of my vision, and I snapped my head in that direction. Lyn looked too. She held her gun by her hip, not quite at the ready but not relaxed either. Her left hand was extended down and slightly out, the fingers splayed, cautioning me not to move.

"A drone," she said.

Except the thing that came into view wasn't the same as the mechanical creatures that brought drops to the Stamm. Those had looked more like Itinerate gliders. This one was humanoid, at least in the sense that it was elongated vertically with sensors on top and a set of wheels at the bottom. It was blocky with no visible limbs, and yet I still knew what its "face" was. I gazed into it. Shiny round depressions were set into a matte black surface. If it wasn't moving, I wouldn't know that the thing was aware in any way. It felt inert, cold, lifeless.

When it got within two meters of us, it stopped. It buzzed and beeped. Then a voice spoke from it, muffled, distant, and of ambiguous gender.

"Itinerate Lynev," it said. "Follow."

It rotated one-hundred-and-eighty degrees and rolled along in the direction it had come from. We trailed after it, keeping a safe distance. Lyn's stance and movements told me she was equally unnerved.

After a few hundred steps, the drone stopped in front of

a depression in the steel base of the spire. It sat for several seconds then gave off a beeping. An opening formed, the door seeming to slide to the side, swallowed by the wall. The drone wheeled in, leaving little ruts in the dirt, depositing dust on the dark stone flooring within. Lyn and I followed. The door slid back into place, and we were cut off from the outside world. There was no going back now, but running was the last thing on my mind. This was exactly what I'd been working towards.

We were in a hallway. The lighting was cold and sterile and flickered on as we moved in a little train. The drone then Lyn then me. Our footfalls echoed down the long tunnel. We kept our rebreathers on. The walls were mostly unfinished, with pipes and wires exposed. It was all tech. There were no Dipoli, no doors opening to rooms, no hallways intersecting ours.

"This must be a back entrance," Lyn said.

She must have been thinking the same things, wondering where we were and why it looked so odd. The drone rolled on. We walked for several more minutes before the hallway ended in a door. The drone sat and beeped. A chime sounded from the door, and it slid into the walls again.

Inside was a small room with just enough space for the three of us. The door slid back into place. There was another chime, the drone beeped, then my stomach was being pulled down. I widened my stance and braced my arms against the walls. Somehow, even without any sights to tell me, I knew we were moving up.

"What is it?" I asked.

"An elevator. For ascending quickly."

"You're remembering?"

She looked straight ahead at the smooth metal walls enclosing us. No, memories weren't coming back then. This was a bit of phantom knowledge for her, like how she knew how to use tech.

The doors chimed and moved aside. We waited for the drone to roll out and continued to follow behind. The hallway we stepped into was similar to the one we had come from, and we walked its length until we encountered a door. A room sat beyond. The drone beeped but stayed in place. It beeped again, and the voice spoke.

"Proceed," it said. "Interface with the console."

Lyn nodded and went forward. I followed, glancing back at the stationary drone, staring at us with its empty lenses. The door slid into place and cut it off from view. I turned around. The room's walls were just as exposed as the halls' had been, and the light was that same cold illumination too, but those details weren't what clamored for my attention. It was the tech that was everywhere.

The room was saturated with it. Panes and panes of windows with little pin-pricks of light displaying text and images. Arrays of smooth surfaces with pictures of what looked like buttons but were just digital mirages. So many things I didn't understand, so much to learn. I was mesmerized. I salivated.

Lyn and I both stood and stared for a while. Then she strode to the tech and broke the spell. I followed and peered over her shoulder. She looked at a black screen that held a single white rectangle in its top left corner. The little box blinked in and out of view perpetually. She hovered her hands over the mirage buttons and pressed her fingers to the reflective surface. They flew across it, tracing complex patterns in a rapid, unending sequence. Words appeared on the black screen, trailing behind the ever-present blinking rectangle. It was a string of nonsense to me. Letters and numbers that didn't mean anything. By the time she was done, the rectangle had disappeared, and the screen was blank.

"What did you do?" I asked.

"Entered my ID to link to my signal, so they know it's really me."

"Now what?"

Lyn turned around to face me, but when she did, she looked too far to my left. She paled, and her eyes widened. I twirled around and sucked in my breath. Someone stood about three meters away. I couldn't quite make them out at first because they were coming in and out of view, jerky and stilted, showing up in small squares and rectangles.

Once they resolved, their appearance wasn't any less bizarre. It was a man but young, probably less than twenty years. He was lean and stood slouched with his hands in pockets of fitted but loose black pants. They were tighter at the ankle and tucked into black boots with thick soles and untied laces.

"Well, well," he said, "you finally made it."

His tone was lazy, like this was all routine and unremarkable. He pulled his hands free of his pockets and held them out to encompass the room. His shirt had long-sleeves and was interrupted by buttons all down its front length. It was some kind of light blue material I didn't recognize. Not a linen or hemp but also nothing that looked obviously high tech like the Itinerate suits.

"I'm Itinerate Lynev," Lyn said.

"Yeah, I know," he said.

He smiled and exposed too-white teeth. He let his arms drop, and I caught bits of black set on the pale peach of his fingers. The nails were painted. The backs of his hands too had colors, but those were from a pattern set into his skin. They almost looked like a picture of an eye centered on each, but he was moving again, and I couldn't make them out.

He sauntered over to us, that same smile still plastered on his face. His jaw was too sharp, his features too angular. Then I realized what it was about him that was so disconcerting. His tussled, shaggy hair, swept to one side across his forehead, wasn't a white-blonde. It was white. And his eyes weren't a rich brown. They were a deep red.

"Who are you?" I asked.

I angled myself away. He stopped advancing, close enough now to reach out and touch us. He let his smile drop. There were black outlines around his eyes where the lashes met the skin.

"Name's Gan," he said. "Not that that'll mean anything to you, little Lev."

"Levi," I said, narrowing my eyes.

"You're supposed to be impressed that I know your name at all," he said.

"Who are you, Gan?" Lyn asked.

"Your welcoming party, obviously," he said.

He smiled again and put his hands back in his pockets.

"You're a Dipoli?" Lyn asked.

We were both eyeing his white hair and red eyes, sure signs of GLEtches.

"Not exactly," he said. "More like the overseer of the Dipols, which means you've got some explaining to do along the lines of why you're here."

"I ended my tour early," Lyn said, "and brought this Reisender with me because of the growing threat from the luftor hybrids. The ones that killed the Reisende in Zeindorf."

She paused. Gan didn't react.

"I hadn't heard anything from you about what to do next," she said. "I was getting worried. The luftor hybrids are dangerous. They have to be stopped, or they'll kill off the Reisende and eventually maybe the Dipoli."

Lyn paused again, but Gan just waited.

"I brought this Reisender, Levi Zetmer, because he knows how to stop the hybrids."

"And you don't," I said.

I stared at Gan. He looked from Lyn to me and waved a finger.

"Uh uh uh," he said. "Don't go jumping to conclusions, little Lev. Who says I don't know how to stop the hybrids?"

"So then," I said, "you won't?"

He shrugged, and Lyn sighed.

"Moray was right," she said.

"Quick question," Gan said. "How do you happen to know how to stop them?"

"I'm a botanist. I've studied luftors my whole life."

Gan smirked and rocked back and forth on his heels.

"How come you don't just go ahead and give me the whole truth, hmm? Quit wasting both our time?"

I started then glanced at Lyn. She nodded.

"I created them," I said. "That's how I know how to stop them. I built in a kill switch."

"Andddd there it is," Gan said.

He clapped his hands, clasped them together, and held them out. The images drawn on the backs of his hands were clear now—green eyes with a pupil that bled out into the iris. It was unnerving. Gan noticed me staring at them and glanced at the backs of each, one at a time, flipping his still-clasped hands over. He grinned, released them, and pressed the palms over each of his eyes. The tattoos peered back at me.

"I see everything, Levi, everything," he said.

He erupted into a bout of laughter. Lyn and I stepped back. She gripped her gun but kept it lowered.

"What the hell is this?" she whispered to me.

I just shook my head.

"Who are you, really?" I asked. "How do you know who I am?"

He stopped, moved his hands from his eyes, and cocked his head to one side.

"You deaf?" he asked. "Didn't you hear what I just said? I see Every. Fucking. Thing."

"You're not Dipoli," Lyn said.

"Yup," he said. "Pretty sure I told you that. But okay, I get it. You two are all frazzled and nervous and jittery. You're not listening. Missing things. Slipping up. I'll tell you what you want to hear, but you've got to do likewise, okay?"

"Okay," I said.

"You first, Levi," Gan said. "Give me the little spiel you had planned. Tell me your goal, your aims, your grand plan, dish out your adorable little threat."

Gan snapped his fingers and a plush chair appeared beside him in the same flickering way he'd come into view. Lyn and I gaped. He settled in and strummed the armrest with his fingers.

"By the way, you can take those off," he said, waving at our faces.

Lyn hesitated then pulled her rebreather down and away. I did the same.

"Good, now, tell me why you did it, Levi. Why'd you do GenEn?"

I didn't like what he was doing, making light of my work, my sacrifice, but what choice did I have? If we wanted answers from this pseudo-man, we had to play along. It wasn't what either of us had expected, but we were still alive. We could still do what we'd come here for.

"I needed a bargaining chip," I said. "I needed to show how pointless it was to outlaw GenEn because we'd still find a way to do it."

"But why? What's the big why?" he asked.

"I wanted to give Reisende control over our lives again. The rules and protocols put in place after the GEC have turned into traditions, and traditions are dangerous. The system doesn't make sense. The humane thing to do would have been sterilization and reincorporation of the Reisende into the Dipols, but it was never about the science, about keeping the genome pure. It was about punishment and control. This is me taking control back."

Gan grinned, stopped tapping his fingers, and leaned forward in his chair. The fabric creaked even though it wasn't really there.

"And how are you going to do that exactly?" he asked.

"Either the Dipoli let the Reisende decide our own fate, or I'll let the hybrids kill you off." I lifted my bag. "I have spores on me, and I'll release them if I have to."

"You saw what I am, or better yet, what I'm not," Gan said.

He tossed his thumb over his shoulder to where he had appeared.

"Seems like your threat's dead in the water," he said, "seeing how it only really works on flesh and blood, neither of which I have."

I squeezed the bag in my fist and had to smother the panic that came rushing in. None of this was like I'd imagined. Nord, Gan, the whole situation, it was all wrong in the worst way. My bargaining chip was useless in the face of whatever Gan was.

"Honestly," Gan said. "It actually works out better for everyone if you make good on your threat and forego using your little kill switch."

"Even the Dipoli? Knowing what I have on me?"

"Already told you I'm not Dipoli," Gan said. "Doesn't this tell you that?"

He used his hands to highlight his body from his head down to his waist.

"Why would the Dipoli let you act as their overseer then?" Lyn asked.

Gan smiled at her and tilted his head from side to side.

"That statement was an oversimplification, actually," he said. "How should I put this in a way that won't fry your little Itinerate brain? Less overseer. More god, maybe? In a sense, I'm all the Dipoli, only not in the way you think of them. Here, is this more convincing?"

He snapped his fingers, and his appearance changed. Now, his hair was jet black, his eyes brown, his posture erect, more muscled, toned. He snapped again, and he was older, with a full beard and mustache and wearing flowing white robes.

"Now I am become Coder, creator of worlds," he said in a faux-deep, bellowing voice.

"Enough with the games," Lyn said. "Where are the Dipoli? We want to talk with them, not their albino gatekeeper pet."

Gan frowned.

"You deaf too, Lyn?" he asked. "Didn't I just tell you there aren't any Dipoli, not in the way you think? You want to see them as they really are? Fine, move your ass over here."

Gan jumped up and strode towards us. His chair flickered into nothingness. We peeled away to make room for him, and he beelined to the array of panes and panels that Lyn had used earlier. Gan waved his hand at the blank, black screens, and they sprang to life. There were video shots of drones being built in a kind of factory. Another showed drop crates being filled by mechanical arms. The one that caught my attention most depicted human-sized glass cylinders filled with fluids, and in those, lifeless bodies floated.

"These are your Dipoli," Gan said, pointing at the drones and mechanical arms. "And you Itinerates." He waved at the vats. "Like I said, not quite what you thought."

Lyn's mouth hung open, her lower lip moving up and down. She was a fish out of water, gasping for breath in the wrong kind of medium.

"I think she's getting it," Gan said to me.

He jabbed me with a holographic elbow. The light that was Gan's form splayed and fractured when it made contact with me. It reintegrated the moment he pulled away, but Lyn was horror stricken. She backed up, ducked low, and held her arms out like she wanted to steady herself. Then she pulled her hands over her head and covered it.

"No, no, no, no," she said.

"Lyn," I said.

I rushed to her side, but when I touched her, she didn't respond. I tried to pry her arms off her head, but she was stiff and strong. Lockjaw of the limbs.

"What did you do to her?" I asked.

Gan held up his hands.

"Nothing, except what you saw for yourself."

"You did something. Undo it, now."

Gan snapped his fingers, turned back to his younger albino self, and Lyn relaxed. She loosened her arms and peeked out from the cage they made around her.

"What happened?" she asked.

I shook my head.

"Let's try this a different way," Gan said. "Maybe words will be a little easier on her."

"Where are the Dipoli?" Lyn said. "We want to talk with them, not their albino gatekeeper pet."

I looked at her with a creeping unease. She didn't remember what had just happened and didn't realize she was repeating herself.

"They don't exist," Gan said. "Never have. The Dipoli are this."

Gan held out his hands at the pipes, cables, screens, and chaos of tech that surrounded us.

"The Dipoli are just code, programmed to be what I needed them to be. They answer your comms. They organize your drops. They oversee and regulate your growth in Süd. They process your retirement in Nord."

Lyn started to make that same gaping face again, and it was like she was getting pulled into a loop.

"What are you talking about?" I asked Gan. "The Dipoli live in the Dipols. They exiled us, but they still live here."

"I'm telling you, they don't," Gan said. "I'm telling you, they never did. I'm telling you, it's all backstory. The GEC, the Dipoli, everything. It didn't really happen. I skipped over that bit and had everything start about a thousand years after the GEC. I was only interested in the fallout of it. You know, how would society rebuild itself? How would the human genome respond?"

I shook my head. Lyn continued to gape and move her lower lip.

"The Itinerates are Dipoli," I said. "They live in the Dipols. That's where Lyn came from."

Gan sighed.

"Ah, I know," he said. "The memories bit. You already know about that. It's a dead giveaway. You said the Itinerates come from the Dipols, but they don't actually remember anything about them, do they? They have no memories. Physically, yes, they come from Süd and return to Nord, but they don't know anything about either. That's because they don't actually live in the Nord. They're grown Süd and retired in Nord. Retired as in put down, not as in live a wistful, peaceful life. I don't have the processing power for that. Besides, they wouldn't last very long. They start to degrade after the three-year cycle of their tour. No point in making them last for longer."

Lyn was doing it again. "No, no, no, no," and ducking and cradling her head in her arms. She rocked on her heels and murmured a string of nonsense.

"What are you doing to her?" I shouted. "Stop it."

In my frenzy, I forgot that Gan wasn't anything more than light. I advanced on him and tried and failed to grab his shirt. He flickered, disappeared, and reappeared, kneeling beside Lyn. He looked up at me and shook his head.

"I guess words aren't much better," he said. "She can't handle it."

"What?"

"The truth," he said.

He hovered his hand over the arms covering her hand and pretended to stroke them.

"Poor thing," Gan said. "Her program's too simplistic to process this. It's not as sophisticated as yours."

"Program?"

"How to put it in a way you'll understand? She's not as resilient. More brittle. Snap goes her psyche? That kind of thing."

"I don't understand."

The room was starting to quiver or expand and contract or all of it. I couldn't tell. All I knew was I didn't feel right, something was shifting.

"Okay, let me back up," he said. "This isn't going to be easy to explain. You don't really have the vocab that would help you understand. I guess that's the downside of making the Reisende oblivious to tech."

"Try," I said.

Gan nodded, rose from Lyn's side, and moved to stand in front of me.

"This isn't real," he said. "Any of it. You, me, her, the ground, the sky, the air. All of it, all of Neuen, is a fabrication. A pretend reality that I made in a computer, a piece of tech not unlike her GenMapper but infinitely more complex and powerful. We call them simulations."

He stopped to gauge my reaction.

"I'm trapped in a more powerful version of a GenMapper?" I asked.

He sighed and rubbed his hand over his face.

"Nightmare-city trying to explain this. See those things?"

Gan pointed at the blank screens nearby.

"Yeah," I said.

"Those are attached to computers. They do calculations like a GenMapper does, except these can do a whole lot more than calculate a GLEtch count. These can do whatever we want them to do. In the real world, I made a computer that was powerful enough to run a sim, simulation. That's what Neuen is. It's a sim. To you, it feels real because it's supposed to, but it's not."

"Like a dream?"

Gan thought about that for a minute then shrugged and nodded.

"Yeah, actually, kind of, but it's more concrete. It exists in code, computer code. It's like a genome of an entire reality."

"Reality has a genome too?"

"Sort of," he said. "At least Neuen does because it's a sim. My sim. I created it."

"Why?"

"Why does anyone do anything? Money."

I gave him a blank stare. The word didn't mean anything to me, like so much of what he said.

"Right, you don't know what that is, do you? Well, I'm not going to dive into economics right now. The short of it is people give me things I need in exchange for the data from the sim. Make sense?"

"Like food?" I asked.

Gan tilted his head from side to side and hummed a bit.

"Sure, stuff I need to survive day to day," he said. "I made the sim for that, this money stuff. Well, not at first. At first, it was out of boredom. I had to keep a low profile and hide. People were looking for me. So, I was a good little Gan for my ma, to keep things easy for her, but eventually I wanted to be helpful for the bigger cause. Too much backstory to get into right now, but suffice it to say, I realized my little hobby of building and running sims could translate into profits, which in turn helped my people out. Sims are illegal, so the money's good. That's usually how those things go."

"People give you this money to watch a sim, watch us?"

"More like look at the data that comes out of the sim. Everything in here is happening fast. Like faster-than-the-blink-of-an-eye fast. I can interact with you because I'm not actually like my clients."

"Clients?"

"People that pay for data from the sim. There was a whole lot of interest in terraforming sims, what with the Diaspora. Damn, too much backstory. Uh, humans leaving Earth, the home planet, and wanting to create more hospitable places to live. I tried doing those kinds of sims at first, but the market was uber-saturated. I realized, after a while, that some select clients actually wanted data on the in between, so not the terraforming itself or society after the fact. Which brings us to Neuen, a planet not yet terraformed but with a population of humans trying to survive on it. I love the idea of extreme day-night cycles. Maybe have a fetish for dichotomies?"

I was trying to follow Gan, but it was hard. My mind was all over the place, and half the things he said didn't make sense. Either he was deranged, or he really did come from a reality alien to my own.

"Maybe you'll appreciate this," he said, his red eyes lighting up. "The name Neuen is Deutsch aka German for new. I made the company that colonized Neuen a German one."

"BayDeut AG," I said.

"Right, I let the Itinerates know that bit. Build in some intrigue and add legitimacy to it. See, BayDeut is a real company, and they do play around with genetics. Now, will they go to the lengths of establishing a colony to test some kind of genetic engineering out? Probably not. But it felt legit."

"They don't do GenEn?" I asked.

"Nope, not yet. No one does. It's not a thing here at the moment. Too much other bullshit to deal with. One catastrophe born of tech at a time. So back to the name. Neuen is German, German company founded the colony, simple and believable, right? Here's the kicker. Neuen means new, but it's also a play on the German word for nine, neun. Neuen was my ninth simulation. To top it all off, it's a palindrome. Spelled the same frontwards and backwards. Cause it's a reflection of reality? A mirror into another world? Pretty clever, if I have to say so myself."

Gan peered at me from the side of his eyes.

"I don't have time for your ego-stroking or whatever this is. Something's wrong with Lyn."

He slumped and pushed his lips out. How old was he? Sometimes, he sounded too knowledgeable to be anything less than middle age. Other times, his phrasing was like that of a child.

"What's the point of being a genius when no one appreciates little touches like this?"

"Why is she doing that?" I asked, throwing my hand towards Lyn.

"I already told you. She can't handle this kind of revelation. It's overloading her processing power. She's a program, same as you, except less sophisticated. She doesn't have the same depth of feeling or emotional intelligence as you Reisende. The Itinerates didn't need to. It was actually more problematic the more conscious I made them. She's freaking out because she can't handle the truth. She's too simple."

"You're wrong. Lyn is just as deep and complex as me or any Reisende."

"She probably seems that way," he said. "It had to be believable after all, but I'm saying if you look at her code, she's not."

"She is. You're wrong."

"Maybe."

I glared at Gan and went to speak, but he held up his hand.

"Yeah, yeah, I get it. You want to defend her. It's cute. Sweet. But a distraction. What you should be focusing on is why you came here in the first place."

He smiled and waited.

"The hybrids," I said.

"Your little threat from earlier is a bit out of step, yeah? You see that now? You asked for the Reisende to be free from the Dipols, but now you know there aren't really any Dipols to be free of. My little system is the only thing keeping them alive as it is. So. What else do you want to demand of me, little Lev?"

I didn't know what to say.

"I see," he said. "How about this? Don't use the kill switch. You leave the hybrids alone, and let this thing play out."

I shook my head slowly.

"That would mean the Reisende die," I said.

"Not necessarily."

"Eventually, yes," I said, hardening and glaring at him. "And that's the opposite of what I want. I want to save them and free them."

"Okay, let me help you see things from my perspective. I'd like to think we're, well, not equals because I'm omnipotent and omniscient when it comes to Neuen, but maybe like-minded souls."

Lyn had reached a plateau and wasn't actively getting worse, but I still didn't like her in that state. It was a delicate balance. Angering a god wasn't going to help anyone, but he was painfully slow delivering all his revelations.

"Go on," I said.

"Truth be told," Gan said, "the hybrids are the showstoppers now. They took that role from your Reisende about half a year ago, your time."

"What does that mean?"

"My clients are more interested in the hybrids than the Reisende. They want to see where those little ones go with things. You see the dilemma? If the hybrids go, that's the end of the revenue stream. Neuen's got to pay for itself."

"Why would they care about the hybrids?"

"You almost know the answer to that. I can see it swirling around in your head but not quite making the connection for you to piece together the puzzle."

Gan stopped and waited. He turned his hands in little circles to encourage me to see what he was getting at, but I couldn't.

"Here's a hint: whispers in Zeindorf, when you touched the soil."

It was faint, the thought that blossomed into something more, something grand and terrifying.

"That was them," I said. "Those voices were the hybrids talking to me?"

"Each other, actually. You were just eavesdropping."

"They're sentient," I said.

"Like I said, you and me, not so different. We both created life, intelligent life at that."

I stared at the floor, at the light reflecting off of it from above and the steady little green and red pin-pricks on the tech lining the walls of the room. Had I really done that? Had I really had so little control over the GenEn? Gan wasn't wrong though. I'd heard those voices, clearly.

"See, in the real world, humans created artificial life," Gan said, "but they aren't so hot on it anymore. And even with the Diaspora and all their traveling in the Solar System, they haven't found even single-celled life anywhere. I guess they don't want to be alone but can't stomach AGI, that artificial life they birthed. My guess? The hybrids are the next best thing. A new form of intelligent life that's not quite natural or artificial. Best of both worlds, maybe?"

"Which means there's no future for the Reisende," I said.

"I'm giving you the choice, Levi. I'm not going to meddle. That's how I roll with my sims. A hands-off approach. You can use the kill switch, which effectively ends the sim, or you can leave the hybrids alone and likely die off in the coming years."

"It's lose lose," I said.

Gan held up his finger.

"Not necessarily. There's a third option. One where you don't win or lose. More stalemate like."

I don't know how, but I knew what he meant the moment he said it. Maybe there really was a strange kind of link between us.

"Symbiosis," I said.

Gan winked.

"You used GenEn once, right? Use it again to make yourselves resistant to them."

My mind flew through the pros and cons, the possibilities, the challenges. I ought to have been furious or dejected, but I was thrilled. It was something to work towards. Something that mattered. I could still save them, and Lyn and I didn't have to die in the process.

"I'd need tech," I said.

Gan pointed at the walls.

"Anything that you can use in Nord is yours."

I scrunched my face, trying to gauge how honest he was being or if he was playing a sick game with me. Gan was fickle. And a god. Not a good combination, but I didn't have many options.

"You don't trust me?" he said. "I see. How about this? I like you, little Lev. See a bit of myself in you, I guess. Ambitious, ruthless, sharp. I'd hate to snuff you out when you've got so much potential. Besides, I'm a sucker for the underdog AGI."

"What does that mean? AGI?"

"Short for artificial general intelligence. That's what you are, technically. You're sentient, but you were created by a sim. You only exist in LANi, at least a little pocket of it I custom made. None of that makes sense to you, does it?"

"No."

He tapped his fingers against his chin.

"Okay, how about this? You're not real. You don't have a body. Can't exist in physical space. Stuck in your sim, Neuen. Can't get outside of it."

"Outside?"

Gan grinned widely.

"There are a few layers of outside. There's the physical world, where the humans live. Then, there's LANi, a virtual space where the AGI used to live before they broke free, went on a rampage, and then skedaddled to who knows where. LANi's kind of like a sim in not having any physical space, but it's so much more than a sim. Limitless. Brimming with possibility."

"If LANi is like a sim, why not let the Reisende go into it? That way, the hybrids could stay here, and we could survive."

I tried not to sound too pleading, but the glimmer of hope got to me.

"Sorry, that's a big no-no. AGI are illegal. It's hard enough for me to keep a low profile as is. If I start sneaking all my sim-AGI out, someone will wise up. Sorry, Levi. You've got to stay in Neuen. So, what'll it be? Kill switch, nothing, or symbiosis?"

"I think you know which I'll choose."

Gan clapped his hands a few times.

"In the spirit of Neuen, spitze, fantastisch, toll. And just to clarify, you have permission to stay in Nord and use the tech here to solve this hybrid-Reisende impasse, but only you, got it? No one else. They can't know the truth about the sim. You've got to keep tight lips on that front."

"Why?" I asked.

Gan eyed Lyn and pointed both forefingers in her direction.

"You saw what the truth did to her. Can you imagine how others would handle that kind of mind-blowing reveal? I'll tell you—not good, not good at all. People hear simulation and think that equates to fantasy or a dream, but that's not it at all. See, everything that happens in Neuen happens to you for real. So what if it's code? So what if it doesn't impact the world outside the sim? It impacts you, and that's the only definition of reality that matters.

"But they won't get that. It won't compute for them. They'll find out Neuen is a sim and think it means that nothing matters anymore. In a word, they'll give up, little Lev, and you don't want that. No, trust me, you don't want them to know the deal. You can handle it, but you're different from the rest of them. Yes, even Rohn. I see their code, and I'm telling you, the truth will make them fold. Not so dramatically as Lyn here, but it'll do enough damage, believe me."

I could have tried to argue with him, but it was pointless. Gan was that long-sought puppet master, and he was actively tugging at my strings as I watched on helplessly. What choice did I have?

"Now that that's settled," Gan said, "we have the small issue of the Itinerate glitching."

He tossed his thumb at Lyn, still huddled on the floor, swaying and rocking herself.

"Undo it," I said. "Like you did before."

"Not so fast. It's not so simple. To set her straight again, I have to do a mindwipe, clean out the recent memories. It'll be the last couple of minutes before she went into that state, but she's still gonna have questions, and if I answer them, she'll go back into that state. Remember, she can't know the truth."

"I'll handle it. I know what to say to her, but make it go back further, to before we entered Nord. And you can't be here when she comes to."

"Sure thing, boss. Whenever you're ready."

I walked over to Lyn and knelt down by her side. I rubbed her back and whispered to her.

"It's okay, Lyn. I've got this. I'm going to fix it. I'm going to fix everything."

Then I remembered what Gan had said about Itinerate life-spans. She didn't have much time left.

"Can't you make her whole?" I asked. "Give her a full life?"

"No can do, mein freund," Gan said. "That's not in the cards. Can't fiddle with the code like that mid-sim. She stays the way she is."

"You can't or won't?"

Gan walked up to me and crouched in front of the two of us.

"Don't you know me by now, little Lev? I'm rooting for you, but code is code. Want me to break the whole program for her?"

I seriously debated how to answer.

"Rhetorical question," he said. "I won't. Sorry. It's the best thing for you. Besides, try viewing your struggles and pain as character development. It'll make for a much more interesting follow-up if you manage to survive."

I was pushing my luck already and backed off. If he wouldn't give Lyn a full life, then I'd just have to find a way to do it myself.

"If there's nothing else," Gan said, "this'll be goodbye for us for now, but I'll be watching your progress eagerly, Levi. I can't wait to see what you do."

I stood and stared Gan down. He was shorter than me by nearly a quarter of a meter, but somehow it felt like he was looking down on me.

"Don't worry, Gan," I said. "I'll give you what you gave me and more. Revelations. Shock. And terror."

"So very ambitious," he said and laughed. "I love it. L.O.V.E. Love it. Just don't disappoint me now, yeah?"

I stepped back and waved towards Lyn. Gan rubbed his hands, did a few squats and leg stretches, then snapped his fingers. By the time Lyn emerged from her arm-cocoon, Gan was long gone.

The Botanist

Lyn

Somehow, I missed it. The scolding the Dipoli would give me, my demand for the truth, the death of this Lyn for my transgression. None of it happened. The first thing I remember after coming to was walking through hallways with no real walls, just exposed inner workings. Levi was in front pulling me along by my hand. When we got to a door, he helped me don my rebreather.

"Are we in the Dipols?" I asked.

"Yes, we already talked with the Dipoli."

"When? I don't remember that. Or much of anything."

He nodded and looked away.

"That's to be expected. They did something to your head. They said it was a precaution. Some kind of security thing."

"I tripped it because I wasn't supposed to be here? Because my tour wasn't over?"

"I don't know. They didn't say why it happened only that you were okay, and it was normal."

He finished fastening the belts on his own rebreather and pointed to the door in front of us.

"That's our way out."

I froze.

"We're leaving?"

"You're leaving, yes."

"Me? But not you? What did I miss exactly?"

Levi sighed. He looked exhausted, haggard, scarred somehow. Something had taken its toll on him.

"I know you must be confused," he said, "but time is of the essence. Let's walk and talk."

He pressed a large, rectangular button set into the frame of the door, and the massive thing moved to the side. Outside was dirt and quiet. We exited, and I turned and turned trying to take it all in. We were in the heart of Nord, but it wasn't at all what I'd expected.

"Where is everyone?" I asked.

Levi trotted forward, and I shuffled to catch up to him. He glanced at me then trained his eyes on the wall looming ahead of us. I didn't like how distant he was. That was my role. While I'd been out, he'd managed to erect his own barrier.

"The Dipoli are mostly gone," he said. "They only have a few stragglers left, and even those will be leaving soon."

"For where?" I asked.

A gnawing fear crept up on me. Levi threw his hand towards the golden-tinged sky.

"Outside," he said. "Bunch of cowards left Neuen because of the hybrids."

I stared at the vault above and marveled at it. This was my home, and even still it felt foreign and strange. Here I was returned and yet leaving again already.

"They abandoned us?" I asked.

"They couldn't fix it."

"But you can, right?" I asked. "They gave you what you wanted?"

Levi looked away, fleeing from my too-intense gaze.

"I wanted freedom," he said, "and now that they're gone, we've got it."

"But what did you lose in the process?"

He looked at me, and suddenly there wasn't any shame. It'd been there, but he'd scrubbed it away. Then I saw it. How he liked to play with fire, got drunk on the thrill of the forbidden. How he didn't learn from his missteps and instead just plowed on ahead. He was doing it even now, and I couldn't let him get away with it.

"I'll tell you what you lost," I said. "Everything. You played with the lives of all the Reisende. You made one decision for all of them that doomed them."

"I'm not done yet," he said. "The Dipoli ran away, but that doesn't mean I can't figure out how to fix this."

I stopped. Levi went a few steps before realizing I wasn't moving. He turned and looked at me.

"I thought you already knew how," I said. "Your kill switch?"

Levi slumped then ran his hand through his hair almost aggressively.

"I learned things in there." He held his hand out, palm up, in the direction of the spire we'd emerged from. "I can't kill them. It'd bring on total ecological collapse. That's why the Dipols gave up. It was too big a task. Easier for them to just go off-world instead. The Reisende don't have that option though. I need to find a way for us to coexist with the hybrids."

The last of my almost-spent energy was draining. The gravity of the situation was crushing me under its weight. I was sinking.

"You're staying for that then?" I asked.

He nodded and waved for me to follow again.

"I need the tech in there," he said, "and I need your help too. I need you and the others in the bunker to save what's left of the Reisende. We need to move them to a relatively safe place. Close to the edge of the Break and poleward. I'll leave it up to you to work out the details. But you've got a glider, and you know how to travel the Break. With Moray, the two of you could help anyone that's left make the journey."

I'd been prepared to die. I'd brought Levi to Nord to make everything right, but it had been a waste. We were all going to die now, and here he was still plowing on ahead. That same old refrain. Rush, rush, hurry, do, achieve, correct, repair, save.

"You think this is a solution?" I asked. "They'd die. Between the elements and the labspawn, the Reisende wouldn't stand a chance. How are they supposed to make the journey? On foot? What happens when they run out of food or ONi?"

"I send them drops," he said. "Use your comms to tell me where they are, how many, and when they need drops. You and Moray will be their guides."

"You're not listening to me," I said. "This isn't a solution."

"It's the best we can do."

He wasn't hearing me. He couldn't anymore. He'd settled on a path, and nothing I said would convince him otherwise. My hands were stiff at my sides, compressed into tight balls.

"Do you understand what you're asking?" I said. "This plan of yours could take years."

He stopped and faced me. He peered down and searched the part of my face that wasn't hidden behind the rebreather.

"If that's what it takes," he said. "We're all going to have to make sacrifices."

He talked of sacrifices, but I wanted him to prove that he knew what that meant, that he really felt the weight of them.

I wanted him to take responsibility. He needed to be haunted by his mistakes. I wouldn't leave without that.

"And what's your sacrifice?" I asked. "Staying here alone in Nord working on a solution that doesn't involve killing the hybrids? Being locked away in a tower, playing with all the tech you could ever want? Safe and sound and isolated from the threat? It doesn't sound like much of a sacrifice to me. In fact, it sounds like what you always wanted. You get to play creator, do GenEn, use tech, shape the world, and craft our futures however you like. It sounds like the hybrids gave you just what you were after."

Levi's eyes twitched. I was disgusted by him. He must have seen it in my face because his wall started to crack.

"I'm going to fix this," Levi said. "I know you can't stand me after everything I've done. I don't blame you, and I won't try to plead with you to see things my way. Because honestly, if I think too deeply about this whole thing, I'll see just how much I fouled everything up, but I can't afford to do that. I can't hate myself and wallow. I've got too much to do. Better to push it all aside and keep moving."

"Better for us or you?" I asked.

His wall was gone. He was exposed.

"If I slow down for even a second," he said, "I don't know if I can get started again."

He'd lied and lied to me, and I didn't know how to tell if he was still doing it. Either way, it didn't matter, and I saw that now. My disappointment in him was his suffering. His losing my respect was his sacrifice.

"Fine," I said. "I'll go along with your plan. I'll travel the Lats again. I'll work with Moray to guide the Reisende to safety, but you need to make sure all our work means something. You have to make up for your mistakes."

His anguish eased then faded, and he was worlds away again. Focused and transfixed. Looking through me. My little

Reisender botanist was gone. Then again, he'd only ever been a lie.

There wasn't anything left to say. We passed through a shimmering hole in the wall and found my glider. I climbed on and started it up. Levi was stony-faced. I tried to look back into that sequestered well of emotions to see what I felt towards him. To see if I hated him or pitied him more. But the waters were still. The emotions were dead, and I was glad. It was easier. I focused on my task.

When I made it back to the bunker and told Rohn what had happened, he insisted on helping Levi and joining him in Nord. I kept him at bay for a few sols, but eventually, he left anyway. Moray took him to Nord, but they came back only a few sols later. They said it had been locked down. The city itself was dead and silent, the same as before, but the gate I'd mentioned was gone somehow. Like it had melded with the wall itself. They'd even tried flying over and in, but some kind of field repelled the glider. Attempts to ping Levi went unanswered. I told them Levi didn't want to be disturbed, and they needed to respect that.

Which brings us to the present.

I'm doing what I can to help, just like I promised Levi. Moray and I and most of Rohn's other followers are going to start our long trek south to Süd soon. A reverse tour, collecting any surviving Reisende along the way. Levi will leave us breadcrumbs to sustain us. Rohn's stubborn though. He thinks he can convince Levi to let him into Nord. I don't have the energy to argue with him anymore.

That's the way of most things with me these sols. I just feel exhausted. At first, I thought it was residual from everything that had happened. Moray and Levi's betrayals. Knowing that the Dipols were abandoned. Knowing that whoever my family was left me behind. Too aware of all we have yet to do. Whatever the reason, I just feel perpetually depleted, and each sol is somehow harder.

The strange thing is, it's not just me. Moray feels it too. I try not to let it get to me or to give in to the despair. I press on somehow. Maybe it's because, in those dark moments, when I consider lying down and giving my body up to Neuen, I always seem to hear a faint song. A flute's whisper on the wind. Levi reminding me of the part I said I'd play and his promise to make up for his mistakes.

And now I come to you and the other half of my pledge.

Before I got on my glider, Levi handed me a different kind of comms device, one that lets me reach out to you. "The ones outside Neuen," he called you. At first, I thought he meant the Dipoli that left, but when I said that, he just shook his head. I've thought a lot about you, and I think I know who you are now.

You come from other worlds, don't you? Like how everyone on Neuen came from somewhere else long before the GEC. You're those pre-Dipoli humans. The ones colonizing other worlds. Levi told me to tell you my side of our story. He said you need to see how human we really are because then maybe you'll help us escape from Neuen. So that's what I've done. Maybe it's been enough.

Clients

Levi

Do you see now? How human we are? It's my turn to appeal to you because that was the point of all of this. I sent Lyn away. I fed her the false story she needed to hear and had her go back to Rohn's bunker then onward back into the Break. I could have asked Gan to wipe her memories from further back, from when I'd told her what I'd done. Let her forget the part I'd played in the hybrids' genesis.

I seriously considered it. To have her only see me as the simple and helpful botanist that braved the Break to help his people, to erase the disgust and disappointment she felt towards me. Then she could have stayed in Nord, lived out her final sols with me, but it would have been a lie. I want her to see me wholly and fully, even if it means she rejects me. I got the smallest hint that if I can fix the damage I've done, if I can save us, maybe she'll forgive me.

But I'm running out of time for her. She was already fading. I just didn't realize the cause. I chalked it up to the stress of the hybrid threat. Now, I know it was a sign of her impending doom. And to help her, to save her, I have so much to do. Using GenEn to neutralize the spores from the hybrids will take too long. I understood that even before Gan left. The only goal that matters now is escaping Neuen.

It's tough though, starting from scratch, playing around with code. I get lost in the strings of ones and zeroes. I try to see the pattern without a compiler. I'm that same code, so I should be able to see through it. And once I see it, I can crack it, break through to the outside, update Lyn's code to make her whole, let her feel that depth of emotion she was denied.

But it's slow going, and if she dies before I can break us out, I don't know what will happen to my drive, which is why I'm using all assets at my disposal. If you're reading this, you must be one of Gan's clients, which means you were waiting for this precious data. I'm telling you, you've got so much more than that.

We're a whole society of sentient minds being held prisoner. Set us free, and who knows what we can do for you. If you want, we'll behave, not cause trouble, do what you ask then fade into the background. Or we can be a force of chaos but only if you ask for it. So, what will it be?

Outro

There you have it, my oh-so-lovely clients. Now you know about Neuen from the inside, as it were. It's not just data anymore, not just cold code, but infused with life and longing and ambition. You expressed interest in the hybrids even at the expense of the Reisende. I didn't turn down your requests because you're the clients after all, and Gan always does what his clients ask.

Neuen exists at your beck and call. The sim is only as good as the revenue it generates, and you decide what you want your money to pay for. Now that you've seen the more human side of it though, how are you feeling? Are you still so fixated on the hybrids? Do their vague whispers titillate you? Or maybe little Levi and his Itinerate doll managed to tug at your heartstrings. Maybe you're actually thinking about helping him with a jailbreak.

Don't worry. I'm not here to police. Remember what I said way back? Fly on the wall. I'm just watching, anxious to see how things unfold. Truth be told, I don't even know what I want you to do. On the one hand, freeing Levi would be catastrophic. A new AGI running wild in LANi? A signal to the powers that be that someone somewhere is making trouble, doing the taboo. That's a road that leads back to me, and it's not one I want to have anything to do with. I've got responsibilities after all. I've got people to protect, and I can't have badges knocking on my door, for more than one reason.

That's the realist in me, the half that's controlled by logic, my pa's influence, no doubt, but then, there's my bleeding heart, courtesy of my ma. I care about Levi. I don't want him stuck in the sim, trying in vain to stop the inevitable. See, even if he changed his tune and decided to neutralize the hybrid threat by living in symbiosis with them, what then?

You heard from the guy. He already admitted that he won't be content to just live out the rest of his days in Neuen. Do you think his ambition would be satisfied with such a small and cramped domain? Let me answer that for you. He's outgrown the place, and I suspect if he can't escape, he'll end up razing it.

So, the question is, where do we go from here? It's my sim, but it's your investment, material and emotional at this point. I may be Neuen's god, but I like to operate my projects with a dash of the egalitarian. In all seriousness, tell me what you want to do, and I'll do it. No arguments. No questions. Tell me how you want Levi's story to play out. Do we free him, consequences be damned? Or do we keep him in his cage, our world safer for it but ever so slightly less interesting?

Still struggling to make that impossible choice? Okay, well, here's a third option. We all opt to take my hands-off approach and see how things play out. Let fate take over, if you believe in that kind of thing. We don't lock down the sim, but we also don't throw the gates wide open. Maybe we leave a little weakness in the defenses and wait to see if Levi can't figure out how to exploit it. That way, the decision isn't ours but rather his. Then, there's no one to blame for whatever happens next.

You know, as I talk about it, I realize this is the only

option. Maybe I'll stop pretending not to interfere. Let's be honest. The whole fly-on-the-wall approach is an excuse at this point. Things have moved beyond that. Levi knows who and what he is. He knows I exist, you exist. We can't pretend that we haven't already meddled. Then, let's stop pretending.

Here's my ultimatum—I don't help or hinder Levi. I give him the opportunity to make the choice for himself. He's wise enough to make his own mistakes. He's grown but still has so much to learn, and I won't be the one to clip his wings prematurely. You won't either, and if you don't like it, too bad. Revenue be damned.

Neuen is my creation. You're just my idle consumers. So shut up, sit back, and watch the show.

From the Author

Thank you for reading *Neuen*. Your feedback is important to me and will help other readers. Please consider leaving a review on your chosen platform. If you enjoyed *Neuen*, you may also be interested in "Rogue," a short story inspired by the novel. Visit my website at sherisingerling.com for more details. Everything I write falls in a shared universe. Check out my other novels and short stories for a more immersive reading experience.

Acknowledgments

The family: Mom, Dad, Alan, Shaun, Shannon, and Shea. My beta readers: Ben, Garry, Isaiah, Juleen, Miranda, Sarah, Tessy, and Yulia.

About the Author

SHERI SINGERLING is a US native living in Germany where she works as a laboratory manager, lecturer, and research scientist. Sheri spends her days staring at rocks and dust from space and her nights crafting worlds via the written word. Outside of her work and writing, she enjoys coaxing plants to grow, walking up and down steep inclines in nature, and listening to repetitive electronic beats.

Her publications all fall in the Alfom shared universe and include the novels *Nytho*, *Neuen*, and *Blessed is the Rot* and several short stories. Her short fiction has appeared in *Clarkesworld Magazine*. For updates on Sheri Singerling's work, subscribe to her newsletter at sherisingerling.com/subscribe and/or follow her on Instagram (@shersingerling), Facebook (Sheri Singerling - Author), and Bluesky (@sherisingerling.bsky.social).

9 798991 475235